If Only They Knew

Megan Foster

One

A crowd of dark clouds trudge across the sky, pulling a dull filter down over the field and making my drawing seem more like a work of fantasy than realism. I sigh and put my pencil down. There's no point trying to change the drawing to match the weather, the sun will be back as soon as I start adding bits in. I learnt that the hard way.

A new subject is added to the scene in front of me and she speeds through the maze of old, wooden tables, trying not to hit other students with her swinging handbag, a few of them yelling as she goes by almost knocking their polystyrene containers full of soggy canteen chips onto the freshly cut grass. Through the chatter, and the riot of a fight breaking out at the back of the field, the seagulls above can still be heard as they cheer her on.

"Did you see?" Cassie squeals when she gets close enough for us to hear. She throws her bag down as she leans over the table, her chest rising and falling at an unsteady rate. "Did you guys see the news!?"

I might as well forget about my drawing, when she gets like this it's near impossible to focus on anything else. I glance at Abby and we both shake our heads.

"Really?" she exclaims, disappointed in us. "Jackson Peters is this months 'win-a-date with a celeb'." She continues when we don't react, "Just imagine. Me on a date with Jackson freaking Peters. It'd be amazing." She looks off into the distance. "I wonder what we'll do. Maybe we'll go to his favourite restaurant. I've always wanted to go to The Royal Port," she sighs, taking the seat opposite me and getting her lunch out of her bag.

I really don't want to be the one to burst her bubble but someone needs to. It's one thing to laugh and joke about winning but that's not what this is for her, she'll get carried away and then be devastated when she doesn't win.

"Cassie," Abby starts, placing her book down and saving me from being the sole destroyer of her dreams. "I bet thousands of people if not millions are going to enter."

"Exactly," I agree. "Plus, he lives in America."

"Yes, but it says it's only open in the UK." She turns her phone to show us. "His UK tour's next month so he's doing the date then." She shrugs. "And I know a tonne of people are going to enter but you have to be in it to win it. Right?" She starts running her manicured nails through her sleek, blond hair, a habit she developed a couple of months ago after randomly deciding to wear her hair down more. I think that was just after her experimental, youtube-tutorialed hair phase.

"No, you're right. Who knows, maybe you'll get lucky," I say with a small smile.

The clouds move on, taking Cassie's worry with them, and I quickly open up my sketchbook, adding shadows and texture to the trees in the background before starting to add Cassie into the picture. She's pulled out her phone and is tapping away violently, probably posting about 'the news'.

"But what about your parents? Are they going to let you go on a date with a famous singer during your GCSEs?"

Abby has a point. Cassie's parents aren't the strictest but it's our final year, and they're not going to let her miss any of it to go and meet some celebrity that's technically a stranger. Even if it is someone she's been obsessed with most of her life.

"Well, we can worry about it later. Can I enter your details as well Lorri? The more entries the better."

"Sure. I bet it's not cheap to enter though?" I ask into my sketchbook as I try to perfect Abby's mousy messy bun. I saw the price to enter last month and thought they were joking. That was for someone I'd never heard of before as well, someone nowhere near as famous as Jackson Peters.

"Yeah but it's for charity," she shrugs. "Remember the dress I made last month? Someone finally bought it, and I have the money that my parents gave me before they went on their business trip. I'll only end up spending it on takeouts otherwise."

"Hey, what are we talking about?" Sean, Abby's not-so-identical twin brother, asks as he sits down next to Cassie. They used to look alike when we first met them at the start of high school but whereas Abby stayed short and plump, Sean never stopped growing and developed muscles so big he became a teenage, slightly weaker, equivalent of Henry Cavill. Not that you'd be able to tell in this uniform or his usual nerdy aesthetic, but it's there alright.

"Cassie's obsessing over Jackson Peters again," I say as Abby grabs one of his cheese and pickle sandwiches, flinging the green slices back onto the foil with a grimace.

He takes his bag off and searches through it until he pulls out a giant book on mechanics. "Ah. So, nothing new," he jokes with a grin.

Cassie lightly hits him and he gasps, grabbing his injured arm like one might do when they've been shot. "I don't talk about him *all* the time."

"No. His name just manages to make it into every conversation by itself."

Cassie tries to argue back as Abby and I fail to hide our amusement.

He laughs and puts his arms up in surrender. "Fine. It shall forever be a mystery how I know everything that goes on in Jackson Peters' life."

This earns him a large eye roll from Cassie before she goes back to her phone, ignoring him as he counts off all the useless facts he knows about the international pop star on his fingers.

Two

It's always a little weird being back on this street, playing spot the difference with the place I called home for as long as I can remember. A car pulls into the driveway, one of those new electric ones. I quickly move from the window before anyone gets out, careful not to see the new happy family that's making memories in the same place mine are held captive, and flop onto Cassie's queen-size bed.

I pick up my sketchbook and let out a sigh at the blank page just as she comes barrelling through the door. She's juggling a stack of fashion magazines and a bag of snacks in one hand, and two rolls of fresh fabric in the other, the bottoms of them leaving a trail in the fluffy carpet. "Do you need some help?"

"No, I've got it," she huffs, dropping the magazines on her desk and placing the snacks next to my overnight bag that's propped against her bed. "Please let me make you a prom dress," she begs as she places one of the rolls next to her mannequin that's wearing half a dress of the same royal blue fabric. "This fabric would compliment your hair colour so well." She turns and holds up the other fabric for me to see.

I instinctively tug at a loose red curl. "You still need to finish your dress, and you need to revise otherwise you won't be able to go at all." The fabric *is* beautiful. It's a heavy-looking silk in a shade of emerald green.

She rolls her eyes and places the fabric with her others before coming over to inspect my non-existent work. "That's not your application drawing, is it?"

I'm supposed to be entering a competition to win a place at a summer camp led by my favourite artist, Vivian Blanche. I've wanted to go for years but it costs close to a grand to attend, and even then your place isn't guaranteed. When I saw there was a competition this year for a fully paid spot, I had to enter. The winner also gets their work in Vivian's magazine next month, it was named the number one art magazine for the last four years, but that's just a plus. It might help if I could actually draw something though.

Her eyebrows shoot up as she realises it is indeed my application drawing.

"I know," I cry, throwing the sketchbook aside. "I wanted to start it ages ago but I have no idea what to do. It needs to be my best work, and it needs to stand out from all the others."

"All your work is amazing. Picasso ain't got nothing on you." She goes back to her desk and starts flipping through her designs. "When's it got to be done?"

"The latest deadline for applications is in a couple of weeks," I groan. "I thought I'd start early, get it done and be one of the first to apply, but at this rate, I'll be lucky if I get it done at all." I grab the share bag of Wotsits out of the snack bag and stuff a handful of them into my mouth, trying my best not to get orange dust everywhere.

"You have plenty of time. If anyone can do it, it's you. I've watched you start and finish multiple drawings in one night and they always turn out amazing, you've got this." She turns to give me a reassuring smile.

I grunt before shoving more Wotsits into my mouth and go back to staring at the blank page.

"Lorri! Lorri wake up! I can't believe it! Lorri…!"

I open my eyes just as a pillow whacks me in the face. I bolt up, my eyes struggling to adjust to the blinding phone screen as it's pushed towards my face. I check the time at the top of the screen.

"Why are you waking me up at half 3 in the morning to show me a photo of Jackson Peters?" I grumble, lying back down. Unfortunately, I can't say this it the first time she's done so.

I feel Cassie come closer before she whispers, "Because I won." I don't need to look to know she has a giant smile on her face.

"Won what?"

She hands me the phone and this time I actually look at it.

It's an email:

~

Dear Cassie,

Congratulations! You are the lucky winner of this month's 'win-a-date-with-a-celeb'! Please email us back as soon as you can to claim your prize. We can't wait to hear from you, and Jackson Peters can't wait to meet you!

~

My mind takes a second to catch up as it goes back a month to when she entered. *She actually won.* I hand her phone back, stunned. "Have you replied yet? Is it definitely them?"

She wafts her hand at me, dismissing my second question. "No, I just got the email. I've only just stopped freaking out. I'm going to meet Jackson Peters!" she squeals, causing me to instinctively shush her.

Rolling her eyes, she continues, "I wonder what he's like face to face? I bet he smells nice. He just looks like he smells nice, you know?"

I slowly nod, my head still fuzzy with shock, as she quickly types out a response and hits send. We both stay there for about ten minutes, listening to the rain hammering the window as she constantly refreshes her inbox. *If she swipes any faster, she'll wear her phone screen away.*

Her phone pings and we both stare at it.

I barely get past 'Dear Cassie' before she gets up and starts dancing around the room, almost tripping over the fabric pinned to the creepy headless mannequin. "I'm going on a date with Jackson Peters!" She stops dancing in front of her giant poster of him and just stares at his face. She sighs and turns around. "I don't think I can do this."

I almost choke on air and strain my eyes in the dim room to make sure it's definitely Cassie and not an alien that's abducted her and is taking her place. "What?" If there's one thing Cassie can do, it's go and feed Jackson Peters' ego for a couple of hours.

"Well, what do I say to him? What if he doesn't like me?" She comes to sit next to me. "What if I'm not good enough?"

"Please, if anything he's not good enough for you. You're amazing and talented and, honestly, you have more personality in your pinkie than he will ever have. If he doesn't like you then there's something wrong with him. Not you."

Cassie shakes her head but smiles, her cheeks glowing. She reads it again. "I can't believe it. I still need to confirm a few things but-" she stops mid read, her face lighting up. "I almost forgot that I get a plus one! You have to come, please…" she begs.

"What about Abby? I'm sure she'd appreciate it more than me. I know nothing about him," I say, crossing everything inside of me and hoping she'll notice my brittle smile and pleading eyes.

"That's not true. You know *some* things about him. I talk about him all the time, and I always have his music on so you must know some of his songs." She must sense that I'm still not convinced because she scooches closer, giving me her best puppy dog eyes. "Please. I need you there. Just in case I run out of things to say."

Cassie is many things, but she is never lost for words.

"Please…"

"Fine," I sigh with a smile. A free meal in a fancy restaurant with one of my favourite people, how bad can it be?

She hugs me tightly before getting up again to do another happy dance. She starts to sing one of his new songs and I laugh as she picks up a teddy and dances with it, whirling around in circles.

It doesn't take long before her dad storms in, wearing one slipper and a pink, silk dressing gown that's just a tad too small, reminding us of the time and telling us to get back to bed.

"Mechanical waves cause oscillations of particles in a solid, liquid or gas and must have a medium to travel through."

Do people understand this stuff? I'm fine in most of my other classes but I've always struggled to understand physics, and the fact I got no sleep last night, thanks to Cassie keeping me up talking about the date on Saturday, really doesn't help.

"Do you want me to send you some of my notes later? You look a bit lost," Sean offers.

"Is it that obvious? Thanks, that'd be great," I whisper back trying not to get either of us caught by Mr Le. "How's your mum? You got a new nurse, right?"

Sean and Abby's mum got sick a couple of years ago and since then they've had to look after her pretty much on their own every day. They get help from a nurse whilst they're at school but after that, they have to take turns so the other one can get their homework done or so Sean can work. As much as they struggle, Sean never asks for help.

He shifts in his seat. "Yeah, she's great. The new nurse is better than the last and she's even offered to come round more at the weekends to give us a bit of a break." His smile doesn't fully reach his eyes and he cringes when he realises his choice of words.

"That's good," I say softly. "I know you've been doing everything on your own for years but it's okay to accept help." I offer a friendly smile.

He returns it before glancing over to Cassie who looks even more confused than me. "So, she really won? And she's going?"

"Yep. Her parents took some convincing but they said it was fine as long as she got a tutor."

He raises an eyebrow. "And *you're* going with her to meet him? I thought you hated him."

"I don't *hate* him, I'm just not a fan of his music. Cassie wants me to go, and it might be interesting to see what all the hype is about."

"I bet he's one of those celebs that are completely different in person, he's way too perfect to act like that all the time. I bet he just does it to make all the girls fall in love with him," he says, glancing at Cassie.

"I guess we'll find out."

Three

"What's wrong with the original one?" Cassie's changed her mind about her outfit at least three times in the last ten minutes.

She glances at the outfit currently thrown on the floor and pulls a face. "It's too basic."

"Oh." Last time I checked my 'basic' tees weren't covered in glitter. "Well, what about the dress you wore to that party last month? It looked great."

"That's not basic enough! I need something simple and elegant but not too boring, you know? I want to make an impression but not the wrong kind of impression." She continues to grab clothes from the wardrobe before deciding they're too plain or too out there and flinging them aside in a heap.

"Anyone would think you're meeting the Queen or something," I say half to myself, going back to my sketchbook.

Cassie ignores me and pulls one of her more recent designs out of the wardrobe, checking how it would look in the mirror before throwing it on. She smooths it out and grabs a necklace and bracelet off her jewellery stand. She checks herself in the mirror once more before opening her arms. "Ta-da!" she says, spinning.

"You look great." She really does. It's a light blue, gingham mid-dress that hugs her figure with a bow rapping around the top as well as rhinestone straps, more for show than for actual structure. "It was definitely worth the hundred-plus outfit changes."

She glares at me before glancing back in the mirror. "Who knows, maybe we'll fall in love and get married." She wiggles her eyebrows at me on the way to her desk to start her make-up. She riffles through her magazines and throws me a couple of older ones. "Have a look at these. Maybe you can learn a few things about him before we meet him."

As soon as I start flipping through them, I come across one of his interviews and quickly scan over it. All he's talking about is how he got his 'chiselled', 'perfect' abs, and how they and his 'charming looks' got him a feature role on a hit TV show. He should be taking himself on a date, there'll be no space for me and Cassie with his giant ego in the way.

I move on to the next page featuring him which isn't that far from the last. This one is all about his 'fashion and latest looks' which if you ask me is beyond boring, every time I see him he's wearing the same top or hoodie in different shades along with his signature skinny jeans. Although, here they've taken photos from red carpet events which seem to be a complete opposite to what he usual wears, in one he's decked out in a full James bond-esque tuxedo except it's been deconstructed in a fashion kinda way that I don't understand. He just looks like he stumbled through an office and got it stuck in the industrial shredder, but apparently it's 'one of the best looks of the year' so what do I know?

Hopefully the next will be more interesting. In this one, he has a whole four-page spread focusing on his speculated past and present love life, including blurry photos of him and the suspected girlfriends at meals or walking through parks. I've never liked the guy but even I can admit this is a bit invasive. I mean, the guy probably can't even pop to the shop without being interrogated. I guess that's the price for being the 'biggest teen heart-throb'.

"I never liked her."

"Huh? Who?"

"Ava-Mae." She pulls a face in the mirror. "She cheated on him and broke his heart. It did result in his best-selling album though so honestly it was probably for the best."

"Oh." How do they know though, it says he denied the dating rumours. I would hate to have my whole life plastered in every magazine for everyone to know.

I finish flicking through the magazines paying more attention to the personality quizzes than the interviews and put them aside.

They don't tell me much about Jackson, just a few surface-level things like his favourite movie is Die hard (of course it is), his favourite colour is blue (not surprising), his favourite meal is a 'proper' beef burger (there's nothing more manly than a giant lump of meat, right?) and that he currently lives in LA in a giant mansion that he owns and 'allows' his parents to share with him, but he says if he had it his way he'd live on his own.

And that's it. I flipped through at least 6 articles about him and that's all I found out. The rest of it is just gossip about potential past relationships or the meaning behind his lyrics (girls, relationships, parents etc. The usual stuff.) Every interview has the same questions worded slightly differently and the answers are the same every time.

I lie back on the bed, the heel of a stray boot digging into my skull, and stare up at the ceiling. *Well, this should be fun.*

We're in Cassie's living room, where we've been for the past hour, waiting to be picked up. I can tell Cassie's stressing about him cancelling, she's been pacing back and forth in front of the window for the past half an hour.

Julie, Cassie's mum, has been coming in every 10 minutes to check she hasn't had a meltdown. "Maybe you should sit down and watch some TV to pass the time. It's probably the traffic, it's always bad on this side of town and he might have to travel far," she says, raising her eyebrows at me when Cassie isn't looking.

"Yeah!" I perk up, taking the hint. "That's a good idea. Why don't we put on that designer show that you like?"

She starts to sulk over to the couch when a limousine pulls up outside. "It's him! He's here! Jackson Peters is at my house!" She runs towards the door stopping as she reaches it. I follow and wait behind her as she takes a deep breath before turning the handle.

Standing in the doorway is an older guy dressed in a plain black suit, holding two small bouquets. "Cassie Ward? Nice to meet you," he starts, handing her the bouquets. "I'm sure you were expecting someone a bit better looking but Mr Peters is a little busy, so he's said he'll meet you there. He wanted me to give you these though." He points at the flowers. "And to let you know he's very excited to meet you."

"This is insane," I whisper as he leads us to our stretched carriage. It's as white as light and so clean and polished that it's just as blinding.

I've never been in a limo before, everything looks so expensive. It has a built-in bar that's stocked full of luxury-looking treats and fancy non-alcoholic drinks, a screen to select the music on, the comfiest seats I've ever sat on and even the ceiling has loads of tiny lights that are starrier than Van Gogh's starry night. I wonder if this is just for the date or if he always travels by limousine.

"Do you think we're allowed to eat the snacks?" She's already searching through them, eying up the Ferrero Rocher.

I grab one and she follows my lead. "So, some flowers and a limo and he's forgiven?"

She knows I'm only teasing but she still glares at me. "He was busy, that's a perfectly acceptable excuse." She shoves a chocolate into her mouth.

"If you say so."

I pull my phone out of my jeans pocket and reread the application form for the competition.

Cassie snatches it out of my hands and shoves it into her purse. "Nope. You need a break. All you do lately is stare at a blank page or a blank application form or research or-"

"Okay, okay. I'll stop but only for the next couple of hours." I'd rather stare at a blank page than regret doing nothing later.

"Good."

The driver takes a long way as he says Jackson's still not ready yet, so we make the most of it and empty the minibar whilst screaming and dancing to music that's way too loud. The driver doesn't seem to mind, and I hate to admit it, but I'm having a good time. Maybe it won't be so bad.

After a while, we finally come to a stop and the music turns off. The driver opens the door and helps us onto the pavement outside of the fanciest restaurant in town, The Royal Port. The front windows are tinted so nobody can see in and airy pastel Amaranthus flowers cascade from above them, a small red carpet leads up to the door and at least twenty people queue to get in. They're dressed up in suits and floor-length gowns, accessorised with jewellery that shines too bright to be anything other than real diamonds.

"I think I'm a little underdressed." I try to smooth out some of the creases in my white off the shoulder top and worn jeans. It's the fanciest my wardrobe could go, and I know Cassie would've loved to dress me up in one of her amazing designs but our styles are just a tad too different for me to feel comfortable in.

Cassie looks like she's ready to burst from a mixture of nerves and excitement as we're led past everyone in the queue, all of them complaining silently among themselves as we're told to go straight in.

We make our way through the busy front of the restaurant, passing a few tables of loved-up couples and one crowded with a group of mums having a well-deserved night off.

The food looks amazing. I try to get a look at some of the dishes as we pass them and everything looks like it came straight from Instagram. In the centre of the room, there's an open kitchen where you can watch some of the chefs work and it's mesmerising. One of them flicks a pan and the whole thing goes up in flames causing the tables nearby to cheer.

We turn a corner and head up some stairs leading to the private garden dining room. I swear as we get closer I can hear arguing, but when the waiter opens the door, we're only greeted by Jackson Peters and his smiling face.

Four

His smile's so wide the forcefulness of it crawls across my skin. It looks so out of place among the warmness of the rest of his face, even his golden curls seem to have a friendly softness to them. His hands are stuffed in his usual skinny jeans and a branded oversized black top sways as he shifts slightly from one foot to his other.

I guess I'm not the only one that's underdressed.

Cassie doesn't move. She's frozen in the doorway with a smile as wide as the Cheshire Cat's and as I nudge her with my shoulder, attempting to break her out of her trance, she only mimics his top, her feet glued to the spot and her face unfazed.

His smile falters, his jaw tightening.

"Hi, I'm Lorri," I rush before he decides were not worth his time.

Cassie's still frozen. Actually, I don't think she's even blinking, should I get her some help? What if she's having some kind of heart attack or seizer or something?

She must feel my stare because she turns her head slowly to meet my eyes, her mouth still halfway to gawping. I widen my eyes and she snaps out of it, finally having that well needed blink. I don't know about 'keys to the soul' but the eyes must have some kind of magic.

"Cassie. I'm a little bit of a fan," she laughs, giving a dramatic reenactment of her previous statue self.

His eyes shift between us and he gives us a quick, "Hey" before taking his seat.

Weird. He could give us a bit more, especially since Cassie technically paid good money for an extra hour with him which we've now lost. She doesn't seem too bothered though, she may have shaken her frozen state but she hasn't lost her crazy grin. I don't think I've ever seen her this happy before, and I've been by her side for the majority of her life.

She watches him pick up his phone with cartoon love hearts in her eyes, and I look away, feeling like I'm intruding.

The room has floor-to-ceiling windows all around and the near-summer sunset shines through, lighting it with tones of orange and pink. It's scattered with vases of various flowers and a few unlit candles. In the centre, there's a big table, but it's not so big that you have to shout at each other, and it has a luxurious silk sheet over it that goes well with the fancy plates and cutlery. It looks like something from a fairytale. I wish I had my sketchbook with me.

He hasn't even looked at her. I get celebs are busy but surely he can spare a few seconds away from his phone to talk to her.

A suited waiter comes and hands us our menus before quietly going to stand in the corner, picking a point outside to focus his gaze on. Cassie and I share a look from behind our menus. With this and the tall, blonde bodyguard outside that searched Cassie's tiny bag for weapons, it really does feel like we're on a date with the Queen.

My stomach grumbles, reminding me of how little I've had to eat today.

"You've come here a lot more than me and I usually just stick to my usual. Is there anything I *have* to try?" Cassie asks, wafting her arms around as she talks.

He continues to read his menu.

She checks with me to make sure she hadn't just imagined the words coming out of her mouth, she no longer looks as happy as she did when we walked in. With knitted brows, I give her a nod and she tilts her head, turning back to the guy that just full on blanked her.

"We're ready to order," he states.

Maybe he didn't hear her. After all, he could be partially deaf from all the concerts and screaming fans. Because if he did hear her, then he would know we're clearly not ready to order. Even if he didn't, it would've been nice of him to ask if we were ready too.

The waiter comes back over and pulls out a small notebook and pen.

"I'll have the carbonara with a side of garlic bread and…" He regards the drink section of the menu, a mischievous grin spreading across his face. "We're trying to have a good night so I'll have a bottle of your finest wine."

I can't remember exactly when his birthday is but I'm pretty sure he's not old enough to order alcohol. The waiter doesn't argue.

I order the lasagne and Cassie goes with the chicken salad, both of us deciding on mocktails instead of wine. The waiter takes back the menus before leaving through a discreet side door. As soon as he leaves Jackson goes back to his phone and starts tapping away, leaving me and Cassie sitting in silence.

Okay, now he's just being rude. I know he's famous but nobody's that famous that just sitting in the same room and breathing the same air as them is worth the money Cassie paid for this. He's going to talk to us whether he likes it or not. "Did it take you long to get here?"

He doesn't even look up from his phone. "No."

"So, you're staying in town?"

"Yep." Still doesn't look up.

I rest my elbows on the cool silk, letting my chin fall to my knuckles. This guy is going to give me more than one syllable even if it kills me. "Oh cool. Whereabouts?"

Cassie kicks me under the table and I glare at her before turning back to Jackson.

He sits up in his seat and for the first time looks me dead in the eyes, allowing me to get a proper look at his. They're hazel, the sunset making them look golden, and despite his glare, they're kind looking, the slight glaze giving a softness to them.

He quickly clears his throat. "I need to make a phone call."

Grabbing his phone, he pushes his chair back so fast it screeches across the floor. He practically runs out the door and we hear him storm down the stairs, the room falling silent. *Well, that went well.*

"Did you have to do that?" Cassie grumbles, tugging at the ends of her hair.

"What?" Why's she mad at me?

"You could tell he didn't want to talk and you still pushed him!"

Seriously, she's defending him? "You won a competition to meet him, the least he could do is acknowledge your existence!" I try and fail, to keep my voice calm.

She must agree because she doesn't say anything else. Instead, she turns to look at the view.

After what feels like forever, the waiter enters carrying a bucket of ice with a shiny bottle of red wine and a tray with our exotic mocktails. He surveys the room with a creased brow, probably wondering where the person paying for all this has gone, before walking up to the table and swiftly placing everything down. "Your food will be ready shortly, would you like me to wait until Mr Peters is back to bring it out?"

Cassie smiles and I can tell she's about to answer yes, so I answer first, "No thanks, he's only popped out to take a call so he'll be back soon." I'm starving and I know he's probably used to everyone waiting for him, but I won't be one of them.

The waiter nods before leaving us again.

I take a sip of my drink, to give myself something to do, and I'm about to ask Cassie if she thinks he's coming back when the door swings open and in he walks. We both watch as he strides from the door to his seat and slumps back down, pouring himself a big glass of wine before downing it. He notices our eyes on him and smirks, "I'm sorry, did you want some?"

We both shake our heads and he pours himself a second glass. So, this is what celebrities are like.

The waiter enters with our meals and places them in front of us, noticing how drunk Jackson already is when he knocks the plate of garlic bread out of his hands, the plate shattering into tiny pieces.

"Oh shit! My bad," he slurs, making no move to help.

What is it with this guy? I thought his fans always gush about how kind and down-to-earth he is, always helping others. That's definitely not this guy. I push out my chair to help the waiter but stop at the small shake of his head. Maybe this isn't the first time he's had to deal with him.

He starts to eat his meal and downs the last bit of the wine. After the waiter cleans up the mess, he tells Jackson that he'll bring him another free of charge. He's almost at the door when Jackson shouts, "And another bottle of that."

The waiter takes the bottle and we all tuck in without making a sound.

He returns with a tight smile and goes to place the fresh bottle into the bucket but it hardly touches the ice before it's snatched from his hand.

Jackson pours another glass before lifting it, "Let's do a toast."

Great. I share a look with Cassie before reluctantly lifting mine to join him.

"Here's to me and my music, for bringing people together. Cheers!"

He rams our glasses together with a loud crunch and glass rains everywhere.

My glass was almost empty, but his was full of red wine and it gushes from his broken glass, streaming down his hand and covering the table. I feel damp on my legs and notice it's not only splattered all over my top but is also dripping off the table and seeping into my only good clothes.

Ruining this 'date' for Cassie wasn't enough, so he just *had* to go and ruin my clothes as well. I'm never going to be able to get the stains out.

"Whoops. Sorry." He takes his napkin and tries to mop up some of the wine on the table. He smears it everywhere, creating an even bigger stain.

"Lorri, are you okay?" Cassie asks, offering me her napkin.

That's it. First, he was rude and refused to acknowledge us, and now this. Cassie might not mind that he's treating us like trash but I do. "No, I'm not okay! My clothes are ruined and he's hardly spoken to you all night. And he was late!"

"Chill, it's just some clothes, buy new ones," he mumbles, taking another fork full of pasta, now completely given up on cleaning up his mess.

"First of all, don't tell me to 'chill'. Secondly, just because you're a spoiled brat that gets whatever you want, it doesn't mean everyone else has the luxury to do the same whenever they please." He scowls at me as I continue, "Just because you're this big superstar with a load of fans and a perfect life, it doesn't mean you can treat pe-"

His chair bangs against the floor as he jumps up, sending it across the room. "You know what? I don't have to listen to this. You don't know shit." He staggers out the door, slamming it behind him.

Five

"I'm sorry, but I couldn't sit here and let him treat us, especially you, like that. He'd be nothing without his fans, and this is how he treats them," I say, assessing my damaged clothes.

She stands, snatching something off the table. I barely have time to register what's happening or wonder if she's leaving because of me before she opens the door and shoots out.

"He forgot his phone!" she calls back when she's halfway down the stairs.

After everything, she's still helping him? If I had found it, I would have dropped it into the bucket of melted ice and watched as he realised he would have to acknowledge the people that were in front of him. Although he'd probably just buy a new one, I wouldn't be surprised if he already had a backup or two waiting to go. I definitely wouldn't be running through the restaurant to make sure he gets it back, but here we are.

It doesn't take long until I'm behind her and we're both running past all the posh couples trying to enjoy their lovely meals. They watch us with disapproving eyes, a couple of them already looking for the closest waiter to complain, but I don't stop to apologize. Right now I need to make sure Jackson doesn't do anything else to ruin Cassie's day. We find him outside the restaurant standing on the pavement. 'Standing' might be a bit generous, he looks like a drunk hunchback of Notre Dame as he sways in the non-existent wind.

Cassie tentatively approaches him and taps him on the shoulder.

He steadies himself. "What? Do you want an autograph or something?"

She recoils, shrinking a couple of inches. "You forgot this," she says, holding out the phone.

"Ah, you want a picture?" He scoffs, "Of course, you do. That's what everyone wants!" He throws his arms out causing him to lose his balance.

A few people in the queue are watching us and there's the start of a low buzz as one by one they realise who's yelling.

"No, I just wanted to give you your phone." The wobble of her voice forces me to step forward. If he doesn't get out of here soon, a picture will be the least of his worries.

"Are you sure? Sure you don't want a picture, or an autograph, or a free t-shirt, or an inside scoop into my love life?" He drags a hand across his face. "Everyone wants something!" he shouts at the sky.

A few gasps arise from behind us and Cassie's eyes start to tear up. This is getting out of hand. "We don't want anything from you. We just want to go home," I try.

He takes a shaky step back, slightly shocked. It doesn't take long before his eyebrows come down again to meet his scowl. "Great, me too." He grabs his phone and shoves it into his coat's inner pocket. There's something clear and shiny already in there. *Is that a bottle of vodka?* "Well, thanks for the date. I wish I could say it was fun but well, it wasn't. Have a nice life and that."

Just as he's about to fall over, the limo pulls up, blocking the view of the passersby that had stopped on the other side of the road.

Hold on, that's the limo we came in. "I thought you were supposed to be our ride home?"

"And I thought you said you didn't want anything from me," he challenges.

If he doesn't wipe that smug look off his face, I'll do it for him. "We need a ride, you can't just leave us here. Wait," The only reason we know he's leaving in the first place is because we followed him out. "You were, weren't you? You were just going to leave without saying anything."

"Ugh." He ignores me and attempts to climb into the limo, the bodyguard from earlier helping him.

"That's right! Just ignore all your problems and they'll go away, right? That must be nice." I start towards him, flinching when he slams the door. "You stuck-up TWAT!" I shout after the limo as it drives off.

I'm suddenly reminded of where I am by the chorus of gasps, stares and whispers coming from the people surrounding us. Even the people who are sitting outside of other restaurants have all turned in our direction. I find Cassie sitting amongst them, on one of the chairs outside the neighbouring bar, and join her.

"My parents can't pick us up, they've already left for their business trip, so I've rung for a taxi. It'll be here in ten minutes," she says, staring at where he previously was.

"I could have asked my uncle to pick us up," I say, picking at the skin around my nails.

"No, it's my fault we're in this mess."

I immediately stop. "You're joking, right? This is all his fault, not yours."

"But we wouldn't be here if I didn't enter the competition."

"True. But none of this would have happened if he was just a decent human being instead of-"

"A stuck-up twat?" she offers with a smirk.

I hide my face in my hands. "Oh, God. Everyone heard, didn't they?"

"Well, you did scream it down the street. I don't think we'll be allowed back to that restaurant any time soon, did you see everyone's faces when we ran out? They were so pissed, and when you were shouting they looked disgusted," she laughs.

I continue to shove my face into my hands, shaking my head, and we both laugh until our stomachs hurt and our taxi arrives.

The taxi stops outside our gloomy block of flats and I hop out onto the pavement. "Are you sure you don't want to stay here tonight?"

"I'll be fine," she replies and I feel my chest relax. "I'll come round tomorrow instead and we can try to get your creative juices flowing for your competition entry. I'll need a bit of math help in return though, otherwise I'm going to fail."

"Alright. Don't come too early though," I warn. Cassie has a bad habit of turning up before the crack of dawn and expecting me to be up and ready, it's never going to happen.

She reluctantly agrees and we say our goodbyes. When the taxi's no longer in sight, I head up the rusty steps to our flat. I pull out my keys and search all my pockets for my phone. Damn, I must've forgotten to get it back off Cassie, hopefully I won't be needing it tonight. As I walk down the corridor my steps slow and my breathing quickens. *Good day or a bad day?*

When I'm close enough to see that the lights are on, I let my shoulders relax and I head towards the door. I prepare myself before pushing it open and let out a deep breath when the smell of cheese on toast hits me. The place is spotless and dad's singing from the kitchen. *Good day.*

"Is that you Lorri?" Dad shouts as he closes the oven and turns his music down.

I take my shoes off, place them on the rack, and walk through the living room. "Yeah."

Our flat isn't big but it's cosy, full of family photos and a few of my drawings dad insisted he framed. We also have a lot of plants. Like A LOT. Dad says they help to bring a bit of life to the room but I think they're just to help with the smell when things get bad.

I reach the kitchen and perch on one of the worn-out stools we found at a car boot sale a couple of years ago. The smell of the cheese on toast makes my stomach rumble, the hole my glass-covered lasagna was supposed to fill now the size of Jackson's obnoxiously big limo.

"He was such an ass!" I say half to myself.

Dad looks up from the giant mound of cheese that he's grating for the second batch. It takes him a second to remember. "Ah. The celeb date thing. That was tonight? So, you didn't have fun?"

"I had fun with Cassie, we got to go in a limo, but he was *so* rude. He didn't speak to us, then he got drunk and then he spilt wine everywhere, including all over me and my food." I gesture to my top and the now dry patches of splattered red wine.

"He sounds awful. I hope he apologised for ruining your top." He takes the first two slices out and loads another round of cheesy goodness into the oven.

"He didn't. Well, he did but he didn't mean it. Even if he did, that's beside the point." He slides a plate over and I take a huge bite. "And then he left us."

"That's celebs for you. You'll find most of them only care about themselves. At least now you can watch the second half of rugby with me."

"It's on TV?" I quickly twist on my chair. It's turned all the way down but I can see the sports presenters talking about the game on the small box in the living room.

"Yeah! It's been a close game, we're behind because Ratchford got a yellow card, supposedly for foul play." He rolls his eyes. *Ratchford would never.* "If we play a bit better in the second half, I think we'll win. Go sit down and I'll make you a cuppa before it starts."

Grabbing my plate, I jump off my chair and get comfy on the couch, turning the TV up whilst making sure my plate doesn't fall off the armrest.

It's been ages since I last watched rugby with dad, we used to go all the time when I was a child. We don't have one of those expensive sports packages so we usually have to wait for the big games that are shown on the main channels. Even then it's rare we both get to watch it.

I smile at the screen as the players run back out to the thousands of cheering fans, remembering the buzz you get when you're there. *I'm glad he left the date early.*

A stray ray of sunlight blinds me as it seeps in from the window and there's a loud banging at the front door. I hear it open and then close a second later. My bedroom door flings open and someone starts violently shaking me. Someone with perfectly manicured nails, freshly washed and styled blond hair that drapes across my face and tickles my nose, and that smells of expensive perfume. I wonder who it could be.

"I thought we agreed you wouldn't come early," I groan, rolling over to face her. The digital clock on my bedside table reads 7:58 am. "Ugh."

"You don't understand...I needed to talk to you..." Cassie says between gasps. She clutches her chest, revealing a sweat patch when she lifts her arm, and leans over, her slightly windswept hair falling forward.

"Did you run here?" I ask in disbelief.

"I couldn't get a taxi and I couldn't wait, so yeah." She takes a minute to catch her breath and then continues, "I saw it last night and tried to message you about it, because I was freaking out, but after my 7th message I remembered that I had your phone. I've hardly slept, I've just been reading them all. It's everywhere!"

Reading all of what? I wait for an explanation but she's busy rummaging through her giant tote bag. Okay, tote bag? Cassie only strays away from her designer handbags when it's a big emergency. "What's everywhere?" I ask, sitting up so fast my head whirs.

She dumps a towering stack of shiny magazines onto my lap and gestures for me to read them. They're all marked with today's date, she must have grabbed them as soon as the shops opened. Has she really not slept all night? What could be so important that she got up first thing and bought one of every possible magazine available and then raced over here to wake me up at the crack of dawn?

The top magazine is upside down, but the front has a paparazzi-taken photo of a couple next to a car. No. There's no way. I quickly turn it the right way, almost knocking the stack to the floor. There's no mistaking my red curls or pink zebra splattered clothes. I scramble through the rest, praying they're not the same. My prayers go unheard as I'm met with the same shot, over and over again, each a little different to the last. Most are of Jackson and me yelling at each other, some also have pictures of me screaming as the limo drives off. One has even zoomed in on my face and put 'who is she?' in big red letters.

"What the…" I say under my breath, still frantically flipping through the magazines. This has to be a wind-up, I don't belong in gossip magazines. I'm a nobody.

"It's everywhere. Every news website, magazine front cover, Instagram fan and news accounts, and even on them gossipy news shows." She rolls her eyes, even though I know she watches said shows. "Also, some people at school are already posting about it. I've had at least three messages already from people wanting details."

I barely listen to her as I read the articles. I can't believe this is happening. "'Teenage heart-throb leaves girl heartbroken.' Please. That's what they get from this?" I hold up the magazine and point at my giant screaming face. I'm not sure what photo it's been cropped from.

Cassie hands me the open magazine that she had been flipping through. "It's only a few that mention you being heartbroken by him. Most of them speculate about alcohol being involved and focused more on that. But…"

I skim over the text. 'Date From Hell', 'Peters could barely stand', 'they must have had a disagreement whilst on their date', 'as you can see in the pictures, Peters was not happy with the guest and couldn't get away fast enough', 'who is this mystery girl and what did she do to our loving Peters?'.

What did *I* do to Peters? Right, because of course, nothing is ever his fault. I bet he could get away with murder. He wouldn't even need a lawyer, they'd just find some reason to let him off and then give him an award. It'd be 'Most angelic murderer' or something and they'd give him a docuseries where crazed fans could obsess over his killings.

"Just ignore them. It's just some stupid gossip mags." She gives me a half-smile.

We both know that's not entirely true. It won't be long until the whole school's talking about it and then I'll be known as 'the girl who was rude to and upset *the* Jackson Peters'. At least I've got the rest of today before I have to face it all.

I push the magazines away as I pull my legs to my chest under the blanket, resting my chin on my knees.

"Why don't we do something? Try and forget all about it. We could see what Sean and Abby are up to, go to theirs and give them a hand or something?" Cassie says whilst shovelling the magazines back into her bag, crumpling them. "I think that's a good plan."

I lift my head. "What have they said?" We both know Sean never accepts help, even on his birthday, so they must have spoken about this.

She stops destroying the magazines and tilts her head. "They said they messaged you? Oh right, here." She searches through her bag and pulls out my phone. "We just think it would be good to hang out, do some revision or whatever. Didn't you need help with physics?"

I'm met with a wall of notifications when my phone lights up. Most of them are from people tagging me in posts and comments, but I also have a few DMs and text messages from people trying to get an 'inside scoop'. I open our group chat to four new messages:

Abs

I just saw all the articles. God, the media suck. Hope you're okay L x

Sean the sheep

I thought you said you DIDN'T hate him?

Abs

Don't listen to him.

Why don't you come over and we can watch a movie? It's been a while since you've been to ours :)

Even though leaving my bed and having to go out into the world is the last thing I want to do right now, I can see how much my friends care so I drag myself out of bed, grab some comfy clothes and type out a reply to let them know that we're on our way.

Six

Once I'm dressed and ready, I leave a note on the counter for dad telling him where I've gone and that I've watered all of the plants, and then we head out the door.

I'm glad I put on my hoodie, even though we're halfway through May, and yesterday everyone was having barbecues, we're still getting April showers. I stuff my hair into my hood, a disobedient auburn curl still sticking out the top, and pull the strings tight so that the majority of my face is protected from the fine rain.

"Ugh," Cassie groans. She opens her bright pink umbrella, almost taking my right eye out. "The weather sucks, it was sunny on the way over."

We shuffle down the rusty stairs at the end of the flats and try not to slip on the wet steps. "Do you think everyone knows?" I sniffle, pulling my sleeves over my hands. "Will people recognise me from the photos?"

Cassie didn't let me watch any tv whilst we had breakfast, and she took my phone back after I messaged Sean and Abby, so I couldn't obsess over what everyone was saying. But I need to know what's going on, I can't just ignore it when it feels as though the whole world is talking about me.

"No," Cassie says, stopping at the bottom of the stairs to face me. "I bet hardly anyone even knows. Sure, people at school will know, because it's school and gossip spreads like wildfire, but most people won't even care." She shrugs. "You never usually care what people at school think."

I don't particularly care about school gossip but it's a little hard to ignore it when it's about you. "I've never had to care what they think."

"It won't last long, they'll be new gossip by the end of tomorrow." Her phone vibrates in her bag and she gets it out, reads the message and quickly types out a response as she starts to walk again. "Sean wants us to grab some snacks, he's specifically requested-"

"Peanut butter and pickles?" I interrupt. She confirms my suspicion with a smile. "I don't know how he can eat that, it's so gross," I say whilst stepping over a muddy puddle.

"I know. Remember that time we went to the cinema for his birthday?" she laughs.

I don't think I'll ever be able to forget. He'd asked us all to get him peanut butter and pickles as presents so we did, and then he ate them all in the cinema and threw up *everywhere.* "He swore he'd never eat them again." I pull a face as I remember the scene. "Oh, that poor family in front of us."

"And the cleaner! I think they were greener than Sean was," she says, laughing harder.

By the time we've stopped laughing, we're both doubled over and my eyes are watering. I wipe at them with my wet sleeves, only adding to the dampness under my eyes, and turn the corner to the front of the flats. When I open my eyes again, I freeze.

I feel Cassie's confused eyes land on me. "What?" She follows my gaze. "Oh no."

Outside our block of flats, there's a group of what looks like paparazzi. I've never seen them in person before but they look exactly how I thought they would. They're all dressed in black and almost all of them are carrying heavy-looking cameras. There's so many of them that they look more like a herd of wild animals waiting to pounce on their prey.

The road's cluttered with big black vans that stick out so much that people have come out of their flats to check them out. Or maybe they just want to get some gossip or have their chance to be interviewed by one of the news reporters that have turned up.

The woman closest to us turns around, looking up from her camera, and a wave of recognition crosses her face. She points at us before we even have a chance to run and yells, "She's here!"

Cassie grabs my arm and pulls me in the other direction. "Come on!"

We sprint to the end of the street and turn right, almost running straight into a child, earning us a scowl from their mother. We shout our apologies as we cross the road and head towards the park, trying not to slip on the wet pavement.

As we near the entrance, I glance back in time to see them run around the corner like a stampede and we hurry through the gate. We run towards the other entrance on the opposite side, ignoring the path and Cassie curses under her breath as she slips on the mud, muttering something about her new shoes. We almost reach the other side but spot a few stray paparazzi behind the gate. Cassie stops and turns to look behind me before grabbing my hand and dragging me towards the bushes.

"Where are we going? We can't just hide in a bush!" I glance behind us and a camera goes off somewhere in the park, the bright flash causing me to see white spots.

"There's a secret exit over here," Cassie replies as she pushes us through the bushes and throws away her turned-out umbrella before throwing her bag through a small hole in the brick wall. "See," she says, smiling at me as she climbs through to the other side. "Come on. Quick!"

I take my bag off and pass it through, hopping over just as the bushes behind me start to rustle. As we're jogging away one of the bigger guys that was following us looks through the small hole, punching the wall when he spots us.

We continue to jog until we reach Mr Lawrence's corner shop where we slip in and head to the back, collapsing when we're out of view of the door window. Cassie grabs a bottle of water from next to us and chugs half of it before offering it to me.

The bell goes and the guy that was at the hole walks through the door. I throw my hand over my mouth in a desperate attempt to hide my lack of fitness as my lungs burn.

"Have you seen two girls?" he asks Mr Lawrence whilst eying up the rest of the shop. His voice is low and there's a hint of an American accent. He looks like a giant next to the much shorter older man.

Mr Lawrence shakes his head and the man turns to leave. "Actually," Mr Lawrence says, "I did see two people run past. I didn't get a good look though. I think they went towards town bu-"

The guy gives a quick nod and rushes out the door before Mr Lawrence has time to finish.

When the door closes, he slowly walks over, making sure the coast is clear. "Was that the police? MI5? Did I just lie to the government?" he shrieks. "I can't get arrested, who would look after the shop?" He gives us a stern look, "What did you do?"

I throw my hands up defensively. "We didn't do anything!"

"Have you not seen the news?" Cassie says at the same time.

Mr Lawrence gasps and claps his hands, "Yes! Another royal baby *and* a royal wedding. It's so exciting isn't it, I can't wait! I hope it's on a weekday, I've been dying for a day off."

Cassie shakes her head. "No, not that." She reaches into her soaked bag and pulls out a damp magazine that's open on a page of Jackson and me. She hands it to him and he stares at it for a moment, scrunching his face in confusion.

"She looks like you," he says after a while. "Ah, I see. I once got mistaken for Brad Pitt, you know. Just tell them they got it wrong"

I'm not sure who told him that but it was either a *long* time ago or they were partially blind. I shake my head. "She looks like me because it is me. Someone took photos of us arguing, because he was rude," I add, "and now they won't leave me alone because they want pictures and interviews or whatever."

He smiles at the photo, "Ah. That sounds about right, you've always stuck up for yourself. I can still smell bananas when that girl walks in."

A couple of years ago, this girl was making fun of Abby's old shoes and the hole in her dress. She made her cry and laughed about it. Throwing my milkshake on her might not have been the right thing to do but it made her stop.

"How do they know where you live?" he asks, passing the magazine back to Cassie.

"I'm not sure." How *do* they know where I live? It's not exactly an easy bit of information to get.

"They could have followed me? They might have seen me when I was getting the magazines," Cassie says quietly, staring at her shoes. "They weren't there when I arrived."

If there's one thing I've learnt about the paparazzi, it's that they're ruthless. "We don't know that for sure. And even if they did, it doesn't matter. They would've found a way," I shrug.

The bell goes again and we all drop to the floor, holding our breaths.

"Hello?" a regular customer calls from the front of the shop and we all pop up at the same time like a broken whack a mole. Thankfully he isn't elderly, otherwise we might've given the poor guy a heart attack.

We leave Mr Lawrence's with a giant bag of snacks courtesy of Cassie's credit card that her parents gave her to use whilst they're away on business trips.

Before we left Mr Lawrence gave us some hats, just in case we run into some more paparazzi. The rain's stopped for now and the sun's coming back out so we take our time as we stroll down the street towards Sean and Abby's bungalow, trying to dry off a bit before we go in.

"Want one?" Cassie asks, holding out a packet of strawberry laces.

"No thanks. How did you know about the hole?"

Cassie lives on the other side of town. I've lived near the park for years and I've never heard of or noticed the hole.

She gives me a quizzical look. "What hole?"

Cassie's never been good at acting nonchalant. "The hole in the wall. In the park."

"Oh, that hole. Everybody knows about it." She quickly glances around. "Oh look, there's Abby. Hey!" she shouts, waving her arm frantically as she speeds up.

"Oh. Yeah."

Seven

Sean and Abby's bungalow isn't that much bigger than our flat but it's a lot nicer inside. Before their mum got ill, she had just qualified to be an interior designer, she'd waited until the twins had been old enough to be left alone before going back to college. When we came over, she was either working or rearranging the whole bungalow.

No matter how busy she was, she would always make sure we were okay and had everything we needed. A lot of the time she'd get us to help with the decorating if we'd done all of our homework. She can't do as much as she used to because of her illness but the house still looks great. Sean probably has something to do with that.

When we go in, we're greeted with a shower of slobbery kisses and are almost knocked over by a wagging tail. Bending down, I take my shoes off and fuss over the giant, almost-white golden retriever running around my legs.

"I swear he likes you guys more than us. Oi, Albert, calm down!" Sean says just as Albert jumps up at Cassie, knocking her over, and smothering her face with wet kisses.

"Aw, it's okay. He just missed us, didn't you?" Cassie replies, whilst ruffling the dog's fur.

"Come on in. Mum's asleep in her room so we'll need to be quiet," he says, taking the snack bag and dumping it onto the sofa.

Sitting on the other sofa, I take out my sketchbook and pencils and place them on the glass coffee table as he searches through the contents. Albert jumps on to the couch, sniffing the treats but as he realises none are for him, he jumps up next to Cassie instead and curls up near her feet.

"What's this for? Where are my pickles?" Sean asks, holding up his peanut butter in one hand and a bunch of celery in the other.

"Sorry. We went to Mr Lawrence's and he doesn't have any, we thought celery might do the job," I answer.

He throws himself onto the sofa. "Celery is *not* the same as pickles."

"Close enough," Abby says as she places some bowls and drinks next to my sketchbook.

"It's gross anyway," Cassie says, earning a stick of celery to come hurtling towards her. She launches it back just in time to stop Albert from eating it.

"It's not gross, don't knock it till you try it." He dumps some of the snacks into the bowls. "I can't believe he still doesn't sell them. I worked out the estimated profit he'd make if he sold them. Honestly, he's missing out on a bunch of cash, especially with me around the corner but he won't listen."

Cassie rolls her eyes and grabs a handful of pink bonbons. "Of course you did. Can we start studying so you can transfer some of your brains to me, please? I'm going to need it if I want to pass anything."

"You're going to do fine," he says softly as he catches some popcorn in his mouth, the corners turning up into a smirk. "But are we really not going to address the elephant in the room."

Here we go. I grab the pillow from next to my arm and aim it at his head. He moves out of the way at the last second and catches it.

"Hey! It's not my fault you got caught screaming at *the* most popular guy of our generation. I've already planned out a speech for when I get interviewed." He clears his throat, straightens an imaginary tie and sits up straight. "I think I speak on behalf of everybody who knows Lorri Johnson when I say that I. Was. Surprised. We all thought she just had a secret crush on Mr Peters, none of us realised she actually despised hi- OW!" He puts his hands up to the side of his face where my second attack hits its target.

Smiling, I pick up the remote and turn on the tv, making sure to stay away from the news channels. Hopefully, we can all move on and focus on something else. This is Sean though so there would have to be an alien invasion for him to change the subject.

"So, what happened? I haven't read any of the articles. I did see the photos and some of the headlines though and they're… not great," Abby says, pulling a face as she opens the dip and nachos.

They're all watching me, waiting for my answer, even Albert. I stroke his butt and he gets up to move over to my side of the couch, attempting to sit on my lap even though he's way too big for that now.

"Nothing happened. He was an ass the whole time we were there and then he took our ride, leaving us with no way home."

"So she yelled at him. In Front of everyone. We got loads of dodgy looks, you should have seen them," Cassie laughs.

"Sounds like he deserved it," Abby says with a mouth full of nachos.

Sean leans forward, his eyes turning to slits. "I don't know. Are you sure it wasn't pure hatred, bubbling up, that you just couldn't hold in any longer? I saw the way you looked at him when we were watching that interview of him the other week." He sucks in a deep breath, "If looks could kill."

He and Cassie fall into a fit of laughter like a couple of giggling hyenas.

I'm used to Sean teasing me, he's like a big brother even though we're the same age. Having no choice but to grow up when their mum got ill, he quickly became the most mature one in the group. Unfortunately, that doesn't stop him from being annoying though.

Cassie's just as bad when she wants to be, but when they're together they feed off each other. Usually, I don't mind, it's only for a laugh, but I'm not really in the mood today.

I lightly hit Cassie with the remote, causing Albert to go into protective mode, and give Sean my best death stare. "Oh, shut up. Are we going to revise or are you going to tease me all day?"

They eventually give in and we start revising.

Around the three hour mark, Abby starts playing with Albert, Cassie starts scrolling through social media, I start obsessing over my non-existing art piece and Sean starts throwing sweets at us to get our attention whilst talking non-stop about quantum physics.

We agree on a break and decide to put on a movie. Abby closes the bright curtains whilst Sean goes to grab a blanket and check on his mum, promising to never speak to us again if we choose another 'soppy romance'.

He returns and we all squeeze onto the main couch like we've done since we were half the size we are now. We watch a film that we've watched a million times and then log into Cassie's Netflix when I notice she's started to drool on Sean's shoulder after complaining that the movie's boring.

By the time the last episode of the new drama Cassie suggested finishes, the sun's starting to set and I have multiple missed calls. Most of them are from people that I've only messaged once or twice about homework, but a couple are from Dad. I go to messages and click on his name.

don't be home late im making fish fingers for tea
you're on the news!?

just saw the news reporters outside the flats. forget the fish fingers we'll get a chippy tea instead

My stomach twists at the confirmation that they're still there. I had been hoping they'd get bored and leave after an hour or two but clearly, I underestimated their will power.

I send a smiley face and let him know I'll be back soon, putting my phone in my pocket as I walk over to the radiator where my hoodie's been drying.

"Leaving already?" Sean asks.

"Already?" Pulling back the curtain, I point to the darkening sky outside.

"Oh," he says, checking his watch. "Well, you could stay for tea? I think Cassie's going to attempt that risotto again."

The bitter taste that stuck in my mouth after spitting it out all over Cassie's kitchen last week comes back and I swollow to try and clear it. "As tempting as that is, my dad's messaged, we're having a chippy tea," I say, smiling smugly.

"Ugh, lucky. Don't tell her I said that," he quickly adds, glancing over his shoulder. "I take it he saw the news."

"Yep. He was going to find out eventually, especially with the news reporters outside the flats."

His eyebrows shoot up and his eyes almost jump out of his head. "They actually do that? Camp outside your home?"

I nod. "They chased us on the way over here as well, we lost them at Mr Lawrence's."

"Damn. Well, good luck for tomorrow. Do you want us to meet at yours to walk to school together?"

"No, it'll be fine." As much as I'd love to not go through that again, alone, I don't want to drag them into it. Hopefully, they'll have someone new to hunt down tomorrow. "Plus, you've got further maths on a Monday," I remind him whilst we walk to the door and I slip on my shoes.

"I can miss a lesson, Miss Jones won't mind." He stands taller. "I'm ahead anyway."

"Of course, you are," I mumble with a grin. I expect to see a similar grin when I face him, instead, he's frowning. I look straight into his downturned eyes. "I'll be *fine*, don't worry. We can meet up before form."

He nods and I go to yell bye to the others before remembering their mum is still resting. "Tell the others I'll see them tomorrow."

We say goodbye and he pushes his leg in front of Albert when he tries to follow me out the door. When it shuts behind me and I step into the last bit of sunlight, I feel the warmth roll over me.

I didn't get much work done but at least I got to take my mind off things for a while. I stroll down the road, heading towards the park and use the hole now that I know it's there.

Maybe they got bored, figured I found a way to sneak past them and went home. Maybe there's already a new story, celebs are constantly in the papers.

Rounding the corner, my whole body relaxes at the sight of the empty street. No people holding cameras searching the street, no vans clogging up the road. I start towards the building, my mouth watering at the thought of the fish and chips waiting for me.

I'm almost at the steps when they emerge from behind the bushes. They try to capture me as I rush up the stairs, going three at a time. *Please don't trip, the tabloids would have a field day with those photos.*

When I reach the top, out of their view, I hear their heavy steps quickly on my chase. I sprint down the hall and slip into our flat. As the door slams shut behind me, they curse, shouting to the others that they've lost me. *If only it was that easy.*

Eight

When I leave for school there's no one outside the flats that shouldn't be there, just the usual neighbours dragging screaming children to school or putting out the bins, looking as if they just rolled out of bed.

I'm already late. Dad slept in and was late for work, so I had to wake him up, make breakfast, pack our lunches and pour him a big flask of coffee. All while trying not to freak out about going to school where there's a huge chance that everyone's talking about me and Jackson Peters.

By the time I get to school, I have a couple of concerned messages from Abby and Cassie asking if I decided not to come in and one from Sean threatening to have a stern word with the paps if they're still bothering me.

Turning the corner, I notice a big black van, similar to the ones that were outside the flat, guarding the school gates. They wouldn't, right? They couldn't. There's no way they found out where I go to school and are camping out at the gates because that would be full on stalking, right?

I inch closer and message the group back to let them know that I'm here as the bell rings faintly, signalling the start of form. Hurrying, I reach the gates and go to slip in as the guy that followed us to Mr Lawrence's comes from behind the van.

My feet freeze, my chest tightening. Why? Why am I so interesting that they feel the need to hunt me down and snap their precious, prying photos? Their precious, prying photos that benefit everyone except the people that are imprisoned within them.

He spots me and his lips twist into a smug leer. He takes a few wide strides and hoists his camera, angling it to capture my shaking features. I turn away before he gets the chance and dash through the gates, running past him with my face so close to the weapon that I feel it when it's triggered.

A few students are still walking through the corridors and they all watch as I barrel through the doors and trudge towards my form. I may be safe from the paparazzi but I'm far from safe, if there's anything worse than tabloid news it's high school gossip.

I pass a girl that I had a class with a couple of years ago and she whispers something to the girl next to her. They both giggle, their eyes still on me when I reach my room. I knew it would be bad but I didn't think it would be 'walking-down-the-corridor-and-having-everyone-laugh-at-me' bad. Maybe I'm just being paranoid, they could be talking about something else and just looking in my direction, right?

I take a deep breath before entering. There's loud chattering coming from the room but it stops as soon as I open the door, everyone's heads turning to face me. Miss Jones smiles and says good morning, and I try to muster a smile back before heading to my seat in the back corner, aware of all the eyes on me as I pass.

I don't usually talk to anyone in my form so I get the whole table to myself. I put my bag on the free chair next to me and get out my sketchbook, trying to ignore the deafening silence. I don't mind, at least I'll be able to get some work done.

Some of the girls at the front start to whisper and a couple of seconds later they all get the giggles. Natasha is sitting in the middle of them. She's the queen bee of our year and with us being the oldest, the school. Last year she chopped some girl's hair off because she thought the guy she liked was flirting with her. She never got punished though because it was outside of school so they couldn't do anything.

I almost forgot that she's in my form, she never usually shows up. I guess when you find out a classmate has made the news for 'attacking' a "teen pop sensation" it's worth coming in early.

Her high-pitched voice is just loud enough to reach me. "Can you imagine being that desperate? I would be so embarrassed, I wouldn't be able to show my face ever again. To be fair, I would never go all crazy over a boy anyway."

The girls surrounding her giggle and nod, flicking back their pin-straight hair when it falls in their faces. A few others around the room join in and I try to hide my face behind my hair as it turns the same colour, blending in.

"Enough! Monday's supposed to be a reading day, not gossiping. If I catch you again Natasha, I'll have to add a point to the system," Miss Jones says before going back to her computer screen.

Natasha cries about only needing a couple more points before she's banned from prom, but Miss Jones doesn't listen, she just hands her a book instead. She turns it over with a scowl before dropping it on the table.

"Can I go to the toilet please?" she asks, already grabbing her bag and pushing her chair back. Miss Jones barely finishes telling her to be quick before she's out of the door. *She won't be back.* She catches me watching as she passes the window next to me and narrows her eyes. I quickly look away before she turns me to stone.

The room's back to silence, everyone's either pulled out a book and started reading or is secretly on their phone. Miss Jones glances up from her screen, giving me a smile with a hint of… sympathy?

I return a tight smile and pull out my pencils, randomly sketching on a piece of scrap paper. Was Natasha just saying what everyone's thinking? Surely not. Everyone that knows me, knows I've never been a big fan of him. When Cassie said she was taking me people were so shocked because they knew that. They wouldn't believe the rumours, even if the photos make them look true.

After form, I have double art, my only subject without any of the others. I start a few pieces, hoping one will feel right to send for my application and leave them on the rack to dry for my next lesson. Paint isn't my strongest medium but clearly, I need to try something else since pencil isn't working at the moment.

So far it hasn't been too bad. No one even whispered the name 'Jackson Peters', although you don't really talk much when you get in the zone. I got a few stares at the start of the lesson but I'm starting to get used to that.

When the bell goes at break I head straight to our usual spot. The sun's out and the heatwave that was predicted is finally here, so as soon as I get outside, I take my blazer off and fold it over my arm, the skin on my arms already burning from the heat.

I spot Abby and Cassie huddled together, sharing worried expressions, and as I walk past the quickly filling up tables, I notice all the heads turning to look at me before whispering to one another.

It'll be over soon. Someone else will do something and then everyone will forget about me before the end of the day. It'll be like nothing happened. I hold my head high and continue to walk towards our table, ignoring the stares and giggles.

"Hey, we've been trying to message you," Cassie says, fanning her face with her maths homework as I take the seat next to Abby.

"How was it? Has anyone said anything?" Abby asks, moving her bag off the table.

I pull my phone out of my blazer pocket, showing them the screen as it powers on. "Sorry, my phone was off. It's been okay, no one really cared. Well, no one except Natasha."

"So, no one mentioned him, at all?" Abby asks again, quickly glancing at Cassie anxiously.

"Nope." My phone screen finally lights up and it practically jumps out my hand. "Jeez! Are these all from you?"

A few of the notifications have their names above but as more and more come through I notice the majority are from random comments on a video. "Why's everyone tagging me? What's happened?"

Cassie leans closer, her mouth set in a grim line. "He did an interview this morning. Have you not seen it?" Cassie asks, already searching it up on her phone.

"He does interviews all the time, I never watch them." Then it clicks, turning my stomach over. "He mentioned me?"

"The whole interview was about your 'date'," Abby says, using air quotes.

Cassie slides her phone over, the screen totally black except for the title in the top corner. *'"Marry me, Jackson Peters!" Peters' recent experience with a crazed fan.'*

I sigh and press play. *How bad can it be?*

"Hi, I'm Alexa Reed, and today we have some juicy gossip as we're joined by the amazing and extremely talented Jackson Peters," the older woman in the seat opposite him gushes.

"Hi, thanks for having me," he says with a charming smile.

"Of course! We're glad to have you back, it's been a while since you were in the UK."

"Ah, I've been working really hard recently on some new music and touring in America, so I haven't been able to make it over. But I love being here, everyone's always so friendly." He smiles and nervously shifts in his chair.

"Well almost everyone," the interviewer says and they both laugh. *"We're all dying to know what happened. There are a lot of different rumours and theories online, but I think the main one is that she hated you?"* She scrunches her brows as if the thought actually baffles her.

Jackson lets out a small laugh. *"The opposite actually."*

"Really?"

"Yeah." He searches the ground as he tries to remember his made-up version of the evening. *"We went and

had a really nice dinner, a good chat and just got to know each other. Everything was going well, but as we were leaving, she said she loves me."

The interviewer's eyes widen and she inches closer, signalling for him to go on.

"I didn't think much of it, because you get a lot of fans telling you that they love you or your music, so I smiled and gave her a hug, like I do with many fans. When I went to pull away, she leaned in and tried to kiss me."

"No!" she gasps, her perfectly sculpted smile so wide it's blinding.

"Yeah," he says, wincing. "So, I had to gently push her away and awkwardly explain that I hardly knew her and didn't have feelings for her like that."

"Then what happened?" she asks, eating up every word.

"Well, as you can tell by the images, she didn't take it well." The screen in between them lights up with one of the photos and his smile falters, just for a second, before he looks away.

"Oh, no. Do you remember what she was saying in these photos?" She points towards the screen, regarding the image as if it was a mouldy banana.

"Not really." Another slight shift. "She started asking me to be her boyfriend and asking for my number but when I said no and my driver pulled up, she got angry and started yelling, but I didn't really hear what she said. I hope she's

okay though. I love all of my fans and I want nothing but the best for all of them." He turns and smiles towards the camera. "Which is why I'm offering her tickets for my sold-out closing concert."

Alexa clutches her chest. "Aww. That's if she doesn't already have one, with her being such a big fan."

He clears his throat and lets out a nervous laugh. "Well, if she did, I hope she didn't burn it after what happened." He smiles when Alexa laughs. "And if she did, the offer's still there."

She matches his smile, sitting up straight. "That's all we have time for, unfortunately. Thank you for coming to have a chat."

"No, thank you for having me. And for letting me clear everything up."

"Anytime. And make sure you come back soon."

"I'm planning my next trip as we speak," he says, smiling broadly.

She turns back to the camera. "Well, you heard it here first. The date went well, maybe a little too well, and she was left wanting more. I'm Alexa Reed and I'll see you next time with some more juicy gossip." She signs off with a wink and the screen goes black.

"Is he for real?" I shout, unable to help myself. He didn't even have to tell the truth. He could have said there was a misunderstanding, he could have avoided the question or just not done the interview. Anything other than throw me under the bus.

"So, you showed her the video?" Sean asks upon his arrival as he slings his bag off his back and onto the floor.

"This is what people have been whispering about?" I ask, wafting her phone in the air. "Oh my god! This is what Natasha was on about," I add, noticing that it was uploaded this morning, a few minutes before school started. "And people believe this rubbish? People really think I tried to kiss him?" I look at them, expectantly, waiting for an answer I already know.

"We don't," Abby says, knowing that's not what I mean.

"People think he's so perfect and they believe whatever he says, if only they knew what he's really like." I hand Cassie her phone and start to fan my face with my hands, the heat now getting to me from getting so worked up.

"Here," Sean says, reaching into his blazer pocket and pulling out one of the famous brownies from the canteen. He smiles and places it in front of me.

Just looking at it fills me with joy. "Thank you," I grin. "You didn't have too though."

"Of course, I did, it's a tradition. If you're sad or having a bad day, you get a brownie. We've done it for years and we're not stopping now."

I open the clear packaging, the familiar chocolatey scent filling my nostrils, and attempt to split it into four pieces as it starts to melt all over my hands. "A 'thank you', for getting me through this nightmare," I say as I hand them each a piece.

"You don't need to thank us," Cassie says as Abby gives me a side hug.

"I will accept the brownie though," Sean says, shoving his in his mouth. He closes his eyes and his whole body melts along with the brownie.

Nine

"So, what are you going to do?" Abby asks, taking a sachet of ketchup from the centre of the table and smothering her chips.

We're at the cafe around the corner from school. Sean works here on Mondays, so we always come straight here to keep him company. And to eat any food that's going spare.

She waves her hand in front of my face and I flinch away from it, losing my staring contest with the window. "Huh?"

"Jackson Peters. What are you going to do?"

"What can I do?" I shrug. "Everyone already believes him, they're not going to listen to me." I take a bite of my cheese and ham panini, throwing it back onto the plate as the scorching insides take off the top layer of my tongue. "Anyway, even if they would, it's not like I could just go on TV like him. Not that I'd do that anyway."

"Ooo, go on TV and then you can be famous," Cassie says, placing three milkshakes down on the table. Thanking her, Abby takes the pink one and I take the yellow one, leaving her with the vanilla.

As soon as I taste banana, my mouth soothes, and I sip another cooling mouthful. "I'm not going on TV, and I don't want to be famous. There's no privacy. I've had my 5 seconds of fame and I don't want anymore," I say, wiping my mouth on the sleeve of my blazer. I can't think of anything I'd hate more.

"That's a shame," Cassie frowns. "If you were famous, you could wear my designs and I'd be the next big fashion designer."

I roll my eyes and she smiles, taking a sip of her milkshake.

"Have you finished your dress yet?" Abby asks.

"Not yet."

Sean darts past our table, wearing his brown uniform and his slightly stained apron, carefully balancing two trays covered with delicious-smelling food and drinks. "I'll join you in a sec."

We nod and Cassie continues, "It should be done in time for prom, I've just been busy. I didn't think Jackson Peters would take up so much of my time."

"Sorry," I say, playing with my straw. I hadn't even thought of how this might be affecting Cassie.

She immediately turns to me. "Don't be stupid, I'm not on about everything with you. Sure, that has also taken up some of my time but I don't care. And it's not like that was your fault, I'd never blame any of it on you," she sighs, twirling her hair. "I spent too much time preparing for the 'date'. Getting my hair done, my nails done, doing my make-up, picking out a stupid outfit and even planning out what I was going to say. Not that any of it mattered in the end." She throws the bit of hair she has hold of and slumps in her chair. "It's just annoying because I wasted so much time that I could have been spending on other things."

"I thought the dress was going well," I say, confused. She's constantly working on it and she's always eager to show it off. She never seemed stressed about it.

Sean arrives carrying a chocolate milkshake. He pulls back his chair just as the bell above the cafe door chimes and a new customer walks in. He fights a groan, "I'll be back. No one touch my drink, I'm watching." He turns to leave but stops as me and Abby glance at the vinegar bottle. "Nope." He snatches his drink, taking it with him to greet the customer.

"It's not just the dress," Cassie says.

Over her shoulder, Seans arguing with the new customer. He's talking quietly, and we're too far to hear anything, but even from over here I can see their challenging scowls. The woman pushes past him and searches around the room, stopping when her eyes land on me. She straightens her suit jacket and marches towards us.

"Lorri, what's wrong?"

"Who's that?"

She heads straight to our table, stopping right in front of me. "Lorri Johnson?"

American? I glance towards the others for help but they look as confused as I feel. Except Cassie, who looks as if she recognises the woman but isn't sure where from.

"Yes?"

She stretches out a hand, smiling wide. "Hi, I'm Sara, Jackson Peters' manager."

This is a prank, right? Or maybe they're a reporter in disguise or just someone trying to mess with me.

No one is saying anything. Sean's standing behind the woman, still looking angry, Abby's staring at her with the same sceptical look that I must have, and Cassie looks like she just solved a really hard maths equation. She catches me studying her and gives me a small nod.

Slowly, I take her hand. She has a confident, firm grip but a soft hand, and she's not as old as I originally thought she was, her face wrinkle-free and glowing. She has a kind-looking face, one that probably makes her and Jackson a lot of money. She could probably convince even me to let

Jackson do an interview and be on the front cover of my magazine. If I owned a magazine.

"Sorry, you're probably really confused as to why I'm here," she laughs. "I'm guessing you've probably seen the interview from this morning. Well, we wanted to make sure you definitely got those tickets. We wouldn't want you to miss the concert, so we thought I should deliver them in person."

"We?" Abby asks.

"Jackson's really looking forward to having you there," she says and Sean scoffs. "Really, he is. They're a peace offering, he's really sorry about all of this with the media."

"Yeah, so sorry he sent you to apologise," mumbles Sean. He makes sure it's loud enough for us to hear.

"I don't want his tickets," I say, earning me a kick to the shin from Cassie. I know if she was in my place she'd jump at the free tickets.

The woman's quiet for a second, debating how to play this to get me to accept her bribe. Placing her bag on the table, she opens it and pulls out an envelope. "Here." She flicks through the contents. "Four tickets for tomorrow's sold-out show." She urges me to take them, sighing when I don't, "Look, I don't know what happened on that date. I *do* know that he can be a little annoying sometimes so I'm sorry if he said something that might have upset you, he probably didn't mean it."

I look away and roll my eyes. *Right.* And the interview where he made me out to be a crazy person? Let me guess, he didn't mean that either.

"You shouldn't let him stop you from having a fun night though, right?" she continues. "They're free tickets for one of the biggest sold-out concerts you'll see for a long time. And they're good seats as well. You could go and enjoy yourselves, forget all about the media and papara-"

"She said she doesn't want your stupid tickets, so maybe you should take them and pis-," Sean says, raising his voice whilst inching towards her.

I grab the tickets before he makes an even bigger scene and gets himself fired, he needs this job to help his mum. "It's okay."

Sean scrunches his face and takes a step back, crossing his arms. He doesn't look away from the woman.

"Thanks for the tickets, we can't wait," I say, trying to fake a smile.

She lets out a small breath. "Great!" Her mouth grows into a wide grin. "We hope you have a good time and, again, we're so sorry about all the media stuff. Nice to meet y'all." She waves and we watch her leave in silence.

When she's gone, Sean finally takes the seat next to Cassie, his shoulders slumping. "I don't like her," he grumbles and takes a sip of his drink.

The cafe isn't small, but it's small enough that the majority of the customers surrounding us heard everything. The table closest to us is full of popular girls from a couple of years below and they stare at the tickets in my hand as if they're the last slice of pizza, and they're *starving*.

"Well, it won't be long now until the whole school knows I have tickets I'm not using." I shove them into my backpack and point at the drooling faces.

Cassie almost chokes on her milkshake. "What do you mean we're 'not using' them."

"Really, Cas," Sean says, stealing half of Abby's chips.

"What? You heard her, we shouldn't let all of this stop us from going and having a good time." Her eyes bore into mine, pleading with me. "It'd be fun. We could get all dressed up and I'll order us a Chinese before we go. We'll have a great time, and then we can have a sleepover at mine."

I guess it would be fun. And when am I going to get another opportunity like this? "I don't trust her. Why does she want us to go so badly?"

Cassie sighs heavily. "I don't know. Because she feels bad and wants us to have fun and forget about it," she shrugs. "Come on, you know how much this would mean to me. I'd owe you big time. Please."

"Fine," I groan. She did stay up all night waiting in a queue to get tickets, just for them to sell out before she could get one. "But there's no way in hell I'm wearing a top with his face on."

Jumping up, she runs around the table and throws her arms around me, squeezing so tight it's hard to breathe.

"Thank you, thank you, thank you. It's fine, I'll only have enough for me, Sean and Abby anyway."

"Absolutely not," Sean barks. "You can count me out, I'd rather go to space without a suit than go to a Jackson Peters concert, thanks." The bell goes and he downs the rest of his milkshake, wincing as the brain freeze sets in and stands to greet the new customer.

"But you have to, it'll be fun. I was only joking, you can wear whatever!"

"Still no," he throws over his shoulder as he approaches the counter.

"Ugh. You're coming, right?" she asks Abby.

"Sure, I've never been to a concert before," she beams. "She did seem a bit persistent but we shouldn't let it stop us. What's she going to do?" *They'll think of some way to use it to their advantage.* Chomping on a chip, she continues, "She's probably hoping we post about it so people can see that there's no hard feelings."

"Exactly!" Cassie says, resting back in her chair. "I mean, it is kind of her job to make sure he looks good in the media." She pulls my plate towards her and takes a triumphant bite of my panini.

She's always been good at winning her case. I guess that's what happens when you're raised by a bunch of lawyers. "You're right. I'm sure it'll be fun, I can't wait," I say, trying to ignore the knot already starting to form in my stomach.

She pushes the plate back to me, smiling. "When am I ever wrong?"

As if on cue, Sean stops at our table. "Most of the time."

She whacks him and orders another round of milkshakes.

Ten

"All of that revision for nothing," Cassie cries as she throws open the heavy double doors that lead to the field. "I was going to pick that case study as well. And now I'm going to fail!"

The exam ended early so we're the first ones here. Marching after Cassie, towards our table, I welcome the fresh summer-like air and the openness, a much-needed change from the gloomy exam hall.

"There wasn't a right and wrong case study, just because we chose a different one doesn't mean you're going to fail," Sean says. "Hey, maybe we'll fail and you'll get top marks." He gives her a side hug and she responds with a small smile.

The bell rings, faintly, from inside the building as we take our seats and Abby gets out her revision cards as Sean continues to comfort Cassie.

"One down, too many more to go," I grumble.

The doors reopen and more people spill out, quickly filling the empty tables surrounding us. There are more people than usual and some stride straight past the tables, settling in groups on the grass to enjoy the sun.

My skin prickles and my stomach clenches. It's a feeling I'm starting to know all too well, someone's watching me. Standing in the doorway, Natasha and two other girls search the crowd. They stop when their eyes land on me and she says something to the others. When she starts towards us, they follow. *Great.*

"Urm, guys?"

The others follow my gaze, their conversation coming to a swift end, and I sense them sit up straighter.

"Hi," she says, flicking her hair. "How did you guys find the exam?"

I swear she empties a whole bottle of perfume over herself every day. "Ugh… Fine," I say whilst trying not to breathe in any fumes.

She grabs hold of my shoulders and drags me into a suffocating hug. "I'm glad that you're okay, you know, with everything going on. Honestly, it's such bad timing. Now you have to worry about exams *and* all of this." Her smile's so sickly sweet that it makes my mouth hurt. "I just wanted you to know that I'm here if you ever need to chat."

Has she banged her head? Or has she finally gone insane from absorbing all the chemicals? "Thanks."

She doesn't leave.

I've only spoken to Natasha once in the whole five years of being here, and that was only because we were paired up for a project and the teacher wouldn't let her switch partners. She kicked off, told me she wasn't feeling well and that she'd speak to me later to finish the project. Three years later and I'm still waiting.

"So, apparently you've got some spare tickets for Jackson Peters' concert tonight. I know that you hate him now, after everything, but it would be a shame for them to go to waste, right?" she asks, batting her lashes.

"What?"

"My sister overheard you telling his manager that you won't be using them. I think it's a shame, really."

I've heard about her sister. She's a few years younger and, from what I've heard, she's following in Natasha's footsteps. She must have been part of the group I saw at the cafe. So this is what she's after.

"Actually, we decided it'll be fun," Cassie says. "So there's no spare tickets. Sorry."

Natasha's quiet and her smile's no longer sickly sweet; it's non-existent.

She's going to lose it. My palms start to sweat as I force myself not to break eye contact to glance at the others for help. The last person that pissed her off is no longer here to tell the tale. And even though there's not long left until we leave, I don't really want her making my life a living hell.

"Oh, you didn't think *I* wanted them, did you?" she cackles. "I bought my VIP ticket ages ago. One of my friends wants to go and I thought since we're friends, and you have tickets you want to get rid of, we could help each other out," she says with the biggest fake smile.

'Friends'. Right...

"Too bad she doesn't want to get rid of the tickets anymore," Sean says with a mock frown.

"It is," she hisses. "What about you, though? You each got a ticket, right? I can't see you wanting to go."

"Oh, yeah." He checks his pockets and she perks up, practically leaning over the table. "Damn," he curses as he comes up empty. "I must have lost it. I hope your friend doesn't mind." He breaks into a toothy grin and she storms off, kicking his bag over as she passes. The others quickly follow.

"Wow," I say, "I don't think I've ever seen her desperate before."

"She looked ready to fight you for them," Abby turns to Sean.

"Oh, she was definitely thinking about it," Sean laughs.

"She would have won as well," Cassie says and Sean pushes her lightly.

We spend the rest of the school day revising before going into our next exam and I have to explain multiple times that the tickets aren't available. Some even offer to buy them from me. I probably would accept if it wasn't for Cassie, one ticket could pay for a whole month's worth of food.

After school, I stop off at home before I go to Cassie's to grab my overnight bag and some clothes for the concert. The flat's empty so I quickly scribble out a note and leave it out on the side for Dad to find.

I told him about the tickets when I got back yesterday and he agreed that it seemed a bit odd. He didn't think I should go, not when the paparazzi have only just started to die down, but I assured him that we'd be careful.

Abby's cries of disagreement float down the hall as I head to Cassie's room. I have to hopscotch over piles of clothes as I enter and try not to burn myself when I catch my ankle on the wire of her hair curlers. I grab onto her dressing table to steady myself and knock off a bunch of make-up products. *I love her, but she's a slob.*

They turn at the thud, both of them stood in front of the full-length mirror as Cassie holds up an 'I heart Jackson Peters' top.

"Hey! Shouldn't Abby wear this?" She's wearing a similar one herself, except hers has a giant picture of his face and says in a giant font 'Marry me, Jackson Peters!'.

It reminds me of the interview and my stomach twists. This is starting to feel like a bad idea. People already believe what he said and if I go it would look like he was telling the truth. But if I change my mind, then it will upset Cassie, and it's not as if I can change people's minds by not going.

Abby mouths 'Help me', cutting my mental spiral short.

"I don't know," I say with a smile. "It's not really her colour." I find a free space on the bed and put my bag down. "It would look great on you though."

She agrees and changes, shaking her head at the fact she even considered the other top. We show off our outfits and take turns sitting at the desk to do our hair and make-up, Cassie doing most of the work.

A while later Cassie's mum knocks and comes in carrying two bags full of chinese food in one hand and some drinks in the other. She complains about the state of the room as Cassie quickly cleans an area for us to eat and she gushes at how grown up we look before rushing off to answer a work call.

We sit on the floor among half of Cassie's wardrobe and tuck into the food, eating it out of the trays and passing them around whenever someone wants a bit of something else.

We're half way through a debate over which Salvatore brother is better when Abby's phone pings. We carry on for a few minutes but when I try to get Abby to back me up, I notice she's too busy smiling at her phone to hear me.

"Who're you texting?" I ask, teasingly.

She almost drops her phone. "What?"

"No! Do you have a girlfriend?" Cassie claps. The half empty rice tray that was on her lap spills onto the floor as she jumps up.

"No, we're not dating. We've been messaging for a few days though." She glances back at her phone, a giddy grin tugging at her lips. "It's Chen."

"Chen Hu?" She's in my art class and I've spoken to her a few times, she helped me out once when I knocked over a giant tub of paint. I got completely covered, from head to toe, and she lent me her spare change of clothes. Her style is way too cool for me but she still insisted that I could pull it off.

"Yeah," she says, smiling at her phone as another text comes through.

"Aww."

Abby launches the nearest piece of clothing at Cassie and it lands on her head, looking like a bad attempt at a ghost costume. We both roll around on the floor, hugging our stomachs, as she struggles to get it off.

After we've calmed down and tidied up the leftover food, I look for my shoulder bag, finding it under a pile of hats. I pull out the envelope of tickets, counting them.

One for me, one for Cassie, one for Abby, and one spar-. "Abby, what's Chen up to?"

"Urm, I think she said she was going to revise."

It really would be a shame for the ticket to go to waste. "Would she want to come with us?"

"Are you sure?" she asks, glancing at both of us.

"Of course."

She thanks me as she runs to grab her phone, and Cassie and I start cleaning the rest of the room.

We hear a knock at the door as we're putting away the last things and we nearly fall over each other as we sprint down the stairs to greet Chen, Abby warning us to be normal.

"Oh my god, I love your outfit!" Cassie shouts as soon as the door's open.

Chen thanks her, turning pink, and follows us into the living room. She's wearing silver hoops, a mesh long sleeve top under a bright crop top, skinny jeans and maybe the coolest trainers I've ever laid eyes on.

"Did you do them yourself?" I gasp, already lowering myself to get a better look.

"Oh, yeah. They took ages but it was totally worth it." She moves her foot around so I can get a better look at them.

She's painted them a similar shade of green as her top and given them a cartoon effect. She shows me the other and I notice it has a little painting of the green character from Inside out. If I didn't know any better, I'd think it was printed on.

"They're really good," I say, slightly in awe.

"Thanks. And thank you for inviting me, I'm a big Jackson Peters fan. But if you tell anyone I *will* deny it."

"Your secret's safe. Just don't tell anyone I gave you the ticket. If Natasha finds out, I fear she might *actually* murder me."

We laugh as we join the others.

Eleven

"We're late!" Cassie cries as we tumble out of her dad's car.

Her dad had a meeting that ran over so he got back later than expected. Then, to add to Cassie's anger, we got stuck in traffic. I think this might be the tenth time she's reminded us that we're late, and that's just during the ride here.

"It's fine. There's still people going in," I huff, trying to keep up with her.

"Don't we have specific seats anyway?" Chen's playing it cool but she's almost overtaking Cassie.

"Exactly! So, can we please slow down? I only have short legs!" Abby shouts from way behind us.

We come to a halt and find the shortest queue, Cassie practically dragging me.

The venue is huge. The ceiling has the most beautiful art on it that must be centuries old, it feels miles away, so far up that either the building was built around it or it was created by a wizard of sorts, one with the most magical technique. I should take a few photos in the hope they can inspire something for my application, which I still haven't done yet. Honestly, at this rate, I can forget about the art program.

Cassie asks if we want anything from the shop, and after taking our orders, she hurries towards the closest stall. As soon as she leaves, Abby and Chen start a playful debate about a tv show and I tune them out when I realise I've never heard of it.

A Jackson Peters song that Cassie plays all the time travels over the buzz and I notice the people in front of us have formed a group surrounding a small portable speaker. There's about ten of them, some tall, some short, and they're all dancing, throwing their heads back to either shout the lyrics or laugh with each other.

A girl from the queue next to us inches closer and she comes alive when the group welcomes her with open arms. Is there anything more beautiful than finding your people?

They cheer as the song switches to 'Home Feeling', the only Jackson Peters song I will voluntarily listen to on repeat. Unlike all his other songs, this one actually has some emotion behind it.

We're almost at the chorus when I hear my name. I stop tapping my foot and turn, along with the majority of the surrounding people, in the direction it came from.

Cassie emerges from behind a couple of girls, her hands full of drinks and her arms stuffed with snacks. She's so focused on not dropping anything that she accidentally knocks one of the girls' arms, spilling some of her drink. She mutters a sorry into the drinks and continues towards us, the girl glaring after her.

"Here," she says, handing me a bottle of water.

Abby and Chen each take one of the plastic cups of Dr Pepper, leaving Cassie with a cup of sprite and a jumbo packet of Wotsits.

The girl's eyes travel from Cassie to me and the corners of her mouth pull up into a smirk. *No, please no.*

"No way. It's the girl in the photos! The one he did an interview about!"

I feel everyone turn, their eyes landing on me like a bunch of vultures.

"No one let her get too close to the stage, she'll try to kidnap him." The girl next to her cackles and a few people around them giggle along.

The group in front of us are no longer dancing; they're also staring at me. Their sympathetic smiles don't manage to reach their eyes.

I don't blame them. After all, Jackson brought them together. He gave them friendships and memories, and countless interviews with insights into his life. I'm just a stranger. They have no reason to trust me.

Abby and Cassie are staring at me too. There's no judgment there, though, just questions.

I'm too tired to try and fight back for the hundredth time this week, to tell them that their idol lied and then watch as they don't listen. "It's fine, *I'm* fine."

Everyone eventually goes back to their conversations. One or two try to take photos but stop once they see Chen, who looks ready to pounce.

The group disappears through the guarded double doors and we're ushered forward. I hand the tickets over to the giant standing before us and he checks them over, his brow creasing.

My heart starts to race as he tells us to wait and goes to speak to the woman standing behind the main desk. *This is it. I knew we couldn't trust her.*

"What's he doing?" Chen whispers.

"I'm sure it's nothing to worry about," Cassie dismisses her.

"Or maybe Sean was right and this is a trap." I need to find the nearest exit, I don't want to be stuck if we need to make a run for it.

The guy strides towards us, the woman quick on his heels. They're going to kick us out. Maybe if we just make a run for it now, we won't get into trouble.

The guy reaches us first and signals to the next people in the queue to move forward. He checks their tickets and lets them in without any hesitation. *Oh no, this is bad.*

"Hi, Lorri Johnson?" the woman asks. She doesn't wait for me to respond before gesturing for us to follow her.

I'm about to question how she knows my name but remember the photos. *Is there anyone who hasn't seen them?*

I can't tell if she's angry with us or not. She doesn't seem angry but the fact she's marching us down a small corridor, and not into the arena, makes me think that we're in serious trouble.

"Excuse me, did we do something wrong?" Chen asks.

We come to a stop at the heavy doors at the end of the corridor and she opens them with her pass. She glances back before letting us through, and we must look like we're being led to our slaughter because her expression immediately softens. "No, not at all!" She puts a hand to her shaking head. "Sorry, it's been a busy day. You guys were just in the wrong queue, I've checked you in now," she says as she continues marching towards another set of doors. "Your room's the closest one to the stage, you'll have the best seats in the house." She smiles at us and leads us through the next set of doors.

We have a room? Abby and Chen look as shocked and confused as me. Cassie, however, looks like she's been given a load of free material and told she has free rein on a dress for the met gala.

"Here we are." She opens the door and laughs at our gawping faces.

No way are we in the right room, this has to be a mistake. There's a seating area with a giant flat-screen TV which I'm not sure why you'd need whilst at a concert, but it's a nice touch. There's also a table spreading from end to end of the room covered with a variety of food and my stomach rumbles as I walk past it despite all the Chinese we ate. There's everything from caviar and a whole-ass duck, to a chocolate fountain and marshmallows.

"Have you seen this?" Cassie yells from the glass doors at the other end of the room.

We hurry over to join her on the balcony and my hand flies to my mouth as I try to contain a gasp. We're in the main arena, right next to the stage. We're so close I have to whisper so the people setting up don't hear me. "This is crazy."

"Not bad, is it?" The woman walks further into the room and picks something up off the couch closest to the door. "These are your passes," she says, handing the neon lanyards to us, "You need to wear them at all times, just in case of emergencies."

"Unfortunately, the toilet here is broken." She points to the door in the corner. "Your closest one is just through the doors so don't forget your passes, otherwise you'll get trapped. Trust me it happens way more often than you'd think," she laughs, walking back to the exit. "The support acts should be starting soon so I'll leave you to it. If you need anything just press this button and someone will help."

"Still think it's a trap?" Cassie teases after the woman leaves. She's come off the balcony and is flicking through a magazine that she's found whilst eating a slice of cheesecake.

I can't believe her. Honestly, I haven't totally ruled out that this is all a prank, and that the police or some media person will come through the door at any second.

"Are these for us?" Chen asks, holding up some overflowing gift bags.

"They must be. Why, what's in them?" Abby replies. She joins us on the couches and we grab a bag each.

They're mainly full of merch (a hoodie, t-shirt, wristbands etc) but they also have a few extra things like coupons for the restaurant we went to on our 'date' and gift cards for some shops in town. His management team sure are pulling out all the stops to try and make all of this disappear. I can't complain though, I'll be able to replace my clothes that he ruined now, and maybe grab some other bits as well.

"Wow, this is the best concert *I've* ever been to, and it hasn't even started yet," Chen says, "Come on. I think we need to take some photos to celebrate." Jumping up she runs over to the balcony, beckoning us over.

Abby and I join her, standing with our backs facing the stage so Chen can get it in the shot.

"Cassie, come on!" I yell through the door.

She's still standing near the bags and I notice her drop her gift cards into Abby's bag. I quickly drop my eyes, a warmth spreading through me.

"Coming!"

The show starts, the support acts blast songs that everyone and their dogs know, and I make a mental note of their names as we scream along with the rest of the crowd and dance like nobody's watching.

When their set finishes, the whole arena starts to protest, but as soon as they mention Jackson Peters and that it's time for him to come on, all attempts at getting them to stay are abandoned.

The lights go out and the crowd roars. Cassie and Chen join in and I have to cover my ears to stop them from destroying my ear drums. There's movement on the stage and the music starts, causing another wave of excitement to flood the arena.

Jackson rises from the bottom of the stage, lit by a warm spotlight, and the fans go crazy. He takes in his view, stopping in our direction. I would think he's looking directly into my eyes if I wasn't aware of the million stage lights blocking us out.

Is Cassie okay? She's screaming and waving her arms so frantically that, for a second, I think a wasp might have gotten in and is trying to murder her.

I have to admit the show's pretty good. Once it properly gets going, there are strobe lights, pro dancers, props, and even fireworks! I'm almost scared to blink. After a few songs I relax a bit more and even join in with the words I know, making sure Cassie doesn't see. I could do without her telling Sean, he'd never let me hear the end of it.

We try to savour as much as we can by taking a million videos and photos, and when Chen's phone yells at her about storage space, we taste-test everything on the buffet table making sure nothing goes to waste. And when we're finished with that, Cassie finds the mini fridge, stocked full of expensive smoothies and flavoured iced teas, and we try all of those too.

His last song finishes and he runs off stage yelling 'thank you' and 'goodnight'.

Finally, I can go to the loo. I really shouldn't have drunk so many smoothies. The show was good and all, but if I don't go soon, the confetti and spilt drinks won't be the only things that need cleaning up.

The arena stays in darkness as the crowd demands an encore, the floor vibrating with their chants. After a minute or two, he reappears in a new outfit, and they go wild. "I want to dedicate this last song to someone in the crowd." The cheering stops, replaced with an excited buzz and he continues, "As most of you know, I went on a date with some fans last week."

I grip the railing, my knuckles turning white. *Please, no.*

"And it didn't go exactly as planned."

Giggles spread across the arena and I feel the girls' eyes on me.

"But they came tonight, so I hope that means we're good," he says, peering up at me.

I hope the lights are dim enough that he can see the daggers I'm sending him. If he thinks dedicating one of his stupid songs to me will make me swoon and forgive him, he has another thing coming. I'm not just another fan that will forgive him just because he wants me to.

He clears his throat. "So L, this one's for you."

'L'?! What, was he too busy to learn my full name?

The music plays, a snort escaping me as he performs the dance moves from the music video and I realise what song it is. Out of all of his songs, he picked 'All is forgotten'. *Of course, he did.* If his management wants me to forgive him for all of this and move on, they need to do a better job of managing him.

"I've forgiven now let's both forget because everything's better when all is forgotten," he sings in our direction, causing the people closest to us to turn.

They try to get their friends' attention as they point at me. Giggling, they aim their phones at us, the flash blinding me.

I can't do this. I have to leave.

I back away, knocking Cassie's arm.

"Hey, are you okay? I'll see if my dad's here." She tries to smile but her eyebrows inch closer together and her hand's wrapped in her hair.

"He's a dick. We could grab the leftover food and launch it at him. We should be close enough," Chen says, picking up the rest of the lemon meringue pie and testing out the weight.

"I'd be down for that," Abby adds. "Should I grab the extra smoothies?"

Chen's face lights up and I quickly tell them I'm fine before they get any more ideas. He's caused enough trouble. As much as I would love to watch a lemon meringue pie hit him in the face as he slips on overpriced smoothies, I would much rather have this nightmare be over.

"You guys stay and enjoy the rest of it. I'm going the loo, I won't be long." I leave before any of them can argue with me and make sure I grab my pass on the way out.

The light turns green, the doors unlock. The corridor on the other side's different from the ones we walked through earlier, it has an echo and isn't decorated like the others. It doesn't look decorated at all, it must be a staff-only area. As long as I find the nearest toilet and don't get into trouble, I don't mind.

There's no sign for the toilets. In fact, none of the doors have signs. *Great, time to check every door.*

I don't have any luck with the first two, which turn out to be supply closets, but the third's more promising.

I switch the light on as I creep in and check no one else is lurking. It's similar to the room we're in, only fancier. It still has the TV and couches, and a buffet, but it also has a dressing table covered in beauty products, a giant mirror on the wall in front of it, and a full rack of designer clothes in the corner.

Not the toilets. But, if the layout's the same as the other room, there *should* be a toilet here somewhere. Whoever's dressing room this is will be back soon so I need to make it quick.

About to give up, I find the door behind the clothes. *Finally!* Waddling, I drag the rack out of the way. If I move it back afterwards, they won't even know I was here.

I wash my hands and reach for the door handle, pulling it open a crack.

"Jackson, great show tonight!"

I slam the door back closed, my heart in my ears.

Crap.

Twelve

The clothes did look like the ones Jackson wore, but his dancer had worn similar outfits. Plus, I would have thought his room would have at least *some* security or his name above the door, that's what happens on TV.

"The new setlist worked really well. You didn't look as tired toward the end." It sounds like his manager. "Maybe we could even squeeze in an extra outfit change next time?"

"Is fifteen not enough?" he grumbles, a little too close to the door.

Can he see the light? It's not that bright, but I'd rather not take the chance. Quickly, I hit the switch and back up until my back presses against the cold wall.

"Sure, but why stop there? An extra outfit means an extra brand deal which means some extra cash." I don't hear a reply but she continues, "I'll make some calls and see what I can do. Get changed and get some rest, we're in the studio tomorrow."

The door clicks shut, everything goes quiet and I let out a breath I didn't realise I was holding. Of course, out of every toilet I could have stumbled into it *had* to be his.

There's shuffling in the room and I put my ear to the door. He's still here, it sounds like he's moving things, maybe packing his stuff. Hopefully, packing his stuff.

His footsteps get closer. He's just getting the clothes off the rack, as long as I don't make a sound, he won't know I was here. And then I can go home and never think about him ever again.

The handle turns and the door presses into my cheek. *Please, go away.*

He tries again, still it doesn't budge.

"Hello?"

It's fine. He'll come to the conclusion that the door's broken or the toilet's out of order, and then he'll leave. And then *I* can leave.

"Hey!" He bangs on the door. "I know you're in there, I can see the shadow of your feet."

Jumping back, I curse myself. Why couldn't this bathroom have a window or air vent I could shimmy through?

"Open up or I'll get security."

I was hoping I'd never have to talk to him again, but being dragged out by security and arrested for being a stalker doesn't sound fun either. I should have tried to hold it and risked peeing myself. It would've been better than this.

Filling my lungs, I slowly turn the lock and open the door. I'm met with Jackson's tanned, bare chest, still shiny with sweat. I'd be impressed if I hadn't already seen his abs more times than I'd like to admit. He really does love showing them off.

"Why are you shirtless?"

"Why are you in my bathroom?"

I try to stand my ground, not breaking eye contact, but it might actually be a good idea to explain why I'm here before he calls for security. "Our toilet's broke."

"Right…" he drags out with a raised brow. "And the only other toilet in this place is the one in my dressing room?"

"Actually, the woman said that there was a toilet down this hall that we could use," I fire back, crossing my arms.

He smirks. "Ah, ok. And mine was the first one you came across."

"Oh, how I wish it wasn't."

He nods thoughtfully, his smirk growing.

Does he really think I hunted down his bathroom and hid in here, yearning for the chance to speak to him again? Yeah, because it went so well last time I couldn't wait to put myself through it again. "Whatever, can I go now?"

He steps to the side, grabbing a folded caramel shirt off the arm of the couch and throws it over his head, his eyes only leaving me as the shirt slides over them. It almost blends into his skin, only a shade darker.

Halfway out the door; halfway to freedom.

He clears his throat. "Did you enjoy the show?" He's sat where his top was, arms folded and voice low.

Yes, before you ruined it. "I've seen better."

He drops his head, a smile playing on his lips. "I'm sorry."

I can't tell if he's being genuine or not, and if he's talking solely about the show or everything else. "What for exactly? The show or the 'date'?" I lean against the doorframe. "Oh, there was the interview as well. Can't forget that one."

He glances at me through his lashes, letting out a short laugh. "I guess I have a long list of things to apologise for." He pauses. "I am sorry about how I acted at the restaurant. I swear I'm not always like that, I'd just had an extremely shitty day and I-"

"And you thought 'You know what, since I'm having a shitty day, I'll make someone else's day shitty too'," I snap.

"No, I-" he starts, jumping to his feet.

"You know other people have shitty days too, right? We don't go around hurting others because of it though."

Red spreads across his face. "You're not listening."

"No, I hear you," I bark, standing straight. "You had *one* bad day so you ruined the evening for cassie and then decided to throw me under the bus to cover your ass and keep up this illusion that you're some sweet, perfect guy who would *never* do anything wrong. God forbid anyone thinks differently." I let out a breath.

He doesn't argue back, his jaw set, and he doesn't even look at me as he walks towards the bag on the dressing table, shoving stuff in.

I should leave. Leave, find the others and never look back. But he doesn't get to dismiss me as if my feelings don't matter. I know I'm not a celebrity but I'm still human. "When you do this to your friends and family do they instantly forgive you, feel bad for upsetting their precious superstar?"

He drops a bottle of face cream into his bag and swings to face me. "Stop pretending you know what it's like for me! You don't know me, you don't get it. I tried to apologise but you don't want to listen," he shouts, now inches away from me. "You wouldn't understand anyway."

"No, I'm just a nobody. I don't have millions of adoring fans, or a giant mansion that I got with all the money I get from touring the world, or any fancy cars and designer clothes that are handed to me on a silver plate because of brand deals." I pause and meet his eyes, hoping my next line hits as hard as I spit it. "How could I possibly understand how hard it must be for you."

His shoulders slump and he takes a step back, his eyes fixed on the ground. "I think you should leave," he says, more to my shoes than my face. "Before I call security."

"Gladly." I storm out, letting the door slam behind me, ignoring the stares from security at the other end of the corridor.

"Spill," Cassie says.

We're back in her bedroom, sitting in a protection circle around the mountain of food and drinks we managed to smuggle before we left the concert. I pick up a packet of popcorn and eat a handful, chewing slowly to give myself some extra time to think.

When I got back to our room, they'd tried to get it out of me there and then but it was too fresh. I knew if I tried to explain it all I'd get myself worked up and we'd be there for hours.

I might as well jump right in. "I ran into Jackson."

Abby and Chen let out a chorus, "What?!" as Cassie makes sputtering noises from inhaling her drink.

"Did you talk to him?" Chen asks.

"I wish I hadn't." I cram another handful of salty popcorn into my mouth.

"Back up, how did you even run into him? I thought you were going to the toilets," Cassie says, her eyes still teary from coughing.

"I was, I did." I mumble, "I just didn't know it was his toilet."

"Woah, I'm sorry. You ended up in *his* toilet?"
"How?!"

"I think you should go from the start."

I start over, stopping every minute or two to answer questions, mainly from Cassie. They squeal when I tell them about opening the door and finding him standing there shirtless, and they join in calling him names when I tell them all the parts of the argument that I can remember.

An hour has past by the time I finish updating them, and the treasure mountain is now relatively smaller than before. We try to squeeze in a bit of last-minute revision for our next exam before bed but end up falling asleep after the first question, drained from the eventful day.

"We have to tell her, right?"

"If we don't, she'll only find out at school or as soon as she turns her phone on."

"At least here she can react to it without everyone watching."

Opening an eye, I find them all huddled near the door, whispering into a phone. I slowly roll onto my other side and wait for them to continue talking before turning on my phone. Is it possible that they're talking about someone else?

As soon as my phone turns on, it's once again bombarded with hundreds of notifications. And here I was hoping last night would be the last of all this.

I immediately clear the notifications. It's probably not a good idea to get sucked into all the rumours. Instead, I open google, getting as far as 'Ja' before multiple suggestions involving 'Jackson Peters' and 'stalker' pop up. I click on one at random, praying it's wrong. Praying that there are no more articles involving me and Jackson.

The screen lights up, loading article after article, all of them mentioning a dressing room. I open the top one, scanning over the text. Then go back and read the next. Then another. And another. And-

"How long have you been up?" Abby asks softly, sitting beside me.

"Is she awake?" Sean's voice comes from the phone.

Cassie spots my phone and sighs. "Yeah."

"Okay. Keep me updated."

They say their goodbyes and she hangs up, coming to sit in between Abby and Chen.

"Nope." She wrenches my phone from my hands, shoving it behind her.

"Give it back. I want to read it." I try to reach around her but she pushes me back. I know it's for the best but I can't help wanting to know what everyone's saying about me. No matter how bad it is.

"How much have you already seen?" Chen asks.

I pick at my nails. "Enough. So taking my phone away won't do anything," I say, glaring at Cassie, aware I'm acting like a child. "I already know what people are saying about me. They're calling me a stalker, claiming I'm obsessed with him, and that he needs to file for a restraining order. At least if he did, I'd never be able to speak to him again. That's a plus."

"How did they find out about it anyway? Did anyone see you go in?" Abby asks.

"I don't think so." There was that group of people in the corridor when I came out but they wouldn't have a reason to do this, not like Jackson. "It has to be him. He was pissed at me last night and wanted to get back at me, so he leaked the story and once again I look like a crazy person and he comes out looking like an angel." Standing up, I walk around them and grab my phone off the floor.

"Surely he wouldn't. I thought he was trying to apologise last night," Abby says.

Cassie frowns. "What are you doing?"

Ignoring them, I open my phone and head straight to my emails. Fifty-three emails in the last hour. Some are just junk, Amazon and Just eat recommendations or my weekly email from one of the art websites I'm subscribed to, but most are journalists wanting an interview.

Last time I ignored them, hoping that this whole thing would blow over after a day or two, but if he's going to play dirty, we can play dirty.

I scroll until I find the name I'm looking for and quickly copy the number into my contacts. Once I do this there's no going back. I'd be adding fuel to the already scorching fire. *A fire that only exists because of him.*

I dial the number and they pick up after the second ring.

"Hi, Alexa Reed?"

Thirteen

The phone goes dead and I turn to the others, just in time to catch the pillow Cassie launches. "What are you doing? What did she say?" she asks, impatiently.

"Can I borrow some clothes?" I ask, already making my way to her wardrobe.

"You're not seriously considering doing an interview, are you? And with Alexa Reed of all people? You know she's like besties with him."

"She's not *besties* with him, she has done a lot of interviews with him though. Which means that a lot of people will see it, and they'll finally know the truth." I grab the plainest outfit I can find, the only thing not covered in glitter or sequins, and shove it into my bag, replacing my school uniform. "It wasn't Alexa on the phone, it was her assistant. She wanted to do the interview as soon as possible and agreed on after my exam."

"You're going to leave to go to an interview? I don't think school will be cool with that," Cassie says as we rush to get ready.

"I'll tell them I have an appointment," I shrug. I wouldn't be missing much. I'd be revising but I wouldn't get much done with all the whispers and beady eyes. I'd rather go and settle this.

"Fine. When are we going?" She's already picking out her own outfit.

"What?"

Abby gives me a look to say, 'Are you surprised?'.

"No, Cassie, I'm going on my own. You have another exam, and even if you didn't, I wouldn't ask you to skip school for this."

She frowns before turning back to the wardrobe. "Meh, who needs business anyway."

I'm not letting her miss out on one of her exams just to help me. She's been here for me almost all my life, it's time I try and do something by myself. It'll be good practice for next year when she's off at the designer school she got into.

"I actually *do* need to do this exam, but you know I'd skip school for you on any other occasion," Abby says, reminding me that even though I won't have Cassie nearby next year, I'll still have her and Sean.

I pack up the rest of my things. "Thanks. I'd do the same for any of you, but no one's skipping any exams. Right, Cassie?"

She finally agrees and we finish getting ready. I leave my overnight bag at Cassie's, only bringing my school bag with the extra clothes in and we head to school, going over some practice interview questions.

Just like I guessed, the tall woman behind the desk didn't ask for any details when I mentioned an appointment, and it didn't take long until I was in the shiny black car with fully blacked-out windows, on the way to the studios.

Half an hour later, we pull up outside of JBG Studios. I've passed it a couple of times when we used to visit the rest of the family for Christmas but it's been a while, and I'd forgotten just how big it is. From the motorway, I always thought it looked like a university campus, but up close it's more of a village, a community. It must be nice to work here, nothing like a regular office job. *All you've got to do is expose other people's secrets, potentially ruining their lives.*

"Lorri, nice to meet you. I'm Jessica. We spoke on the phone," a petite woman in a casual skirt suit says. She's carrying a tablet and has an earpiece as well as two phones.

We shake hands and she leads me through the gardens, explaining that the building for Alexa's set is at the back of the studios. She takes me around like a tour guide, going over the history of each building and of the more well-known celebrities that have been in each one.

We reach one of the smaller buildings and she lets me in. The smell of freshly baked croissants hits me as soon as we enter, the whole of the ground floor a hang-out area. I can't believe people get to sit in floating dome chairs whilst playing video games and call it work. They're being paid to be here but I'd come for free.

"Come on, we don't have all day," Jessica says from the elevator. "It took me a minute to get used to it all as well."

I follow her down the corridor and into one of the side rooms. It's full of bright lights and expensive cameras, all pointing at the familiar beige backdrop and stiff, velvet chairs. I can't believe I'm here, it's like I've climbed through Cassie's TV screen. I feel a pang at the thought, she'd have loved to see this.

"You can get ready in the bathroom," Jessica says, showing me the way. She lets me know that Alexa's on her way and walks me through the interview, "She'll introduce you and then talk a bit about what's happened, just to clue people in, and then you'll get to tell your side of the story."

I nod, feeling my shoulders relax. *Finally*.

"Just don't let her get under your skin. She's a journalist, her job is to get the answers she wants. I don't always prepare guests but I'm guessing this is your first interview, and Alexa can be very…" She searches for a word that won't get her fired. "Persistent when it comes to a good story."

I've seen quite a few of Alexa's interviews over the years so this isn't news to me. She once made a guy cry because she wouldn't stop interrogating him until he admitted to sleeping with someone else the night before his wedding. But that's different, they were celebrities. She'll go easier on me, right?

"And I'm a good story?" I ask, raising a brow.

"One of the best."

"Are you ready?" Jessica shouts through the door.

"Yes," I croak as I take a last look in the mirror.

I don't look bad. I'm having a good skin day and the dry shampoo I covered my hair with this morning has made it look as good as new. None of this comforts me, though. It should, considering this interview will be watched thousands, if not millions, of times by people all around the world. I can't stop thinking about what Jessica said and how Cassie reacted. Am I crazy for doing this? Maybe I could climb out of the window, we're only on the second floor. If I'm lucky I'll only break an arm or two.

There's a young girl dressed in black, carrying a clipboard and some wires, waiting outside of the bathroom. She explains she needs to mic me up and before I can ask any questions she attaches it to my collar, shoving the wire down my top.

I wonder where Alexa is? I scan the room, reaching the door at the exact moment she struts in, hair freshly styled in loose waves and make-up flawless. A tall guy runs after her spraying a stream of hairspray, nearly choking the girl carrying a make-up bag behind him. I bet she gets free clothes and brand deals too.

"Okay, two minutes everyone!" someone from the middle of the room shouts, putting everyone up a gear.

I'm not entirely sure what I'm supposed to be doing but I guess since no one's come to talk to me, I'm ready to go. I walk over to the set, trying not to disturb the people rushing around, and take a seat in the chair that I remember the guest usually sits in, waiting for whatever comes next.

Alexa joins me, the guy and girl still working on her already perfect hair and make-up. She doesn't look at me. Instead, she looks right past me, focusing on a spot just above my head.

Is there something wrong with my hair? Maybe I should run my brush through it once more, just to be safe.

"Thirty seconds!"

Or maybe not. I take one last frantic look around the room. There's no one guarding the door to the exit or the bathroom, I could still make a run for it. No one would even have to know, I don't think they've advertised this interview. No one would know if I chickened out at the last minute. Cassie will still be having lunch, I could see if her mum or dad could pick me up. They wouldn't mind, not if it's an emergency, and even if they're busy, she'd probably send a taxi.

I could leave. I should leave. I need to-

"Going live in three, two..."

Fourteen

"Hi, I'm Alexa Reed and today I'm joined by a *very* interesting guest. Lorri, it's nice to finally meet you," she says, smiling ear to ear, a contrast to the expressionless look she gave me a second ago. "I think I speak on behalf of every Jackson Peters fan when I say I've been looking forward to this."

"Thanks for having me." I've watched enough of these to know that's my line.

"So, for the people watching, you went on a date with the talented heartthrob that we all know and love, and, well, it didn't really go to plan, did it?" Shaking my head, I open my mouth to speak but she goes on, "A couple of days ago we managed to get Jackson on to hear his side of the story and now we're ready to hear yours." She flashes me another

Hollywood smile. "Let's start at the beginning with the date. What really went on in those photos? We heard something about love?" She playfully raises an eyebrow.

I startle myself by letting out a short laugh and quickly try to cover it by clearing my throat. "I'm not sure where that came from. The truth is, I've never really been a fan of Jackson, you can ask anyone that knows me."

"Then why go on the date?" Alexa cuts in before I have time to explain.

I smile and continue, "My best friend, Cassie, is a big fan. She won the competition and asked me to go with her, she was excited and nervous to meet him for the first time. If I had known what he was like I would've never gone."

She tilts her head slightly. "Oh, what do you mean by that?"

"Urm." I shift in the hard seat, my eyes flitting to the red light next to the camera. "He was rude, not what we thought he would be like, that's all." They don't need to know about the drinking, that's not for me to share.

"Ah, he didn't get the door for you on the way out?" she giggles to herself.

I force my lips into a tight smile. She's just looking for a reaction. Something to paint me the way she wants. "He wasn't rude like that. But if I'm being honest, no, he didn't get the door for us. He didn't speak to us much and when we tried to talk to him, he seemed very stand-offish. And he walked out halfway through the meal, taking our ride and leaving us with no way home."

"If that's the case then," she says narrowing her eyes just enough for me to see, "how did the photos come about?"

"Well, we ran after him be-"

She flies forward, like a frog trying to capture it's next meal. "Why?"

If you let me finish. "Cassie noticed that he left his phone on the table, so she went to give it back to him, and I-"

"And you ran after him to tell him you loved him," she says, smirking at the camera.

Can she let me finish just one sentence? I unclench my jaw. "Actually, I just wanted to make sure my friend was okay. And I'm glad I did because when I reached them, he was yelling at her, and *that's* why I yelled at him."

She raises an eyebrow, letting out a loud laugh. "Yelling at a fan for returning his phone? That doesn't really sound like the Jackson we know."

Maybe you don't actually know him like you think you do.

She continues, "Hmm, two completely different versions of events, I guess we'll never know which one is the truth." She shrugs at the camera.

"I mean, you could ask Cassie or anyone that was there and they'd confirm what I've said."

"Right, I'm sure your friend would," she says, smirking. "Anyway, enough about that, that's old news." She dismisses it with a flick of her hand. "We want to know what went down at his concert. We heard he dedicated a song to you? That's so sweet of him!"

Again, I have to try my best to cover up a laugh. What does she want me to say? Is she hoping I agree, so she can continue his lie that I'm madly in love with him? Or does she want me to break so I look crazy? It wouldn't take much.

I sit up in my chair, the camera now fully on my face. I came to tell my story, I don't need to play nice and answer her questions, I just need to say what I came to say. "I went to his concert because we were given free tickets and I wanted to have a good time with my friends. Our toilet was broken so we were told to use the one down the hall. I went to look for it and ended up in Jackson's dressing room."

She opens her mouth. *Nope, my turn to speak.* "I didn't know it was his," I hurry on. "I needed the loo and that was the first one I saw. Should I have checked if I could use it first? Probably. But the show hadn't finished yet and I thought I had time before anyone came back." I take a breath, leaning back in the chair. "However, I was wrong and he came back when I was there. He tried to apologise for the 'date' and everything else."

She's watching me intently, her brow ever so slightly furrowed.

"But I didn't think his reasoning for how he acted was good enough." I pause. Was it? I wouldn't know. I've been thinking a lot about our last chat, I didn't really give him much chance to explain properly before I started to bite his head off. "Or maybe I just didn't want to hear it because I was still mad about everything. Either way, we ended up arguing, clearly loud enough for someone to hear, and here we are."

Alexa uncrosses and crosses her legs, her eyes flitting at the cards in her hands. Is it possible that I broke Alexa Reed? She flicks to the last card and sits up straight, throwing them on the table next to her chair.

"It seems you've covered most of it," she says, smiling thinly at me, "But I'm sure everyone is dying to know, what *was* his reason? The one that you say wasn't good enough."

"He said he'd had a bad day." As soon as it leaves my mouth, I know she's got me. I'm not just a stalker, I also like to kick people when they're already down in the dumps. Perfect.

She smiles, wide this time, and turns to the camera. "Damn. So the poor guy had a bad day and you decided to make it worse by yelling at him." She sucks in a breath. "In front of the paparazzi as well."

I should have seen it coming. If she can't make it look like his story is true, then she's going to twist mine. "We all ha-"

Alexa glances past the camera and nods before once again cutting me off, "So sorry but that's all we've got time for."

I look to the spot where she nodded. *Of course, there's no one there.*

"Lorri, it was lovely to meet you. I'm sure this won't be the last we'll see of you," she laughs into the camera.

It better be.

"And there you go. The truth, so she says, about what *really* happened between her and the lovable Jackson Peters."

I roll my eyes. I no longer care if the camera catches it or not.

"I'm Alexa Reed and I'll see you next time with some more juicy gossip." She sits, beaming at the camera until the red light goes off and someone from the back of the room signals that we're no longer live.

Everyone starts to move around again, turning off the big lights and checking cameras, and I notice Jessica in the corner in a deep conversation.

I pull my phone out of my back pocket. There are 6 new messages in the group chat:

Cass

You did great! X

Abs

Damn, she's tough.

You did amazing tho :)

Sean the sheep

Congrats on keeping it together. I was screaming at Cass' phone. If she had interrupted me that many times, I would have lost my shit.

Cass

She's like that with everyone don't take it personally x
And remember NO SOCIAL MEDIA!!!

I thank them and wish them good luck for their exams, adding that I know they'll do amazing anyway. I promised Cassie I wouldn't check social media, not until she, Abby and Sean had a look but as I exit my messages, watching as the small number in the corner of my social media apps' folder rapidly increases, my finger hovers over it. I know the majority of the responses are going to be bad, and I know I shouldn't look, but I can't help but wonder if it worked. I allow myself to open the folder and I head straight to Twitter. I might as well get the worst out of the way.

"Lorri."

I quickly shut the app down and find Jessica now in front of me. She's quieter than before, her tone softer. "We should go. We'll get you de-mic'd and then George," she says, pointing over her shoulder to a muscular guy, dressed in black, near the exit, "will walk us out to the car."

Did I do something wrong? Do they think I'm going to rob the place or something? Maybe they really do think I'm a stalker and that I'm currently on the lookout for a new target so they're simply trying to protect their staff and guests. HR at it's finest.

The same girl from before takes care of my mic and I throw my bag over my shoulder before following George and Jessica.

"You did great, by the way," Jessica says, as we walk across the grass. "Try not to worry about what others are saying about you, some people will only ever hear what they want to hear, no matter what you tell them."

So, people still don't believe me. What will it take? For me to swear under oath? If so, throw me a bible. I give her a small smile, hoping she can tell I appreciate how kind she's been.

We pass a fountain and the people sitting around it stare at me as we walk past, a couple offering me a sympathetic smile when I make eye contact.

I fiddle with the strap on my bag and take a deep breath. "Is it that bad?" I ask, quietly.

She stops walking. "Sorry, I thought that you'd already had a look online, I thought that's what you were looking at on your phone."

I explain the pact we made. "I almost checked, though. I'd just opened Twitter when you came over. I should thank you, after all, curiosity killed the cat. At least now I know to avoid it."

Her forehead creases. "I should warn you that people know where the studios are." I don't say anything and she continues, explaining slowly, warmly, as if I'm a six-year-old that doesn't understand maths, "So people know where the live stream was, where you are."

So? It's not like there's a hit out on me. I'm not going to exit the studios and be met by a group of tiny red dots, all fighting to get to my heart. At least, not that I know of.

She sighs, "I've been told that a small group has gathered at the entrance. We've got George so we should be fine. I mean, if he can't fight off a few teenagers then we'll need to invest in some better security," she tries to joke and I glance at George. He's turned away from us, talking into his radio.

She continues, "It'll be fine. George is just here to help us get through the crowd and to the car, I'm sure there won't be any fighting. They *may* shout things though and, unfortunately, George can't protect you from that. I know it's easier said than done but try not to listen to them." She places her hand on my shoulder, her face full of sympathy.

I wonder if she has to do this often, console people after an interview with Alexa and then prepare them for the aftermath. She's good at it, she is. But she's wrong, it won't be fine. No matter what I say, it'll never be fine.

Fifteen

Their shouts hit us as the doors slide open and I half expect pitchforks and a huge mob, not a handful of girls all around my age. An extra security guard has joined George to stop them from spilling into the building. Or, I guess, to stop them from getting to me.

George cranes his neck, shouting back, "Ready?" He's trying to stop a very determined child from getting past him. I think she's a second away from taking a chunk out of his leg.

"Mhm."

I doubt he can hear me but they move forward anyway, creating a path as effortlessly as a snowplough through a carpet of fresh snow, and I trail behind them, Jessica close by.

Where's the car? All I can see are signs held by angry people. People who are angry at me. And for what? For speaking the truth? I did nothing to them. I didn't call them names or harm them. I don't even know who they are. They don't know me. And yet here they are.

My chest tightens with each insult that hits. I can't make out the full sentences they're yelling, but I catch the fragments injected with extra venom. "Crazy", "Stalker" and "Desperate" are the most frequent ones.

The car comes into view and my chest lifts, my shuffling quickening. Just focus on getting to the car. These people don't mean it, they're doing what they think is right. Just get to the car and leave them behind.

Something hits my chest, right over my heart, and falls into my arms. A ball of paper? I grab it and glance in the direction it came from. It could've been anyone. I feel like a rabbit caught in headlights, one that accidentally stumbled onto the wrong road.

There's a flash. Then another.

Is it not enough for them to humiliate me, hurt me, they have to document it as well? Share it with the world for others to join in.

"Come on," Jessica shouts, grabbing my arm before I have time to hide my face. She pulls me towards the car, the two security guards blocking us off as she opens the door and shoves me in.

The door slams behind me and the silence is deafening. The only noise my thumping heart.

We can't be more than fifteen feet from the building yet, somehow, it feels like it's a world away. Thank God I remembered my bag. As much as I love it, I wouldn't go through that again to get it back.

I'm still holding on to the paper and I open it as the car distances us from the crowd.

DIE

The irony of it causes a manic laugh to escape me. *If only they'd thought to use red paper.*

I tried. I thought I'd be making it better, I thought people would listen. It's not fair. I never asked to be in the spotlight, to go on a date with Jackson Peters, to be hated by millions just for standing up for myself.

I crumple it up, throwing it aside as a tear runs down the side of my face. It drips off my chin and splashes onto my phone as I open Twitter, ignoring the rapid incoming notifications and heading straight to the settings, hitting deactivate.

I do the same with Instagram before turning my phone off completely. One of the others will notice and I'm not really in the mood to talk about it yet.

Resting my arm on the door, I rest my head on top and watch the world pass by. I don't bother answering the driver when he asks if I'm okay. Nor do I bother wiping my arm when it starts to stick to my face.

The smell hits me first. The sour air filling my lungs. *Not again. Not now.*

I drop my bag onto the couch, noticing the flies circling the forest of beer bottles and spilt food containers on top of the coffee table. The remains have mixed, a picture drowning upside down in the centre, and it drips off the edge in a stringy waterfall, sinking into the worn-out carpet.

The curtains are still drawn, the only light coming from behind me and the TV that's on standby.

How did I miss it?

The floor creaks outside as someone's footsteps get closer. I yank my keys out of the door, quickly shutting it. We're not friends with anyone around here but the last thing Dad needs is for people to gossip about him.

Including the smashed one that's shattered all over the shelves next to the TV, I count eight beer bottles. And one half-empty vodka bottle. *Crap.*

I make a move toward my dad's room, holding my breath and pinching my nose as I hop past the puddle of sick in the hallway.

The door's ajar and I knock twice before opening it fully, not waiting for a reply. The stench is worse in here, the air thick from the heat, and my hand shoots to my mouth and nose in a poor attempt to block it as the door swings open.

I can only just make out Dad, lying on his back on top of the covers, still wearing the clothes he had on yesterday morning, only now they're decorated with sweat patches and other splotches of unidentified liquids. It's so similar to the last time that my breath catches, getting stuck in my throat. "Dad?" I shout, unsuccessfully missing the second puddle as I dart to the side of his bed.

He doesn't even stir.

My ears start to ring and I swear I can hear them again. All I wanted to do was help him but eight-year-old me didn't know what to do, he wouldn't wake up.

"Dad?" I shout again, louder and shake him with my trembling hands.

I blink and the ringing gets louder, turning into clear sirens, and the paramedics jump into action behind my eyelids.

I take a deep breath. *I know what to do this time. It's not the same.*

I push him into the recovery position and check for a pulse. My breath finally escapes my throat when I find one and I swipe under my eyes.

"Dad, wake up!" I walk to the curtains, throw them back and open the windows as far as they'll go.

He groans at the light and rolls over croaking, "Lorri?"

I rush to the other side of the bed, missing the puke this time. "Yeah, it's me. Are you okay?" Of course, he's not okay, he drank a stupid amount of alcohol and threw up everywhere. What I'm really asking is 'do I need to grab some hangover recovery things or should I ring 999 and Dr Hayes'.

He lets out a ragged breath and attempts a smile. "I'm fine. Nothing some water and sleep won't fix."

Sure, maybe if you were someone else and this was a normal hangover. "Good," I say quietly and make my way back through the corridor to the kitchen.

The sink and side are full of yesterday's dishes along with some new ones, including dad's favourite bowl. As I get closer, I notice it's full of shepherd's pie that's more the colour of charcoal than anything resembling food.

Even though it's burnt to a crisp, the smell still takes me back. It's funny how certain scents can do that, I hardly remember anything from before, but I don't think I'll ever be able to smell shepherd's pie without being taken back to that house when Dad and I would sit around the kitchen table eagerly waiting for Mum's famous dish. Dad would tell jokes that would make me laugh so hard my drink would come out my nose and Mum would watch us lovingly from the other side of the room, occasionally joining in so I could taste test the new recipes that she would be working on whilst waiting for the shepherd's pie to cook. It was her favourite. She'd make it almost every night, and no one ever complained. She'd pull it out of the oven and set it on the table as dad and I groaned but we'd both be smiling, and she'd tell us, for the millionth time, how healthy it is and how it's full of the best ingredients, including her secret ingredient, love.

I snatch the dish, scraping the insides into the overflowing bin. *I always thought it was missing something.*

Grabbing a few things, I leave the kitchen tap on low and let it fill up. "Here," I say, handing him some water and paracetamol. I place a slice of dry toast and a banana on his bedside table.

He drinks most of the water and nibbles on the banana. "Don't do that, I'll sort it," he mumbles, wafting his arm in my direction.

I continue to pick up the rest of the knocked-over things on the dresser next to the door. "It's fine."

He sucks in a breath as he sits up, putting his glass down. "No, it's not." He lets out a deep sigh. "None of this is okay. You shouldn't have to come home and find me like this. You shouldn't have to clean up after me either."

I stand up the last photo frame, it's a picture of us from my first art exhibition. It was a week after Mum left and I was heartbroken because I thought she'd gone on holiday and forgotten about my big moment, but Dad came and made a big deal of it. He bought me the biggest bunch of flowers and kept bragging to all the other parents that his daughter was going to be the next Van Gogh. Even though he knew where she was and he was struggling, he still showed up.

"I'm sorry. You should be out with your friends, not worrying about me. I'm such a bad parent, a disappointment. I'm sorry. So, so, sorry." He sniffles and I turn in time to see the tears start to roll down his face. "I understand why you'd want to leave too."

The picture in the living room. It was the one from the back of the shelf next to the tv, the only one left including mum. *I miss her sometimes as well.*

"You're not a bad parent." He used to spend months saving for birthday parties and take millions of photos of me on the first day of school wearing my giant backpack full of supplies, including a homemade emergency period kit. He's not a bad parent, far from it. "You're ill. You need a bit of help and that's okay, we all do sometimes." I look away, my gaze landing on my twisted hands. "Maybe it's time to speak to Dr Hayes."

It's so quiet I'm afraid to breathe.

He meets me with a hard stare. His jaw clenched, eyebrows drawn and eyes squinted. *Here we go.*

"You're doing your best, and I know that." I take a deep breath and a tiny step back. "But Dr Hayes-"

"Dr *Hayes,"* he spits, "knows nothing! I *was* ill, but I got better. Yes, she helped me, but I don't need her help anymore."

He reaches for the glass and the corner of his duvet absorbs some of his puddle. *Clearly.*

"She said I was still broken but I was perfectly fine. I still am! This," he says, gesturing to himself and the rest of the room, "is just a blip."

I'd believe him if I hadn't heard him say it multiple times before.

"I'm fine, honestly. I don't need her. You were gone and it made me realise that that's what it will be like when you go to the summer program. You'll make new friends and work late on your projects in their fancy art studios, you won't have time for your old dad. And that's fine, I'm so, so proud, I am." He sniffles, "I'm just going to miss you."

This is about me? I take a seat at the end of the bed, keeping enough distance that the stench of the sick doesn't burn my nostrils. "I'll ring all the time and I could see if I can come home at the weekend. I don't need a fancy art studio to do my work in, I've got all my supplies here." It would be a dream come true to be mentored by Vivian Blanche but it wouldn't be worth it if it made Dad ill again. "I'm not just going to up and leave. I'm not-" He gives me a stern look, cutting me short. "Anyway," I continue. "That's even if I get in." At this rate, I'd have more luck trying to go to space.

"What? Of course you're going to get in. Where's this coming from?"

"I still haven't sent in my application," I admit, lowering my head. "Maybe it's for the best, though. The chances of me getting in are already slim and I could stay here instead." I shrug.

"No," he says, sitting up straighter. "You're not staying here to look after me, you've worked too hard. I thought you applied ages ago, you said you were applying early."

"There's so many people applying, my drawing has to stand out otherwise I won't win." I sigh. "It's not like anything I've done isn't good enough, I just haven't done anything. I can't, I've tried, but nothing comes to me."

"Can't you send in one of your old pieces, they're all great." He grabs the plate of cold toast and takes a big bite, holding the side of his head whilst he chews.

"We're not allowed. The new sketchpad they sent has QR codes for them to scan so they know it's a new piece. There's also the prompt, 'All I'll ever need'." I sigh again, taking his empty glass. "I'll come up with something. And if I don't, it won't be the end of the world, I'll still be able to study art at college. More toast?"

He shakes his head at his lap, thinking, and I grab the banana peel too before turning to leave.

"Lorri?"

I stop in the doorway. "Yeah?"

"Try not to worry about it. The more you stress, the more stuck you're going to be. You'll do something great, you always do."

Sixteen

I put my shoes on the rack next to Dad's clean work boots and tidy up the bottles. It takes me almost three hours to get the living room, kitchen and hallway looking anywhere near normal, and most of that time I spend trying to scrub gunk out of the carpets. When I'm finally somewhat satisfied with my job, I check on Dad one last time before switching on the tv and grabbing some snacks.

Two episodes of Superstore later and an advert for a daytime show comes on raving about an exclusive interview with Jackson. Seriously, has anyone witnessed him and the

Queen in the same room because the way they're hyping this up, they might well be the same person.

I should turn my phone back on. I'd rather not, it's been nice not having it go off every minute, but this is the longest I've gone without speaking to the others. Plus, I know Cassie will have been freaking out over my missing socials.

I mute the tv as my phone starts up. There's no buzzing or notification chimes, the silence is bliss. A second later it goes off with a handful of notifications, most of them from Cassie. I'm about to press call when another comes in from Sean.

There's only so long I can hold Cass back, she's about to start a witch hunt for you.

Then a second, straight after.

Seriously tho, we're worried. Everything okay?

School would've finished an hour or two ago, Sean's shift starting half an hour after. I can almost picture them, sitting around our usual table at the cafe, worried expressions on their faces as they tap away at their phones and take turns ringing me.

I find Cassie's name in my contacts and hit call. It barely rings once before I hear her voice on the other end.

"Finally! Are you okay? We've been trying to get hold of you for hours. What happened to your accounts? They've all vanished! You didn't look at them, did you? I told you not to! Not until we'd checked them. We thought you were still meeting us here, we got worried when you never showed. Are you at home? Sean said he can get off early and we could come around? Only if you want us to, obviously. Or you could still come here? Sean says he'll give you a free brownie." She stops to catch her breath and Sean yells in the background, claiming he 'never said such a thing'.

They start to argue and there's the sound of multiple hands on the phone.

Maybe I should say something. Although, I'm not sure they'd hear me at this point.

There's a bang and then silence, just distant chatting and a bit of quiet jazz music. "Right. Now everyone can talk to her. Lorri, are you still there?" Abby shouts into the phone.

"I'm here. And I'm okay, just needed some time," I add quickly, before they ask again.

"Are you sure? We saw the videos from after the interview. Scum, the lot of them," Sean says banging, what's probably, a chocolate milkshake onto the table near the phone.

"Yeah, I'm fine." *As fine as someone receiving death threats can be.* "I'll be fine, don't worry about me. It's all good. Over." Not entirely true. I'm sure people at school are still talking about it and the headlines won't magically go away, but it is over, for me at least. No more Jackson Peters for as long as I can help it.

"So, you saw it then?"

"Cass!"

"Sorry," she cries. "I held off as long as I could. If I had waited any longer I would've exploded."

Is it possible that they're referring to someone else, something more newsworthy than me and Jackson? As much as I'd love that, I highly doubt it. "Saw what?"

"Oh. Nothing," Cassie says, her voice vanishing into a squeak. I swear I can hear her twirling her hair around her manicured nails.

She has to tell me now. "Cassie."

She's silent and I start to pick at the little balls of fluff on my socks, waiting for someone to clue me in. Is there another photo? Maybe there was a secret camera in the dressing room or maybe someone's sent in a fake 'tip' and I'm in the headlines yet again. Why can't they just leave me alone so I can focus on my exams and application?

"He apologised," she says so quickly it takes me a minute to figure out what she said.

"He stood up for you too. It was on his Insta," Abby adds.

Yeah right. He 'apologised' last time and look how that turned out. His apologies don't mean anything, they're just a PR stunt to cover his back so that his precious little fans don't stop giving him money.

"I wouldn't call it an apology per se, that would require him to actually admit that he was in the wrong and own up to his mistakes," Sean says, his scowl present in his voice.

I knew it. Jackson Peters' apologies have as much meaning and empathy as a unicorn taking a dump. It's a stinking, hot pile of shit, no matter how nice you dress it up.

"L? You still there?" Abby asks.

"Yeah. I'm just... Not that it means... I deleted my accounts. What did he say?" I ask, unsure that I even want to know.

"You deleted your accounts?" Cassie gasps. "I'm sending a screenshot now. We'll have to set up a Finsta for you now you're all famous. Of course when I say we, I mean me. Which one are you feeling more; Bob Ross or Micheal McIntyre?"

"Why are they your two options?" Sean asks, his voice full of judgement.

"Well. Bob Ross is obvious, she's an artist. And Micheal McIntyre because... Micheal McIntyre."

"Sure, but there are way better people to base you're Finsta off of," Sean claps back.

"Name them."

I pull the phone away from my ear as he starts his list and open the new message from Cassie. It's a screenshot of Jackson's Insta story, posted a few minutes after I left JBG Studios. He must have been watching the interview. Who am I kidding, of course he was watching the interview. If not him then at least someone from his team, so they can get a head start on damage control. That's probably what this is, some phoney attempt at an apology to cover Jackson's back, posted by his team.

There's no photo, just a black screen with his paragraph on top.

I would like to apologise to Lorri. No human being deserves to be treated the way she was today outside of the studios. It was awful, especially since she's done nothing wrong. I hope the people involved know that they're no fans of mine. My fans are kind and caring, and I saw none of that in those videos. I really am sorry Lorri, not just for today but for pulling you into all of this.

I don't know what I was expecting but it wasn't that. I reread it a few times, making sure I read it right. That's definitely what it says. I stare at the screen, chewing my thumbnail.

He actually sounds… sincere? Sean was right, technically he hasn't admitted to anything *but* he did say I've done nothing wrong *and* that he pulled me into all of this.

That's even if this was him. I'm still not ruling out that this is a PR stunt, especially since it's all very beat around the bush. Nothing incriminating, it says all the right things to put this to an end and bring everyone out smelling, somewhat, of roses.

"Mnmnhhmnhnh"

Huh, what's that?

"Lorri!"

I snap the phone back up to my ear, remembering the others, and the hum of the cafe makes me feel like I'm there with them. "Yeah, I'm here."

"Have you read it?" Abby asks, the sound of the cafe getting quieter in the background.

"Yeah. A few times. Are you guys leaving?" It's still early, Sean should still have a few hours of his shift left.

"No, I just had to get out of there. You know what they're like." The bell above the door goes, the sound of the cafe completely disappearing. "We *can* leave, though. We could come, talk about this. Roy's said Sean can leave early because the cafe isn't busy so we were going to hang here for a bit but we could go to Mr Lawrences and grab some snacks then head to your-"

"No," I say quickly, my eyes lingering where the puddle of sick was just a couple of hours ago. "Urm, I mean... It's fine, honestly. I have a lot of revision to do for tomorrow, you guys have fun."

"Oh. Well, we could bring our revision. Or we could revise here, I could really use the help to be honest," she says, not picking up on the change in my voice. Or maybe she has, it wouldn't be the first time she's nudged me to open up.

"I'd love to but I'm really tired. I think everything from today has just tired me out," I nod to myself. "Actually, I'm realising *just* how tired I am so I think I'm gonna go and take a nap," I stifle a fake yawn. "I'll see you guys tomorrow though, before school?"

She's quiet. Probably debating whether or not to go along with my bullshit. She will, they always do.

Cassie's known from the beginning, walking in on one of the 'bad days' and helping me clean up whilst Dad was chucking up his breakfast. That was before it got really bad. We never spoke about it, not even when he went into the hospital. I stayed with her for a few days and we just pretended that everything was normal, or as normal as someone being rushed to the hospital could be, and I was thankful for that. We haven't spoken about it since, there hasn't been any point with Dad getting help and getting better.

I think she knows it's happening again, though. I try to hide it from her so we can keep not talking about it, so it can still be just my burden, but she knows. I see it in her eyes when she asks, 'how's your day been' or 'how's your dad'. She says it casually but her eyes go wide in that serious kind of way.

It's different with Sean and Abby, they've never seen anything. They came into my life after Dad got help, they saw the 'best version of himself', fresh out of therapy. But he started to slip, and I started to hide it from them. They'd ask why I wouldn't invite them around anymore or would make playful jokes when I worried that he wasn't texting me back or picking up my calls, then one day they stopped and they got that same look in their eyes. I know she told them, I'm not mad at her for it, I'm grateful. This way I don't have to.

"Sure, we'll see you tomorrow. Message, *or call*," she adds quickly, "if you need anything. You're not alone."

"Yeah." I clear my throat to stop my voice from breaking. "Yeah, I know. It feels like the whole world is with me. What with all the comments and the news articles," I say with a short laugh. I know she's not talking about Jackson but talking about Jackson is so much easier than addressing *that*. "I'll see you tomorrow."

She doesn't laugh back, just lets out a quiet breath. "Yeah. Bye."

I can tell she's hurt that I won't open up to her, but I can't. They have enough going on with their mum, they don't need to worry about me and my dad as well.

The screen's back on the screenshot of Jackson's Insta story. I read it once more, still not quite believing that it might be over, and launch the Instagram app. *Finsta it is*.

Seventeen

I decide to go with @BobLorRossi for Cassie's sake and use a funny photo of Michael McIntyre for my profile picture. The first thing I do is follow Abby, Cassie and Sean. Hopefully, they'll take it as a sign that I'm okay and stop worrying, and Cassie and Sean can stop arguing. I can almost hear her victory cheer now.

Before I do anything else I head into the settings and make the account private. I doubt anyone will find it but I'd rather not take the chance, not with the luck I've been having.

Once it's fully set up, I search for Jackson, looking for the verified account among the thousands of fan accounts, and head straight for his story. I'm met by five slides, each one a link to a new interview or article.

It ends and his profile pops back up. *Huh? Where is it?*

I click it again, taking my time to check I'm not missing anything. Nope, definitely not here. Just two links for the same interview posted yesterday, and three new posts, all uploaded in the last hour or two, with links to other interviews and photo shoots. No mention at all of me or what happened earlier.

My friends wouldn't lie about something like this, that's not something they'd do, it *was* on here at some point. I sit up and lean into the screen, going full detective mode.

Thanks to Cassie, I know that fan accounts like to repost anything and everything about their idol so his tagged photos are my best bet. Lots of them are fanart or edits but after scrolling for a few minutes, just when I'm about to give up, I spot the familiar black photo. There's a wall of them, reposted by tens, maybe even hundreds, of accounts. *Gotcha.*

I know Cassie would kill me if she knew, but I read a few of the captions anyway. Most of them are apologies on behalf of the people who harassed me or comments about how nice it is of him to stand up for me but when I scroll to the next one, the caption's addressed to me directly. It's an apology on behalf of not just themself but everyone else in the fandom. The next one's the same. And it only takes me a few seconds before I find another, then another. *Maybe it truly is over.*

Still, where did it go? It shouldn't have disappeared yet, not unless it was deleted. Maybe he deleted it after finding out his PR team posted it, but surely he'd want this to be over too. I know they say 'there's no such thing as bad publicity' but I don't think your name being all over the news because your fans attacked someone is exactly 'good' publicity.

Whatever, it doesn't matter who posted it or who took it down, people saw it, and they've apologised so hopefully this nightmare is finally over.

My dad stirs and a few coughs come from his door.

I quickly scroll to the top of the page and hit 'follow' as I grab another glass of water from the kitchen. I debate pressing the button again before hitting the bell icon. *Just in case he posts anything else.*

The next couple of days are somewhat normal and school's fine. Sure, you get the odd person that won't drop it and continues to ask questions or give me the side eye, but it's much better now we've moved. We had to exchange our usual spot outside for a dark corner of the school library. Cassie keeps complaining about the lack of sunlight but it's a lot quieter which makes it much better for revising. Abby hasn't mentioned our phone call like I knew she wouldn't, only mentioning Jackson's post once.

Cassie's invited us around to hers, claiming we all need some 'well deserved relaxation time' and that her parents' outdoor bar and hot tub is the best place to do it. I didn't mention the fact that we're finally starting to feel the effects of summer and that it's at least twenty-five degrees in the sun which is way too warm to be getting into a hot tub, especially when you're ginger.

"You came!" she shouts as she opens her front door.

"Of course I came. Why wouldn't I?" Maybe because I tried to make every excuse as to why I couldn't come. It's not that I don't want to be here, of course I want to hang out with my friends, but I didn't want to leave Dad on his own, not this soon after a bad day.

Uncle Joe phoned yesterday, though, and I think he could tell something was wrong because he invited us around for tea tonight. We don't see him often because they moved just outside of town when my second cousin was born and we don't have a car anymore. I was definitely tempted by the mention of a sausage casserole, but I knew coming would mean a lot to Cassie. Plus, Dad might talk to Uncle Joe if I'm not there.

Cassie opens her mouth and then closes it. "No. Obviously, you came," she says, moving to let me in. "Sean and Abby are already here, they're making cocktails in the back. Well, Sean's *attempting* to make cocktails. Honestly, the guy's a genius but I don't think he'll be adding cocktail making to the list of things he's good at."

My laugh echoes through the empty house. "It's good that he's found something he's bad at, it'll humble him."

"Exactly. It'll remind him that he's human, like the rest of us," she says, smirking as we exit the sliding kitchen door.

"I will never be one of you mortals!" he bellows from behind the bar. "I shan't stop until I've mastered the art of cocktail making." He grabs his shaker and tries his best to hide a smirk. "What can I get for you, ma'am?"

"If you value your life you'll say 'nothing'," Abby mutters from the side of the hot tub, sipping a can of Foster's.

"The last one wasn't that bad! Right?" He takes a sip of a green liquid before rushing to spit it into the sink, taking a big gulp of his can. "Cider?" he coughs at me.

Cassie rolls her eyes as he opens a bottle and hands it over.

Accepting it, I take a seat at the edge of the pool and try my best not to get my shorts wet as I dip my legs in.

Abby jumps in and the splash only just misses me, the droplets tickling my knees. She emerges and floats on her back in front of me.

"How's your mum?"

"She's alright," she tells the clouds. "Good, actually. When we got back yesterday, she was really excited to tell us what she did with the nurse. She was able to go out and watch the sunset at the park, and I think it was just nice for her to be able to hang out with someone closer to her own age." She stops floating and swims to the side next to me. "I think it upset Sean though. Because he couldn't be the one to help her," she whispers, staring at her can. "We can't always do things on our own though, can we?" she says, locking her eyes onto mine. "It's okay to accept help when it's needed."

I know what she's trying to do, it's not happening. I give her a small nod, "I'm glad she's good. Is she with her tonight?"

There's a moment of disappointment, one so small that if I'd blinked I would've missed it. "Yeah, she's going to be here for a few hours every night."

"That's great," I say, my voice as warm as the water.

So much of their time is spent looking after their mum. I know they don't mind and they love spending time with her but there's only so much they can do. And now with exams and college, they need all the help they can get.

"Shots time!" Cassie shouts from behind me.

I jump, only just stopping my bottle from polluting the clear pool.

"Why are we having shots again?" Abby asks, elegantly lifting herself out of the pool.

We walk back over to the bar and share a look when we're handed tall shot glasses full to the top with a bubbly dark liquid. I take a sniff, confirming my suspicions. "Is this Coke?"

"Okay, so, my mum took all the strong stuff, *but* she poured some vodka into a bottle of Coke for us." She spots Abby, Sean and I smirk at each other and throws her hands up. "Look, I know it's supposed to be straight vodka but this is the best we've got."

We hardly ever drink. The only time we've gotten drunk was two years ago when Cassie stole two bottles of wine from her parents' collection. We were ill the whole of the next day and ended up missing a mock exam because we couldn't go to school, our parents were furious and grounded us. It was over Easter break so we couldn't use school as an excuse, we didn't see or talk to each other for the whole week. That, mixed with everything that's happened with my dad, is enough to put me off alcohol for life. The only time I drink now is when everyone else is, and even then, I never finish my first bottle. "Why do you want to do shots anyway? What's the occasion?"

"No occasion. I just wanted to try something new," Cassie says, looking at us expectantly. "Oh, come on. Just one so we can say we've done it. Together." Her voice catches.

There's only a couple of months left before college starts. Only a couple of months left until she leaves.

I nod and tap Cassie's shot with mine. "Okay, count me in."

Abby and Sean follow my lead and we cheers, take a big breath and then down the shots. It's not as bad as I thought it would be. Actually, it's not bad at all. Everyone else seems to have the same reaction too, all of them wearing the same relieved look I'm sure I have on.

"Huh," Cassie says, eyeing the glass suspiciously.

Abby lifts hers, sniffing the remains. "It tasted just like-"

"Normal coke," I say and Abby nods. "Are you sure your mum put any in?"

Cassie looks sharply at Sean. "You used the open bottle, right?"

He opens his mouth in an 'oh' shape before quickly shutting it, trying to hide a grin. "Well, you just said to pour some of the coke from the fridge into the shot glasses. I thought the fuller one would be fizzier so I went with that."

Cassie glares at him and he throws his hands up in surrender. "Hey, you didn't say which one!"

Sometimes he makes it really hard to believe that he has an IQ close to Einstein. Maybe he's more of a Newton and has had too many apples fall on his head. I catch Abby's eye and we try to hide our amusement as Cassie smacks his arm.

Grabbing his wrist, she takes our glasses and starts to drag him toward the back door. "Come on, you can help me get the real shots. We'll grab some ice lollies as well."

When they reach the door, he playfully mouths 'help' over his shoulder and we stop trying to hide our giggles now that Cassie's out of view.

Abby turns to me as the door shuts. "So, when will we be able to see your finished masterpiece?"

"What do you mean?" I know exactly what she means.

She tilts her head. "*I mean* your drawing for your application. You know, the one you're always working on?"

"Well, do you have any plain paper?" I say into my bottle.

She gives me a quizzical look, answering slowly, "No, but Cassie'll have some."

"Good. If you go and grab a piece then you'll see my amazing *masterpiece*." I add jazz hands for extra emphasis on just how screwed I am.

She finally gets it and whispers an "oh" whilst sitting down on one of the fancy sun loungers.

I join her, sitting on the one half-shaded by the outdoor bar. "Yep. 'Oh.'" I take a big mouthful of my drink and place the bottle on my legs, letting the cool condensation drip onto my already red skin.

"But you always say it's going well."

"Correction, I said 'getting there'." It wasn't a total lie, at times I did think I was getting *somewhere*. But, if I'm honest, I was probably just trying to kid myself into thinking I was 'getting there' so I wouldn't have a meltdown. "I don't know. I had ideas and I thought they were good, but when I put them on paper they just seemed wrong, not good enough, so I scrapped them halfway through. Now I can't even come up with a stupid idea."

"You've had a lot going on, what with 'he who shall not be named' and your… school stuff," she quickly catches herself, giving me a sympathetic smile. "It's no wonder you have stuff on your mind."

I nod, watching a new drop roll down the glass and sink into my skin. Maybe she's right. Sure, I was already struggling before I met Jackson but I'd been stressing a lot about Dad. Consciously, I told myself that he was fine and I was worrying over nothing, but subconsciously, I recognised all the warning signs. That, mixed with the stress of exams, was enough alone, but now with Jackson on my mind, there's no space left to think about my application. As soon as I get my pad out and stare at the blank page, my mind replays images of Dad unconscious or wanders to Jackson and all the messages I received.

"Hey," she says, turning to face me. "Maybe you need to draw it."

"What?" All I've been trying to do is *draw it.*

"Draw whatever's on your mind. You know, get it out of your head and onto paper. Then, maybe you'll have a clear mind to focus on your application." She shrugs. "I'm not saying you have to draw the actual thing, because I know you'd rather never send in your application than draw a photo of Ja- you know who, just draw how you feel, how everything in your head makes you feel. Let it all out." She smiles for a second before adding, "You could even burn it after, or shred it. No one has to see it. It's worth a shot." She finishes with another shrug.

"Yeah, maybe." I fake a smile as my bottle meets my lips, thankful for the advice but praying that it's over. As much as I want to finish my application, I'd rather not open that box and let all of my feelings and emotions spew out with the possibility of someone seeing. And I definitely do *not* want to draw Jackson's smug face. *No matter how annoyingly symmetrical it is.*

The sun jumps out from behind a cloud and I'm hit with the heat, my legs becoming increasingly more lobster-like by the second.

"They've been gone awhile," I say, reaching over to grab the bottle of factor fifty out of my bag. I smear a big dollop onto each leg, the skin instantly soothing and my mouth waters at the thought of the promised frozen ice pop.

"Sorry, Sean's fault. He dropped a glass and we had to clean up the mess, luckily it didn't smash, though." She comes over carrying the four shots and takes a seat on the end of my sun lounger, passing one to me and Abby.

"Uh, yeah, sorry," Sean mutters, taking a seat at the end of Abby's lounger. He passes out the ice lollies, giving us each our favourite flavour, and then takes his glass off Cassie.

Neither of them look at the other whilst they exchange goods, both of them finding something much more important to focus on in the areas behind each other and on the patio next to them.

Did I miss something? I check if Abby's also picked up on the weird vibe but she just smiles, holding her glass up to toast.

"Here's to forgetting the past week and looking forward to the future, wherever it may take us."

"I'll definitely cheers to that," Cassie says, raising her glass.

I lift mine to meet the others. "Me too."

I glance at Sean but he's lost in thought, cradling his shot glace like it's a cup of hot chocolate on a cold winter's night. I nudge his foot and he flinches, breaking out of thought.

He looks at my concerned face and instantly breaks into a wide grin. "Cheers!"

Eighteen

"One extra hot mocha and a complementary cheese scone for our favourite customer. Careful, they're still hot."

"Just the way I like them. Thanks," I say, briefly turning away from my work to offer Zac a smile.

"No need to thank me, just remember us when you're a famous artist. You know, post on the socials or drop our name in interviews when you're asked about your first paid gig." He adds a wink and a smirk as he goes to help his husband with the three steaming trays of baked goods that he's trying to juggle.

I've been coming to Zac and Seth's coffee shop since Cassie's obsession with iced tea. She must have drunk her whole body weight, twice over, of it that summer we were here that often.

One day Zac walked past our table when I was finishing a drawing and he instantly demanded I repaint the cafe, giving me free rein to do whatever I liked. I kept it simple on most walls; light dusty teal with little silver coffee beans here and there, and then on the wall opposite the door, I did a painting of the couple so it's the first thing people see when they walk in. Cassie helped with some of it, suggesting we add a few facts and quotes on the blank walls. That was when she was in her calligraphy phase. I have to hand it to her, she did an amazing job. They paid good money for it too, especially with it being my first gig, and now they repay me for it every time I come in. Let's just say I'll never go hungry so long as they're here.

I take a bite of the cheese scone, letting the plate catch the crumbs, and drop it when my fingers can't take the heat any longer. It melts in my mouth, the cheesy lava dripping from my lips as the bell above the door chimes, and I close my eyes. *Is there anything better than melted cheese?*

"Hey. Can I get a mocha, please? Oh, and a pain au chocolat? Thanks," says an awfully familiar American accent.

My eyes fly open as it echoes around the empty room. There's no way. Out of all the coffee shops in this area, there's no way he found mine. I can't say I've ever ran into any other Americans around here though.

Wiping my mouth with one arm, I quickly run the other through my hair.

What am I doing?! Although, to be honest, wherever he goes the cameras aren't that far behind.

I wish I took longer picking out my outfit this morning instead of throwing on the same shorts and top I wore to Cassie's yesterday. I had to make sure I was ready before Uncle Joe came to pick Dad up though, otherwise I would've had to walk in the heat.

Pushing my messy hair over my shoulder, I slowly turn to catch a glance of him, being careful not to make it too obvious.

There he is. Standing in front of the coffee counter is none other than Jackson freaking Peters. I almost don't recognise him in his baggy brown pants, graphic tee and brown baseball cap, I probably wouldn't have if it wasn't for his usual designer sunglasses. Well, that and his voice.

If I didn't know it was him, I might've said he looked good.

I mustn't be doing a good job of hiding my curiosity because Seth eyes me as he hands Jackson his order and, noticing my failed attempt to spy, raises an eyebrow, completely blowing my cover. Jackson turns and I snap my head back towards my sketchbook, cursing. His footsteps get closer and closer, and I continue to swear under my breath in an almost prayer.

I quickly start to shade an area of my drawing that isn't supposed to be shaded and stuff half of my cheese scone in my mouth. You can't spy, eat and draw and the same time, right?

"Wow," he says, coming to a halt next to my table. "That's really good."

"It's nothing," I reply between struggling bites, the words barely audible as I blow out hot air whilst also trying not to blow out chunks of half chewed dough. My face reddens and I throw the cover over my work, remembering what it was I was working on before I got distracted.

"It didn't look like nothing." He gently takes the seat opposite me, waiting for me to object. When I don't, he places his things on the little area of the table I'm not using, careful not to disturb my things.

I could tell him to piss off. Scream in his face for causing so much drama and throw the remaining piece of my cheese scone at him for upsetting Cassie- although that wouldn't be fair on the cheese scone- or I could just glance at Zac or Seth and they'd chuck him out. We had a quick catch-up when I came in and they wanted all the juicy details on all things Jackson Peters. Of course, when I say they I really mean Zac, Seth listened too but he was more preoccupied with the pies.

He takes a tentative sip of his coffee as he tries to avoid my gaze, his golden eyes cast down in an attempt to act casual as if his sitting with me isn't out of the ordinary. *What harm can he do?*

"It's personal. It's not really for anyone else to see," I say, my sketchbook now secure under the weight of my crossed arms. I decided to listen to Abby in the end. It only took another wasted night of staring at a blank page to realise I might as well try. I started it first thing this morning, throwing all my thoughts and feelings about Dad, and Mum, into it. I doubt anyone would be able to understand it but still, I'm not ready for people to see it, it would be like them peering into my brain.

"Oh! I'm sorry," he says, placing his coffee back down on its saucer, "I didn't see much, I promise." He seems genuine, the corners of his mouth pulled down slightly as he finally meets my eyes.

What is happening? I'm sitting in a cafe with Jackson Peters and he's gazing into my eyes. This isn't real, right? This is some weird dream that I'm going to wake up from and think 'Huh, what a weird dream' and then tell Cassie about over a cup of real coffee. Cassie, that's it! We were at Cassie's last night and were drinking. I'm probably hallucinating from the alcohol poisoning or I've died and this is hell. Although, I don't think hell would be this tolerable or feel this friendly. Obviously, that's thanks to Zac and Seth, not Jackson and his brown eyes. *Or are they more hazel, golden?*

His eyes dart from my face to his forgotten pain au chocolate as he clears his throat and I try to find something, anything, else to look at other than his face. They land on my cup of coffee and I instantly pick up, taking the longest sip of my life.

The room shrinks as the silence grows and I rack my brain to think of literally anything to say to make it less awkward. I try another sip of coffee as my brain fails me and we continue to sit in silence, avoiding looking at each other.

I go to prepare myself for another unwanted sip but he looks up, the urgency almost knocking me off my seat. "I'm glad I bumped into you." He waits for me to respond, or maybe he's debating whether or not to continue.

I pry my hands away from my mug and drop them into my lap, picking at the bit of skin near my thumbnail. Why on earth is he glad he bumped into *me*? Surely, he has better things to do with his time than sit in silence in an empty cafe with someone he hardly knows. He's just finished his tour; does he not have parties to get to or holidays to jet off on?

"Um, I just mean, now I can try and apologise again. Properly." He waits for me to object but I let him continue.

I'm not sure why considering how well it went last time.

"Well, I don't know if you saw but after the interview you did I posted an apology on Instagram, taking full responsibility. I saw what they did to you when you finished the interview, it wasn't right."

When he doesn't continue, I state, "My friend sent me a screenshot."

His whole face softens. "Good, good. I was scared you wouldn't see it, especially when my PR team deleted it. You'd *think* I'd be able to control what I say but..." he trails off, raising his eyebrows as he frowns.

So, he did post it. And he wasn't the one who deleted it. Huh.

"Anyway," he says, snapping his head back up, "I'm really happy you saw it. And, again, sorry for everything." He finishes with a smile, clearly chuffed with himself.

That's it. *That's* the big apology he's been dying to say to me. I've heard better apologies from people who've cut in front of me in a queue. He could've at least given me some form of explanation as to why he acted like a total ass, or why he had to humiliate me at his concert, or why he did the interview, claiming that I'm madly in love with him. If just *one* of those things hadn't happened it would've been a lot better, but no, he just had to keep going one step further and making it worse, and I don't even get an explanation for it.

"Wait, did you really think that rubbish you put on your story would instantly fix everything?" I basically throw the last words at him.

His face drops, his smile now a ghost of what it was. "Urm. Yes?"

I cross my arms and sit back in my chair, raising an eyebrow. I don't care if this is the first time he's ever apologised without his PR team holding his hand, it's going to take more than that.

"Well, everyone has backed off. They're all apologising too. And the media should leave you alone now as well which is good, right?"

"Oh, okay. So, everyone else has moved on, forgotten about it or found a new story to focus on, so I should do the same? Just like that." I sit up, snapping my fingers.

"Uh…" He shifts uncomfortably in his chair, frantically glancing behind me, where Zac and Seth are no doubt watching from behind the counter. "I just thought that you'd be happy now that I came clean and told everyone that you did nothing wrong, and because everyone's leaving you alone."

"Well, I'm not. Because you didn't *come clean*," I say using air quotations, "not really. Sure, you said I did nothing wrong but you didn't tell the whole truth." He tilts his head slightly, his brows knitted as I continue, "Oh, so you didn't tell the world that I was '*madly in love with you*'?" I place my hands over my heart, feigning admiration.

"I didn't want to do it. I told them it wasn't fair to bring you into this to cover my mistakes, I stood up for you!" he shouts, leaning slightly over the table.

"Aww, my hero." I clutch my chest again and flutter my eyes.

"Whatever. I tried to help, sorry it wasn't good enough."

"Yeah, well, too little, too late." I think back to the crumpled piece of paper as I re-fold my arms. I glance down at my lap and take a steady breath before meeting his stare, hoping he can't see the tears threatening to run.

He searches my face for a second too long, causing my eyes to dart to the window.

"I'm sorry, really, I didn't mean to upset you, I just wanted to apologise. To try to make it right."

I want to yell at him, point out the fact that he still hasn't fully apologised or given an explanation and that, because of that, it will never be 'right', but the tone of his voice stops me. It's so quiet that I bet Zac and Seth didn't hear him, even with the empty cafe and the music on low. He sounds so genuinely hurt that I have to check it's still me he's talking to.

"I'll stop bothering you," he says standing, quietly pushing his chair back. "I was just looking for a quiet place to get away from everything and focus on some writing." He pulls one side of his mouth into a sad smile and tilts his head towards my sketchbook. "Great minds think alike, huh?" He rakes his hand through his hair when I don't answer. "I'll find somewhere else. Enjoy your coffee."

His half-full mocha and pain au chocolate stare me down from the far corner of the table, begging not to be wasted. Was I too harsh? Once again cutting our conversation short before he even has the chance to begin an explanation.

"Wait," I say, my eyes still glued to where he was previously sitting.

Out of the corner of my eye, I catch him pause in front of the door. The sun comes out from behind a cloud and suddenly the paths alight outside the window, the reflection blinding me. The heat makes me feel like, and probably resemble, a tomato growing in a greenhouse in the Sahara Desert.

I suppose I could do with some fresh air, and maybe if I fix things with Jackson, I'll finally be able to get my drawing done.

"I might know a place."

Nineteen

We've been walking silently for the past ten or twenty minutes, although maybe it hasn't been that long considering we haven't made it far.

"I could've paid for my own things," I say, taking a sip of the red berry smoothie. I decided we should grab some drinks to take with us to make sure we don't die of dehydration in the heat, and some snacks because snacks are always essential, no matter the weather.

We've finally reached the small gate at the end of the long road and he pushes it open, walking through first. "You know, most people would just say thanks," he smirks, holding the gate for me. It falters as I make no move to join him.

"Actually, I think I saw a new cake on the menu that I haven't tried before." Not particularly true, I've had everything on the menu at least three times, but he doesn't know that. "You can find your own way, right?"

I take another pointed sip and turn to leave, ready to head back to the cafe and leave him here, but something warm tugs at my arm. It slips down, settling in my palm.

"Sorry," he says when I look at where our hands are intertwined. He pulls his hand away just as quickly as he put it there, leaving mine oddly cold. "Just, please, don't leave," he begs softly. "I'm sorry, obviously you don't need to thank me, *I* was trying to thank *you* for giving me a second- or maybe even third- chance. If I'm honest I'm not even sure why you decided to come with me, I thought you hated me." He looks down at a small pebble on the dirt path and knocks it with his trainer.

Why does he care what I think? I give my arm and head a quick shake as I step through the gate. "Yeah, well, maybe I have my own reason for coming with you," I say, offering a small smile as I walk past. I carry on walking further down the track, still sipping my smoothie.

After a second of watching, he jogs the short distance between us. "Oh yeah, and what's that? You planning on taking me into the middle of nowhere and murdering me? Should I be worried?"

"Very. It's far worse than that," I say, joining in with his playful tone. "I made a deal with the paps, you for me."

He jumps back, his eyes wider than I've ever seen them, his hands grasping his heart as if I just told him a terrible story of a gruesome death. *I guess in a way I have.* "And here I thought we were becoming friends."

"It was all part of my master plan." I shrug as though it's a business transaction and he's just collateral damage.

He drops his arms and his mouth pulls into the charmest of smiles, little dimples coming out of hiding on both sides. "I guess I kinda deserve it. Just, if people ask, tell them I put up a fight."

I surprise myself by letting out a chuckle. "Sure."

He turns at the sound, his crinkled eyes burning me more than the sun, and I don't need to look at him to make out the big, toothy grin he's wearing.

Stop it. You're only here to get your drawing done, and then get back to your normal life. God, a couple of minutes ago you were arguing with each other, pull it together.

I give him one last smile before quickly carrying on down the narrow dirt path. We probably just have heatstroke, we'll be back to hating each other once we're in the shade.

As we walk further into the woods, we fall into a comfortable silence and he keeps a watch on the surrounding wildlife, scanning from side to side as the borders turn from brambles and thorns to the most vibrant of wildflowers.

I've always wondered why they left it like that. I thought it was a shame no one knew of its hidden beauty but maybe that's the point. I guess it's true what they say, you never should judge a book by its cover.

A dragonfly flutters past my head as we reach the first field. It retraces our steps, gliding from me to where Jackson's stopped. He doesn't even flinch when it almost lands in his hair, his eyes glued to the red sea. I don't blame him, this field's always been one of my favourites, it's packed full of wildflowers but each year the number of poppies doubles. It won't be long until the whole field is dominated by them.

He's amazed when I tell him this isn't the place I had planned and asks if he can take some pictures before we leave. I ready myself to become his personal photographer and try to calculate how long it would take for his fans to find out where this is and infiltrate, but after a few clicks of the field he just says, "Let's go", not taking a single selfie.

We walk past a few more fields just as equally beautiful and serene as the last and cross the rickety bridge over the stream. Jackson offers to go first and points out the slippery spots from where the water has splashed up from the rocks below, offering his hand when I accidentally slip on one.

I hear it before we even round the corner, the chirping birds and low hum of the grasshoppers drawing me in like a beacon guiding me home. We finally reach the clearing and my chest lightens, even as my breath is sucked out of me.

I throw my arms out. "This is it. My quiet spot."

It's a cove with green walls made of tall trees and bushes of wildflowers, creating shadows of all different shapes and sizes, and the middle glows as a stream of light floods the grass floor through a break. It cuts through like a spotlight highlighting the main feature; a small pond lying peacefully under the opening. The water's so still and pure it resembles a large mirror, glowing from the sun above. On the other side are more serene fields, except this time, it has the full attention of the sun above, setting it alight. It sways in the gentle breeze creating a sea of magical, golden fire.

"Wow." It barely comes out as a breath as he steps out, wandering over to the pond. As soon as he steps into the spotlight his whole face lights up. His hair glows with shades of gold, creating a godly halo effect, and his skin glistens, accentuating his angular features.

"It's beautiful," he gasps.

Yeah, it is. I take the few steps to join him and stop on the rock next to his. "I come here whenever I need to get away from things or to think about things. Or just when I need a bit of quiet."

"I get that." He turns to watch me, his eyes glistening.

"I actually used to come here a lot when I was younger." I glance out at the field, the image almost identical to the first day I saw it. "My parents found it. Then every week after that, we came and had a picnic. We did it for years." My mouth waters as I remember the taste of Mum's special pasta and Dad's Victoria sponge, one of the only things he's ever successfully baked, and it draws up into a sad kind of smile as I hear mine and Mum's laugh at Dad in a heap on top of the trifle after claiming he could do a handstand. "The last time we came together feels like a lifetime ago, but I still come. I don't think it gets many visitors and it's too beautiful not to be seen."

I'm not sure why I'm sharing my family memories with a total stranger. Actually, I'm not sure why I brought him here at all, I've never shown it to anyone, not even Cassie.

A little robin skims across the surface of the water and perches on the opposite bank. It looks around before digging into the earth. I sense Jackson's gaze on me and it sends a phantom shiver down my arms, the hairs standing on end. The robin pulls out a small worm and skips back the way it came until it's out of view.

"Well, this is it. I usually sit here." I point at the big slab of rock beneath his feet. "But we could sit on the grass or somewhere else if you want." I'm not sure why I'm giving him the privilege of choosing where we sit considering this is my spot and I really want to sit in my place.

He gestures to our feet and the space in front of us. "Here's perfect."

We both fling our bags off our backs, flopping down to the rock, and I've never been more grateful to feel the cold slab on my legs. I bet both of our shirts are glued to our backs with sweat at this point. Plus, if we had to walk any longer, Jackson might've actually ended up dead with the number of times he's tripped over things.

I get out my water bottle and sketching stuff, and Jackson removes his snacks and notebook, and within minutes we're both lost in our work, the only occasional noise a distant aeroplane or Jackson fighting with his crisp packet for something to chew on while he stops to think. I start a new sketch of the view in front of me, including Jackson, putting all of my feelings towards him onto the page.

About an hour later I think he's clocked on to what I'm doing as he keeps glancing in my direction. He does it again, peeping up from behind his notebook like a meerkat, and I realise it's not me that's caught his attention but my water bottle.

I secretly search over the contents of his bag that I can see from where I'm sitting, noting there's no bottle in sight. "Did you not bring a drink?" I ask, the concern annoyingly clear in my voice. Today's not the hottest the UK's ever seen but it sure is warm. Too warm not to have a drink on you.

"Urm, no," he admits, rubbing the back of his neck. "I forgot to grab one when we left the cafe. It's fine, I'm used to dehydration with all the concerts, rehearsals, photoshoots etc. It's normal to forget to do usual human things like drinking water, sleeping or just breathing sometimes," he half-jokes.

"Maybe you should talk to someone about that. Because I actually heard once that water's, like, *extremely* important for you."

He chuckles and it sounds so familiar, yet it's so far from all the fake compulsory laughs he dishes out in interviews. It's nice and contagious, making it hard for me to keep a straight face.

I grab the bottle, offering it to him. "Do you want some? Sounds like you could do with the extra hydration."

"Oh, no. I'll be fine." He waves a hand in front of the bottle as if is trying to magic it away.

"I really don't mind. There's more than enough for both of us." I'm only offering to make sure he doesn't die on me. I'm sure the media would have a field day, I can see the headlines now: 'Jackson Peters rushed to hospital as crazy stalker lures him to the forest to murder him'. I'd rather take the risk of sharing DNA.

"Well… If you insist." He smiles and accepts the bottle, chugging a mouthful or two before returning it. "Thanks," he says, wiping his mouth with the back of his hand.

I place it in the space between us as a sign that he can help himself, and go back to my work.

A while later I'm pulled out of my drawing again by an annoying tapping. It starts low and slow at first until it quickly turns into a much louder rhythm.

Jackson's no longer writing in his notebook, instead, he's absentmindedly using it as a drum whilst staring out across the field, his gaze fixed on one spot. I try to block it out but it's soon accompanied by humming.

It's not a tune I recognise, though, I usually only listen to the same couple of songs in my playlist. He stops and restarts the tune again, and then again, each time slightly different, better. With his eyes still locked on that one spot, the humming slowly becomes quiet words, then full sentences. Something about light having many colours but they're hidden.

He's either forgotten he's not alone, completely enveloped in his craft, or he doesn't mind me hearing.

"Did you write that?" I ask before I can stop myself.

My voice breaks him from his trance, finally allowing him to rip his eyes away from the golden flames. "Oh. Yeah," he says, his cheeks slightly reddening. "It's just something I'm working on."

"It sounded good. It's different from your others, I thought it might've been someone else's."

"Yeah…" he trails off, looking back down at the pad resting on his knees and then back at me. "I don't usually release these ones."

I rest my arms on my knees, pulling them towards my chest, almost mimicking him. "How come?"

He shrugs, turning back towards the pond.

"Well, maybe I'd listen to your songs more if they were all like that," I say with a small smile.

He hugs his knees, letting his pad fall to the stone next to him. "So, you listen to my music," he smirks, his eyes sparkling in the sun.

"I didn't say that."

"You know, I'm sure I saw you singing along at the concert. Actually, I've been meaning to tell you, we got some noise complaints from the surrounding fans, next time if you can you be a bit more mindful of others before screaming the lyrics that would be great. Don't worry," he throws his hands up in surrender, "I get it, It's my fault for making such epic music." He flashes me another swoon-worthy smile, earning him an *epic* eye roll.

I let out a small chuckle despite myself. "I think you're getting me confused with someone else."

He leans back, resting on his palms, and closes his eyes, the sun washing over him. "No, it was definitely you. The stage lights were pretty bright but even then, I could still see your fiery mane."

Was that a compliment? Maybe I'm just overthinking it, he could just be taking the piss. It wouldn't be the first time someone's used my hair as a punching bag. Or maybe it was nothing, why do I even care?

He opens an eye and studies my expression, trying to read my thoughts.

Is he starting to blush? It's probably just the sun, it must be midday by now so it'll be in full swing. Heck, I've probably been 'blushing' since I left the house. I rack my brain for a joke to ease the tension and open my mouth, hoping that something not too embarrassing will tumble out.

We're interrupted by ABBA as 'Money, money, money' blares from his phone.

Thank you ABBA. I promise to never again complain when Mama Mia!'s on TV for the third week in a row. I whip out my discarded drawing and pretend that the last bit of our conversation never happened.

The ring tone doesn't last long, cut short by Jackson before he shoves it to the bottom of his bag.

I consider saying something, letting him know that it's okay if he wants to take it, but something about his body language tells me he's in no rush to do so.

"I'm sorry-" A short laugh escapes him and he shakes his head. "I don't think I've said sorry this many times to one person before." He shakes his head again and continues, "What I was trying to say is, I saw that you had to delete your accounts. I'm sorry you had to do that just to escape them."

He noticed that I deleted my accounts? Well, maybe his team noticed and let him know. That's the sort of thing PR teams would do, right?

Oh, no. For my birthday last month, we dressed up as Marvel characters but on a budget since the new Avenger movie was playing at the cinema and we took a photo just before we left to watch it, doing our character's poses. *I really hope it's something his PR team would do.*

I shrug, adding a slight shake of my head. "It's fine, I didn't use them much anyway. I mainly used Insta but only to post stupid pictures of me and my friends. They actually told me to set up a Finsta." He raises his eyebrows. "I know it's a little extreme, it's not like I'm a celeb or on the run from the government or anything, but now I can still use it to stay in touch with friends."

"I didn't know people actually do that. It's not a bad idea, though." He points to the bottle of water and I nod.

"Oh yeah. It's great, no one knows it's you," I say, accepting the bottle back and taking a sip of the warm water myself.

"Maybe I should make one. Then I could actually post what I want to post without it going through ten team members first."

"Yeah! You could add me, @BobLorRossi." I joke and wiggle my eyebrows, proud of my Finsta name that took less than two seconds to come up with.

"No... BobLorRossi?" he whispers, a grin growing across his face. "*That*. Is honestly amazing."

"Thank you, thank you," I say, grinning, and take a half bow.

His phone rings again, muffled this time.

He sighs, digging his hand into his bag. "Hello?" he answers the phone, his tone on the edge of pissed off. He listens for a second before his face pales and he jumps up, almost knocking his bag and notepad into the water. "Okay. I know! I'll be there as soon as I can. Tell them I'm sorry and I won't be long. Bye."

Twenty

I follow his lead, shoving all my things in my bag. "Everything okay?" I try, but fail, to keep the worry out of my voice.

With his hand on his head, he turns to me, his belongings now collected in his backpack. "Urm, yeah. Well, no, not really." He sighs, wiping his palm down his face. "I forgot about an interview. A pretty big interview. One we've had in the works for months. I'm supposed to be announcing my next tour *and* two new albums."

"Can't you reschedule it?" He goes to pass me the water that I forgot to pick up, but I refuse. "You need it more than me."

He mutters thanks as he shoves it in his bag, a ghost of a smile on his face. "The interview's live so we can't reschedule, unfortunately. It starts in," he checks his watch and his face crumbles as he strides towards the way we came a few hours before. "Fifty minutes! I'm not going to make it, it took that long to find this place."

I pull my bag over my shoulder and rush after him. I'm about to point out that he's over-exaggerating and that it was only a twenty-minute stroll but he continues.

"We've been hyping it up all week, hinting at the announcement. My fans are going to be so disappointed, they've been commenting like crazy about it. I can't let them down, even if I have to run there and go on stage looking like a hot mess. I can't let them down." He picks up speed and I struggle to keep up.

"Hey, it'll be okay. I'll call for a taxi, they shouldn't be busy so you'll have plenty of time to get there. It'll be okay, just, breathe." I put an arm out in front of him and slow my speed, feeling his sculpted abs under my palm as I pull him back.

His brows knit together in annoyance and confusion and I slowly bring my arms up and down in front of me in an exaggerated deep breath until he finally copies, rolling his eyes.

"Good," I say, pulling my phone out of my backpack's side pocket. "Now, let's find a taxi."

"How long did they say?" he asks, jumping impatiently from one foot to the other.

The first five minutes waiting he spent pacing back and forth, not knowing which way it was going to come from, and creating quite a nice breeze. I much preferred that to this new development, it may have been a tad annoying but it was the only thing stopping me from melting.

I take a seat on the pavement, instantly regretting it as the burning tarmac scorches the back of my thighs. I curse under my breath and jump up. "They said twenty minutes on the phone, which usually means more like half an hour, and I rang…" I check the time on my phone. "About twenty-five minutes ago. You can tell when the traffic's bad because this road gets really busy but it's empty, so chill. It'll be here any minute now."

He nods, his face no more relaxed despite my attempts. He goes to sit in the spot next to where I previously fried myself and I grab his arm before he touches the ground.

"I wouldn't." I point at the ground. "It's like lava."

"Thank-"

"It's here!" I cut him off as a car comes around the corner, a big sticker across the doors.

He smiles from ear to ear, checking his watch as the car pulls up in front of us. "I think I might make it! What would I have done without you?"

I let out a small laugh and shake my head. "Well, you probably wouldn't have ended up in the middle of a forest so you wouldn't have forgotten about it in the first place. But I'll take the compliment."

He laughs, opening the back door of the taxi and throwing his bag in. "I really need to get going if I want to make it but thanks for today, for showing me this place and for letting me hang out with you," he says, massaging the back of his neck. "I had fun."

"Me too, surprisingly," I say before I realise my mouth is even moving. I guess he did make me laugh, and we had multiple conversations without me wanting to punch him. *Plus, he's not the worst person to look at.* Blushing, I lower my head to hide it from him, realising I meant what I said.

"Well…" he trails off.

He's searching my face. We lock eyes and my heart betrays me by tripping over itself. His face softens and his lips part, about to say something and I lean closer, eager to hear what it is.

"Are you getting in, I don't have all day!" the driver yells, beeping his horn in three continuous beeps.

Jackson clears his throat, checking his watch, and his face hardens again. "Crap, yeah I'm coming! Maybe I'll see you around sometime?" he asks, eyes wide.

I quickly nod, "Sure, but you need to get going or you're going to be late." I spin him around and start ushering him into the back of the taxi.

"Okay, okay. I'm going," he grins, surrendering.

I close the door behind him and wave through the window. He starts to wind it down but he's too late, the car speeds away leaving me alone on the pavement, the only sound the birds chirping in the trees behind me and the occasional car driving past.

Weirdest day of my life. And I've not even had dinner yet.

I take the longer way home, walking back through the forest and past the fields instead of going back to Zac and Seth's. I crank up the volume of my earphones, 'Lavender haze' playing as the backing music for my stroll, and enjoy the start of the summer weather.

I might as well pick up some milk from Mr Lawrences since it's on the way. I push the door open, shoving my earphones into my shorts pocket, and wave to Mr Lawrence who smiles in return.

"Ah! I'm blessed by two of my favourite customers at the same time, what are the chances?" He nods his head to the other side of the shop at my confused expression.

A blonde head hovers above the last row of shelves, it bobs to the end of the row and Cassie's face comes into view. She jumps slightly when she sees that it's me, almost knocking the peanut butter out of her arms. "Oh, hey! What're you doing here?"

"Getting some milk. What're *you* doing here?" I know Cassie *loves* to gossip with Mr Lawrence but surely she didn't come all the way here just for a good old chinwag.

"Oh. Well, I was going to yours but my mum's actually just messaged me. She needs my help with something. Quick actually, so I should really hurry up," she scrambles as I grab a big bottle of milk and a bottle of strawberry water from the fridge.

She scurries to the till, throws some money on the counter, grabs a lollipop from the container and heads for the door. "Keep the change. Thanks, bye!" The door slams behind her.

Well, that was odd. I pick up a cheap chocolate bar and go to pay.

"I might be able to open a new shop soon, thanks to Cassie," he says as he scans my items.

Thanks to Cassie? I know whenever we come in here she always goes overboard and we end up taking away half the shop, but we haven't been coming as often as we used to do. In fact, the last time we were here was the first time in a while.

He looks at me as if I'm being stupid. "She's been in here almost every day. Honestly, I've had to restock three times as often as I usually do, if she didn't tip so well I'd start charging her for making me do so much overtime. And don't get me started on the extra order of peanut butter I had to make, the guy on the phone made me sound like a weirdo for requesting so much, but I had to keep up with the demand." He takes in my surprised expression. "Oh, I thought you would've known?"

"No…" If she's been coming in every day, then she must have been lying about coming to see me. I suppose she could've been spending more time with Sean and Abby, it'd make sense with all the peanut butter, but why not just tell me? Why don't they want me there with them? I guess it has been all about me and Jackson recently…

"Oh, no. I didn't mean to make you upset. Here." He shoves some of my favourite sweets from under the counter into one of the little paper bags and hands it to me. "Have these, on the house. Or on Cassie, considering she's the one funding said house."

"Thanks," I say with a faint smile. "It's fine, I've just had a bit of a weird day. Well, a weird week to be honest."

He places my things in a bag and passes it over the counter in exchange for the change in my other hand. "Ah, I saw. It's died down now, right? Or is another hulk-like man going to come barrelling through the door again and give me another heart attack?"

The image of Mr Lawrence trying to fight off the paparazzi that followed us flashes into my head, the giant man towering over the older man, and I don't bother hiding my smile. The poor guy wouldn't stand a chance against Mr Lawrence. "No, no more paparazzi, thankfully. It's mostly over now, Jackson made a statement and it's not as bad anymore."

"There you go, I knew it'd all work out in the end. Gossip never lasts long. So, he apologised?" he asks, sitting on his stool behind the counter, making him an inch or two taller.

"Yeah… He kind of apologised in the statement. But I saw him today and he wouldn't stop apologising," I explain.

"Oh." He raises his eyebrows and gets the same sparkle in his eyes that he gets from gossiping with Cassie. "You saw him today?"

I pass the heavy bag to my other arm, shifting my weight from my right leg to the left. "We just bumped into each other at the coffee shop," I say flatly.

"Right. You know, you sure do bump into him a lot to say you're not a stalker." He wiggles an eyebrow, teasingly.

If he's this bad I don't want to even think about what Sean will do if he finds out. "He bumps into me, not the other way around."

"You don't seem to mind," he says with a smirk.

The bell chimes and the new customer heads towards the bread section near the back of the shop.

"Well, turns out he's not as bad as I thought he was." I pick at my nails, listening as the woman's steps get closer. "He was actually okay company."

Mr Lawrence lets out a snort. "What a compliment! I'm sure he'd love to hear that he's *okay company*," he says, adding air quotes.

I roll my eyes and try to keep a straight face as the woman's steps come to a halt behind me. Taking my cue, I make a move towards the door before he can carry on teasing me.

"Remind me to never ask you what you think of a new haircut."

I wave his comment away as I open the door and step out, shouting back, "Bye Mr Lawrence," in a sing-songy way.

"Bye Lorri! Come back soon," he says, the scanner beeping in the background. I'm about to close the door when he yells, "Try not to do any more stalking!"

I smile as the door clicks shut, blocking out his giggles, and head towards the flats.

Dad's still out so after putting the milk away I go to my room to finish the drawing I started of Jackson, deciding I should probably do it whilst the image is still fresh in my mind.

An hour later and it's finished. There were only a few little finishing details I had left to do, but I ended up spending twenty extra minutes redoing parts of his face. I hold it up and it sets alight as the sun from the window opposite my desk hits it, creating a similar effect as the beam of light from the cove. *Not bad.* It might be one of the first pieces I've done in a while that I don't hate.

A warm, proud feeling comes over me as I place it back safely onto the desk. I should get something for Abby as a thank you for the suggestion and for reminding me that drawing doesn't have to be stressful all the time.

I head to the kitchen to make a sandwich and my stomach rumbles at the thought of food, the hole that the chocolate bar filled slowly coming back. I quickly check my phone as I grab some bread from the bread bin, hoping to find an explanation text from Cassie about our weird encounter earlier. My arm stops mid-air, the bread not making it to the plate. There's nothing from any of my friends, but I have one new follower on my Finsta account and a message request.

@HughJackmanSon

Hey! This is amazing, no one knows who I am. Why didn't I do this earlier?

I smile, placing the bread on my plate. I hit accept and grab the butter and ham from the fridge.

No way! The son of Hugh Jackman followed me, I think I'm going to die!

Does Hugh Jackman even have a son? What made you pick that anyway, Wolverine fan?

Exiting the chat, I go to his account and follow him back. He's got three posts already, all photos from today. The first one's of the field of poppies we stopped at, the second's the little bridge we crossed and the third's a close-up of both of our feet on the rock next to the lake. I mustn't have been paying attention when he took it but I'm glad he did. They look as if a professional photographer took them, using the light and shade perfectly to capture satisfyingly beautiful images. I had no idea he was into this sort of thing. If he ever needs a backup plan, he could always do this for a living.

None of them have captions, they've just been posted to simply exist, as a way of saying 'I'm here' to anyone who cares to find them. I double-tap them all and take a screenshot of the third one before I can think too much about it.

I pick up my plate after throwing the knife into the sink. My screen lights up and the plate slips, landing on the side with a small thud and only just missing the sink. It said that he messaged me an hour ago, he couldn't have gotten back already.

Apparently, he does, who knew? I've actually never watched wolverine before. The Greatest Showman is my favourite movie though.

I tried to think of a better username but we can't all be geniuses like you.

I go around the flat opening all the windows as I think of what to message back. I take a bite of my already warm sandwich and reread the message. I don't remember 'The Greatest Showman' ever appearing in his interviews.

I thought your favourite movie was Die Hard.

I almost choke on my food as I realise what I've done and frantically try to delete it. Too late. *Great, now he really will think I'm a stalker.*

You've been researching me, huh?

No.

I start to sweat despite my efforts to cool the room down and take another big bite of my sandwich, hoping it'll feed my brain so it can come up with something to use in my defence.

Don't believe everything you read.
Especially in the media.

Well, I might be safe from a restraining order for now, but these days the chances of it happening are scarily high. Whipping the sweat off my forehead, I take my plate to the couch and sprawl out, praying the breeze from the window will be strong enough to reach me.

Didn't you say it though? In an interview?

Dots appear, disappear, then re-appear, and I finish off the rest of my sandwich as I await his answer.

I did.

Oh. So, he has a habit of lying in interviews.

The dots appear once more but this time his message has no hesitation.

Can I call you?

Twenty-One

Ignoring the weird feeling in my stomach, I reply with 'sure' and await his call. I stare at my screen and a few seconds later my worried face stares back, making me jump up and almost smash my plate for the second time. *Video call, crap.*

I sprint to the full-length mirror next to the door, shoving the abundance of old coats, scarves and other mysterious articles of clothing we haven't used in years to the side, the top layer falling to the ground.

My hair's almost at max frizziness, now triple the size it was when I last saw him, and my face is all blotchy and moist thanks to the heat and early stages of sunburn. I knew I should've applied more sun cream, not that it would've made much difference. I can't answer looking like this, not when he always looks so perfect. *He models for god's sake!*

The annoying ringing stops and I glance at where my reflection was just as our conversation pops back up with a new message.

You missed a video call from @HughJackmanSon

I speed walk to the bathroom, figuring that running won't do me any good, and quickly fire back an apology before he tries again.

Sorry, one sec.

Throwing my head under the tap, I splash water over my face, running the excess through my hair in a frantic attempt to somewhat tame it. I pat my face dry, already looking more like myself, and grab my extra bobble off the side to push my hair back into a cute-enough ponytail. I check my reflection once more before hitting the video call button. I should probably leave the bathroom before he thinks I was messaging him from the toilet, I've had enough embarrassment to last me a lifetime already, thanks.

It doesn't take him long to answer and by the time I reach the end of the corridor, his smile fills the screen. "Hey. Are you busy? We can chat some other time?" It looks as though he's in a hotel room, a big luxurious bed lying behind him, and he's changed into a different graphic tee, one much more faded and worn out than the previous.

"No, now's okay."

"Good." He pauses, nibbling at his lower lip. "I thought it would be better to just talk to you about this than try and type it all."

"Okay…" I say, waiting for him to explain. With all the stress of the video call, I've forgotten what we were on about in the first place.

He shifts on whatever it is that he's perched on and takes a deep breath. "So, basically- the thing is…" He sighs, smiling wryly as he collects his thoughts. "I've never told anyone about this, I don't even think I'm allowed to so if anyone asks, I never told you." He tries to say it in his light, joking tone but I can sense he's still nervous.

Oh, no. Is this where he tells me he's part of some weird cult that drinks people's blood or something? I smile back, encouraging him to continue.

"It's like I said, don't believe everything you see in the media." *Right, he was telling me about his lying addiction.* "Almost everything I put out has been prepared by my PR team. Or if I somehow manage to convince them to let me be me, it has to be checked over by at least half the team. And even then, when it gets back to me and it's ready to go, it doesn't even sound like me anymore." He lets out a breath, as if just by telling me it's lifted a weight off his shoulders even though it doesn't really change anything.

So, it's all fake. Everything he claims to have said, he never did, not really. I wonder who it is Cassie thinks she's in love with; his sixty-year-old PR leader Rob with the coffee breath or the baby PR intern Jessie who's only taken the job because it'll look good for her uni application.

He hasn't noticed that I haven't responded, either riding the high of finally telling his truth or shocked he's finally let it slip and is now thinking about what would happen if I told anyone. I can't see his fans being particularly happy that everything they thought they knew about him was lies. I ask the only thing I can think to say, "Why?"

He finally looks at me, softening when he sees my face and I wonder if maybe he thought for a second that I might react differently. "I guess because I was really young when I started they thought that they could mould me." He looks away as if mentally combing through the last five years or so. "Into, like, some kind of perfect popstar. And because they've stuck with me all this time, it's just become normal. They've become family so I can't say no, I wouldn't any way they wouldn't listen. Or maybe I'm just scared of what the fans will think." He goes quiet again, fighting over whether or not he should finish his thought. "What the fans will think of me." His eyes meet mine through the screen. They're glazed over in a way I don't think I've ever seen them, fuelled with so much distraught and disappointment, not for the situation or anyone else but towards himself.

Actually, now that I think about it before I met him, I don't think I'd ever even seen him frown. Some would say that his recent bad mood could have something to do with me, but maybe not. Maybe he's just not allowed to, not when he's playing his role.

"They're not my fans," he continues, "Not really. They're Jackson Peters, teen heartthrob's fans, but that's not me. What if I finally get to show them the real me and they hate him." I swear I see a tear roll over but he turns almost as quick as it falls.

"What if they love you?" I ask quietly, bringing his attention back to me. "They clearly care about you, I don't think that'd change because they find out you lied about your favourite movie or your favourite colour." He starts to object but I stop him, "I don't like you." He looks as if I climbed through the screen and slapped him. And then murdered his puppy. And insulted his grandma. "Not the media you," I explain. "I think he's rude and so far up his own ass that I'm surprised there's any room left for his fans."

He chokes out a laugh. "He is his biggest fan."

"This Jackson though," I gesture to him. "This one's pretty good. This one's worth knowing."

He blushes, rubbing the back of his neck. "Thanks," he says looking more like himself, more relaxed. "You're not too bad yourself."

We chat for the next half an hour over the most random of things. He explains that he's always been a big fan of musicals, ever since he watched Charlie and the chocolate factory as a kid, and that Augustus Gloop was the song that got him into singing. He tells me through tears of laughter that he would break into song and dance for months after watching it and there was nothing his parents could do to get him to stop other than take him to see a different musical. When I demand to see his rendition, he doesn't object, getting up before I even finish the question, he proudly sets his phone on the side and gives me the best performance I've ever seen. I miss most of the ending because I have to wipe the tears out of my eyes but what I do see is definitely… interesting.

We somehow move on to sport and I'm just about to convince him to watch a game of rugby whilst he's here when voices come from outside the flat. A shadow goes past the window, stopping outside our door. It sounds like Dad and Uncle Joe but I didn't think they'd be back this early.

"I'm not sure, sports aren't really my thing. Maybe if you cam-"

"I have to go," I blurt out. "Sorry. I think my dad's back."

"Oh." He freezes, his mouth stuck in the 'o' shape.

The door handle starts to turn just as his mouth pulls into a tight smile. "No, of course," he says, shaking his head. "No need to apologise. Urm, I'll message you later?" he half asks, his voice jumping an octave.

"Mhm," I nod. "Sure, bye." I hang up just as the door flies open and I jump up from the arm of the sofa where I subconsciously decided to stay when we started the call.

"Who was that?" Dad asks as he walks into the flat, closely followed by Uncle Joe.

They both look as if they just had to walk through the Sahara Desert and then around the whole coast of England to get here. My dad's top has the same amount of sweat patches as my old coat has holes and both of their hair is glued to their forehead.

"No one," I lie, moving the pillow back to where I'd knocked it off the couch. "Just the TV. What did you guys get up to?"

He glances at where the TV is, turned off, as Uncle Joe speeds past and heads straight down the corridor yelling back, "I'm dying for the loo."

"Uh, actually," he starts when the bathroom door closes, sounding nervous.

He shuffles to the kitchen and I follow, grabbing a glass. "Water?" I offer.

"Please. They had water there and I almost drank the whole thing, but I still feel like I could drink an ocean." He leans back against the counter, wiping his face on a tissue. "God, I was a wreck."

What's happened? I thought they were spending the day at Uncle Joe's or going shopping, something fun and relaxing not anxiety-inducing.

"Thanks," he says accepting and downing most of his drink.

I grab two more glasses and fill them up, placing them on the side. "Where was that?"

He takes a big gulp to finish off his water and knocks the side of his head with his empty glass. "Sorry, I'm not with it today." *You're not the only one.* "We passed Dr Hayes' office on the way into town and Joe convinced me to go in."

"I wouldn't say convinced," Uncle Joe chimes in as he reappears. "Dragged, maybe."

"You went?" I'm thankful I put the glasses down otherwise I don't think they'd still be here.

He nods. "She'd just had a cancellation for tomorrow and asked if I wanted the slot. We had a quick chat too before her next client."

Uncle Joe lowers his head, taking a sip of his water. *How very convenient that they took the long way to town that passes her office and got there just as she had had a cancellation.* He catches my accusation and smiles.

"And everything was okay?" I quickly ask, remembering all the arguments he's had about her.

"Yeah. She wasn't as bad as I remembered and it felt good to talk."

"So, you're going again?" I ask, getting my hopes up for the first time in a long while. There's still a bit of doubt, gnawing at the pit of my gut, that causes my voice to waver.

"Of course," he says, pulling me into a bear hug. "I told you, this is it. I'm going to get better, I promise."

I hug him back, fighting the tears threatening to fall. I've heard this before, multiple times, but never sober and never after seeing Dr Hayes. I believe him, whether or not it happens I'm not sure, but right now I know he really means it. And I know this is mostly Joe's doing but Dad still had to decide for himself, I learnt that the hard way. "Thank you," I whisper, barely loud enough to hear myself.

I hug him tighter and stop resisting the tears, letting them turn from fear to relief.

We end up watching rugby. We're playing a dirty team and we scream in unison at the screen whenever the ref misses a high tackle.

At half time, Uncle Joe decides to stay for tea and insists on paying for a takeout to celebrate the start of Dad's new journey. We search the drawer under the TV that we always shove random bits and bobs into for a menu, deciding we'll order from the first one we find.

We're halfway through emptying the contents when Dad's hand shoots up grasping a crinkled pizza flyer as if it's the golden snitch that's just won him the game. It's so old the colour's faded and the numbers are only just readable, but as we already spent ten minutes searching, we take our chances and dial what's hopefully their number.

Half an hour later, and just over halfway through the second half, we're chomping on the greasiest pizza I think I've ever had and its heaven.

This morning didn't go exactly to plan, I definitely never thought I'd be bumping into Jackson again, but right now I'm happy. And the more I think about it, today wasn't that bad. Sure, Jackson was annoying at first but maybe he's just not used to speaking to people without hiding behind the mask that is Jackson Peters, teen heartthrob and international popstar.

"Give him the ball! Give him the ball!" A bit of pepperoni flies out of Uncle Joe's mouth as he screams.

"There's no one there! Pass him the ball!" Dad joins in.

One of our players is trying to run the whole length by themselves with multiple opponents after them. A wall of yellow and red is closing in on them on both sides but they decide to plough on despite everyone's protests. The player in front of them trips, taking their own players down and creating an opening. Our player only just makes it through and we all let out a sigh of relief.

There's only a minute left! And we're two points down! I join them on the edge of my seat, gluing my eyes to the screen and begging them not to blink in case I miss anything.

He keeps running, making it past the halfway line, the group of players tailing him.

Thirty seconds left. "Come on," I whisper, gripping the sofa.

There's another yellow and red jersey waiting for him at the thirty-metre line. He's so close to our player with the ball that if he offloaded it we'd be guaranteed the try.

"Pass it!" I scream, dropping the crushed pizza crust I'd been unknowingly clutching.

Fifteen seconds. The opposing player jumps at him, he doesn't collide but he catches the back of his top, pulling him back and stopping his stride. We all gasp, along with the crowd as he gets dragged into touch, our hopes of winning the game following him off the pitch.

"I can't believe it!" Dad yells, throwing his hands up in defeat.

"Why didn't he just pass the damn ball?" Uncle Joe shakes his head, mimicking our other players on screen.

The hooter sounds, signalling the end of the game, and the other team celebrates, creating a mountain of yellow and red.

"Great," I say, grabbing a cold slice of pizza and taking a big bite.

Uncle Joe decides to stay over and sleep on the couch, saying he'll drive Dad to the therapy session in the morning, so before I go to bed Dad asks me to grab the extra duvet from the top of my wardrobe. After I've handed over the blanket and said goodnight, I get ready for bed and slip under the covers feeling drained after the strangely eventful day.

Before I let my eyes fully close, my phone lights up. I haven't checked it since I spoke to Jackson and I haven't messaged the group all day. I grab it off the side and rub my eyes. It's not completely dark yet but my eyes are too tired to be looking at a screen. A new Instagram message?

@HughJackmanSon

Why is he running it by himself?

Is he not allowed to pass it to the other guy?

Never mind, I think the commentator just said he could?

There's people everywhere! Why isn't he passing it?

He needs to pass it!

HE HAS TO PASS IT!!!

NOOOOOOOOOOOOOOOOOOOOO!

…

Okay.

Maybe I could be a rugby fan. That was entertaining.

Annoying.

But entertaining.

Sorry for the spam. Enjoy the rest of your evening.

Goodnight x

Twenty-Two

Last night I was too tired to reply to Jackson's message, and I figured he'd be asleep anyway, so I thought I might as well leave it until this morning. Although now I'm sitting at the breakfast bar slurping the last bit of milk in my bowl of cereal, already dressed and ready for the day, and I have no idea what to send back.

Dad's alarm and the sound of him frantically searching for things around the flat woke me earlier than I'd like and I wasn't allowed to go back to sleep until I'd looked over five different outfit choices and picked the most 'I-know-I'm-in-therapy-because-my-life's-falling-apart-but-it-can't-be-too-bad-because-look-at-how-great-and-put-together-my-outfit-is' outfit. Dad's words, not mine. I think he might have had a mug of coffee or two already before I got up.

He's gone now and I'm all alone. Well, I would be if my phone wasn't staring at me from the other side of the counter. I told myself I'd message him back once I got dressed, and then once I'd done my teeth, and then after I said bye to Dad and Uncle Joe, and then after I'd had breakfast. It wasn't too bad after the first bowl but now I'm three bowls in and I'm starting to feel a little sick.

Pushing the bowl aside, I lunge for the phone. *Screw it.*

Morning x

I hesitate, delete the kiss and then add it back, hitting send before I make a big fuss over nothing. *People send kisses all the time.*

I told you you'd like it!

I quickly shut off my phone and swap it for my bowl. Finally, I can stop forcing myself to eat a whole box of off-brand Cheerios. After I've washed my dishes and put the box in the bin, I check my phone twice for a reply, each a minute apart. This is stupid, I need to do something to take my mind off of Jackson. I send a message to the group chat checking if anyone's free and when I don't receive a reply after a couple of minutes, I go to my room in search of things to do.

Revision would be the sensible choice but if I don't start on my application drawing soon then I can kiss the summer program goodbye. So instead, I head to my old wooden desk and pull out a new sheet of paper, placing it on top of the drawing of Jackson.

Taking a deep breath, I pick up my favourite pencil, one out of the little fancy set that Abby and Sean got me for my birthday. I tried to argue that it was too much but they insisted I have it, saying they wanted me to have the same chance to get into the summer program as all the rich kids that would be entering. Before today I still wasn't sure if they'd wasted their money on me, but as soon as my pencil hits the paper, I start to sketch out a picture that I'm finally happy with, one that feels right.

The theme is 'All I'll ever need' and I'm not sure why it took me so long to see that even though I might not have a lot material wise, I'm spoiled when it comes to relationships. My friends and family are all I'll ever need, they're what keeps me going and who are there for me when I'm stuck. I don't think I would have gotten through the past couple of weeks without them.

My name comes from the living room and a second later my door cracks open, Dad's head popping around the corner. "Oh, you are in. I thought you would be out by now, enjoying the sun," he says, pointing to the window where the sky's now significantly darker than it was when I started. He grows a frown when he sees it's open.

"I'll close it," I quickly grumble.

"You better, I'm not spending another night cleaning up leaves."

"Promise. I was just doing my application," I say, covering my half-finished drawing. "It's going really well, but no one can see it yet." I shoot him a warning glare.

He holds up his hands in surrender. "I know, I know. You don't like people looking until it's done. I promise not to snoop."

"Yeah, you said that last time."

He draws a cross over where he thinks his heart is. "So, you're not going out? Because we're going for a picnic at the park near Joe's with the rest of the family if you want to come?"

"Urm." I haven't been to a big family gathering since Christmas a few years ago when the turkey somehow ended up on the roof. It would be nice to see everyone again. I grab my phone and kick myself at the ignored new messages. I'd got so focused I forgot all about my pleas for entertainment from my friends. "No, sorry, revision emergency," I say, showing him the wall of messages screaming my name. "I've been summoned."

"No worries. I think we're going to make it a weekly thing so you can come next time, no excuses. Hey, bring the others, I haven't seen Sean and Abby in a while. And I know your grandma would love to see Cassie again," he says as I pick up my bag and stuff some revision books in.

I quickly swing my bag over my shoulders as I realise the messages were half an hour ago and I'm already late. "We'll be there. Oh." What with getting lost in my picture and then the rush of being pulled back out, I almost forgot where he'd been. "How was it?"

He smiles thinly as he scratches at where his beard would be if he hadn't shaved this morning. "Not bad. She was glad I finally went back."

"Me too," I say, giving him a quick hug.

"Me three." He squeezes me back. "Okay, go on. Get studying," he says, ushering me down the corridor and out the door, handing me a fiver for some snacks which I pocket. I'll use it to replace the cereal and milk later.

"About time!" Cassie shouts at my arrival.

I return Abby and Sean's waves as I walk to the back of the cafe and take my usual seat. "Sorry, I was doing my application and lost track of time." I glance at Abby and she offers me a knowing smile which I return, hoping she understands how grateful I am for her help.

"Nothing new there," Sean says with a big grin, automatically placing a cheese and ham panini in front of me as if it's been waiting.

"Thanks." I gesture to the spotless table. "I thought this was a revision session?"

"We didn't want to start without you," Abby says, pulling her hair into a messy bun, the shorter bits around her face falling down. She pushes them behind her ears and takes a sip of her drink.

"Yep. We need to start soon though because I've been freaking out all day over these stupid Macbeth quotes and I need all the help I can get if I'm going to remember any for tomorrow." Cassie fans her face and copies Abby, pulling her hair back into a sleek ponytail.

We all empty our bags, spreading workbooks and revision cards across the whole table and wait for Sean to finish his round. Once I've finished my panini, he collects my plate and, after a quick glance around to check he's done everything he should, he takes a seat too and we begin. We use Sean's revision cards since his have twice as much writing on as the rest of ours, and he tests us until we've each had a go at every card at least twice.

"Okay, I think it's time for a break. There's only so many times I can hear the meaning of 'out damned spot' without losing my mind myself," Abby says two hours later.

Sean wraps his cards up and shoves them back in his bag. "Fine, I should go and check on the customers again, see if they need anything." The cafe's not as busy as it usually is due to the good weather but there's still a few customers that Sean's had to get up to serve during our study session and a couple of them keep glancing over. "Did you bring your scrooge cards?" he asks Abby as he gets up, adjusting his apron. "Yours are better than mine."

Abby thinks for a second before searching the table, finding a small stack of cards hidden beneath Cassie's empty glass. She holds them up triumphantly and Sean nods before heading to the counter.

"I need the loo before we start," Cassie says, grabbing a tampon from her bag. "Won't be long."

Abby waits until they're both out of earshot. "So, you started the drawing?"

"I did, thanks to you," I reply, putting my phone down after checking Instagram for the hundredth time.

She shakes her head. "You would have figured it out anyway." I open my mouth to remind her just how close it is to the deadline and how screwed I was but she continues, "Glad I could help though."

Sean places some chips in the middle of the table and plops back down next to Abby, wiping his brow. "It should be illegal to be inside in such heat. I promise next time we'll hang out at the park or something." He uses his apron to wipe the whole of his face whilst simultaneously downing the rest of his lemonade.

"Well," I start tentatively. "My dad actually invited you guys to a picnic next Sunday. Most of my family will be there so I totally get it if you don't want to come or if you're busy..." I trail off. Maybe my friends don't want to spend their precious free time hanging out with my grandma.

"Hmm, I don't know. Hang out with you all day," Sean says with a disgusted look. I throw a soggy chip at him which he catches, smirking as he chomps on it. "Kidding, obviously we'll come." He looks expectantly at Abby.

She looks a little shocked at the offer, not that I'm surprised considering I hardly speak about my family let alone invite my friends to meet them. "Of course. I can't wait," she says with a genuine smile.

"I think I'm supposed to be working but I'll get the day off, it's not every day you get to meet the Johnsons," he says.

"Who's meeting the Johnsons?" Cassie asks with wide eyes, stopping behind her chair.

Sean lifts his head, meeting her eyes for the first time since I've been here. "We are if you're coming?"

He sounds weird, his question more loaded than the extra loaded French fries on the table next to us. Cassie hesitates, just staring at him.

It's not the first time today that I've noticed them acting a bit weird towards each other, they've both been a lot quieter than usual. Abby never mentioned it so maybe it's nothing, maybe I'm just imagining it. Or maybe it's just the weather, it does weird things to people. I should know.

"I'm going to see Grandma Johnson?" Cassie squeals, her face lighting up so much I'm surprised a boat doesn't smash through the window. I don't think Cassie even gets this excited to see her own grandparents.

I nod, causing her to literally jump with joy. "We're having a picnic next Sunday and you're all invited. We don't have to sit with them, we can just grab some food and then chill on our own. Oh, why don't you invite Chen?" The more the merrier, right?

Abby's eyebrows shoot up and she starts to inspect the chip that only made it halfway to her mouth before I pulled her back into the conversation. "Oh. Uh, I don't know."

"They broke up," Cassie blurts out as if it's old news.

What?! But they seemed really into each other. Plus Abby doesn't exactly look like the face of heartbreak. Sean nods, confirming Cassie's answer. When did this happen and how did I not know about it?

"It only happened yesterday," Abby says, reading my mind. "And we didn't *break up* because we weren't dating in the first place. We thought it was something more but it wasn't." She shrugs. "We decided we're just good friends so we're going to keep it that way."

"Oh." Yesterday? So, Cassie *was* on her way to theirs when I saw her at Mr Lawrence's.

"She could still come as a friend?" Cassie offers, looking at me for reassurance, snapping me out of my thoughts.

"Yeah," I reply, a little too enthusiastic. I clear my throat and continue, "It'll be fun. Well, as fun as hanging out in a park with a load of adults can be."

"Uh, sure." She nods, slowly, still on the fence. "We were on about starting a martial arts class together and I think there's one Sunday morning. So I suppose we could go to that and then come straight after."

"Martial arts?" we all chorus, completely shocked.

I don't think I've seen Abby try to fight off a hungry gnat, never mind another human being. She's always been the type that would rather chill on the sidelines than get involved in any kind of physical sports.

"That's great," Sean says, his voice climbing as he struggles to hide his surprise. "But I don't think we have enough money right now to try out new hobbies."

"It's a community class, it's only a pound donation a week," she says, shaking her head as she laughs at the state of our faces. "Is it really that hard to think of me beating people up?" *Yes. Yes, it is.* "Okay, so I'm not the most aggressive person," she carries on when she doesn't get an answer. "I think it'll be fun, plus it'll help if I ever need to defend myself." She adds another shrug and leans back in her chair, picking up a new chip.

"It sounds good," Sean starts, his voice still on the wary side. He takes a second to chew it over before breaking into a grin. "Are you sure you'll be able to reach the other people though? Is there not a height requirement?" He pats her on the head and immediately jumps up to avoid Abby's swinging arm. "Sorry! I take it back!" He retakes his seat as Cassie and I try not to fall off our chairs with laughter. "You'll be fine. As long as they're sitting down, you'll reach."

Abby picks up her half-empty glass and angles it towards him, partnered with a deathly stare.

"Oh, look. Another customer!"

Twenty-Three

"I'll walk back with you and get a taxi from yours," Cassie says as we pack up our revision and get ready to head out.

I smother a fresh layer of suncream over my arms, face and legs, offering the others some whilst we wait for Sean to hang up his apron. It's late now but the sun is still high in the sky and even though it's significantly cooler than before it still feels like an oven out.

"Okay," Sean says, his eyebrows drawing together as he watches Cassie tie her jacket around her waist. "Ready to go?" he asks, quickly averting his eyes as he catches me watching him.

There's definitely something up with them. Maybe they had an argument when she went over yesterday? I'm sure one of them will tell me eventually, although if they've been hanging out behind my back then maybe they won't, maybe they don't want me to know.

We grab our stuff and head out, down the road towards home. Sean and Cassie continue their odd quietness, both of them on the outside as far away from each other as possible. Abby seems fine, smiling away, so I don't question it.

"Did you hear about Jackson's new albums and tour?" If there's one thing that will get Cassie talking, it's Jackson Peters.

She looks at me as if I've just told her she's won the lottery. That she never entered. "A tour?!"

"Yeah. I thought you would've known by now." I can feel my cheeks start to heat up. It's not every day I know something about Jackson before Cassie. Heck, it's never a day that I know something about Jackson before Cassie. Luckily for me, my face has been as red as a stop sign all day so I don't think any of them notice.

"Cassie not knowing the latest on Jackson Peters. I never thought I'd see the day." I'm surprised when this comes from the shorter of the Crawfords.

Is Sean still with us? As I glance over, he stares at the ground, his eyes distant.

"When? When was it announced?" Cassie asks, already tapping away at her screen.

"Urm, in some TV interview he did yesterday." I try to find something to look at in the distance so I don't seem any more interested than I usually would.

The tapping stops and I glance sideways, expecting a happy Cassie, instead, she's stopped a few paces behind us, her head tilted causing her frown to represent a bracket. Now we just need Sean to tilt his to close it. "I watched that interview. He announced the albums but he said nothing about a tour."

Crap. "Are you sure?" I ask as if maybe she somehow passed out for a minute or two of the interview.

"Yes," she says, deadpan.

"Oh, I must have read something online and got confused," I add a laugh hoping that will stop them from looking at me like I just grew a third arm on top of my head. I could have sworn he said he was announcing a new tour.

"I think you almost gave her a heart attack just with the thought of not being the first to know," Sean says, sounding a little more like himself.

"The FOMO is real guys," she says, coming to join us again.

We walk on for a bit, the topic moving swiftly onto other things, and I wait until they're all occupied to discreetly pull out my phone. No new messages from Jackson and I can't help but feel a little disappointed when I see he's left me on read. Maybe he woke up this morning, no longer suffering from dehydration, and decided he never wants to speak to me again. I'll send one last message and if he ignores it, fine.

I start to type out multiple messages, not sure if I should ask about the tour or not, then delete them all, sticking to a simple:

Hey.

I'm not expecting a reply back, especially not in the next hour or so, so I exit Insta and go to turn off my mobile data. My phone vibrates and the Insta logo appears in the corner of my screen. I almost trip as I rush to click it.

Hey!

Sorry, I thought I replied before. I've been busy with photoshoots and studio sessions all day, I haven't had time to check my phone.

I can't help smirking as I type out my response.

I hope you got in those water breaks.

His response comes straight away.

I may have forgotten and now I fear I'll look like a dried-up prune for all eternity. Will you still be my friend even though I'm a giant prune?

I'm not sure, it might ruin my image if I'm seen with a giant prune. No, I'm sorry but it won't work.

Ouch, you've broken my heart. I'd bleed to death if I wasn't so pruney.

He adds a gif of a dancing prune and then another of a prune drowning in what looks like plum juice.

"What are you laughing at?" Cassie asks, leaning over my shoulder.

"Nothing!" I jump, pulling my phone to my chest and angling my body away from her almost on instinct.

"Right…" Abby says at the same time Sean says, "She's definitely up to something." He smirks at me in that annoying way that tells me he's enjoying this.

"You were flirting with someone!" Cassie squeals down my ear, almost causing premature hearing loss.

Sean, now fully engaged, practically skips over. "Well, now we have to know."

I quickly shove my phone into my bag, making sure it's buried as far down as it will go, and hold my hands up in surrender before he can wrestle it off me. "I wasn't *flirting."*

"You were definitely in someone's DM's," Cassie says with a pointed look.

"That doesn't mean I'm flirting with someone," I say, returning the look with my head held high.

"But everyone you're following and that knows about your account is here," Sean says, his voice laced with amusement. He really is enjoying this, isn't he? Next time he gives me a reason to mock him I'll be thinking of this very moment.

"Actually," Abby says, holding her phone up so that the others can see. "That's not true." They huddle around her phone to look at the account. I already know it's Jackson's, it's the only other account that follows me.

"That's the account she was messaging! I didn't see the full username but it looks the same."

Why couldn't I have been paying more attention when I was messaging him, or just waited until I'd gotten home? I could have avoided this mess of an interrogation.

"So, who's HughJackmanSon? I take it he's not actually the son of Hugh Jackman," Sean asks.

"I wouldn't know. Never spoken to them." I'm not giving in. Maybe if it was anyone else it wouldn't be so weird to talk to them about, but I know I won't be able to escape the teasing if I tell them who it really is. Trust me this is nothing compared to what it would be like.

"Lorri?"

"Yes," I drawl as Abby continues to inspect her screen.

"Aren't those your shoes?" She once again turns the phone for us to see.

This time I get a glimpse of the screen before they swarm it, and I spot the photo that I saved, the one of Jackson and me at the pond.

Cassie gasps. "You have a secret boyfriend and you didn't tell me?"

"I don't have a secret boyfriend. If I did though and I told you then it wouldn't be a secret, would it?" They all stop, their eyes bulging out of their sockets. "But I don't! Look, I bet hundreds of people have the same shoes, they're not those expensive red bottoms or anything. I see people wearing them all the time."

"They're called Louboutin's," Cassie says, crossing her arms.

Of course, that's what she focuses on. I share a look with Sean and Abby, all of us shaking our heads.

"Not important, I know," she says, throwing her hands up in a bit of a fit. "Fine, I'll choose to believe you, for now."

"Me too," Abby says before pulling Cassie over to look at some video.

"Me three," Sean chimes in, in a lighter tone. "Although, I only remember drawing on *one* pair of old Converse," he whispers.

My head snaps in his direction so fast I'm surprised I don't get whiplash. He couldn't have seen the dinosaur, right? Our feet weren't that close to the phone and I'm sure it's on the other side. It is on the other side, right?

A few years ago, we had a project for school where we had to create a poster. We stayed in Cassie's bedroom all day working on them and needless to say, it got boring very fast as does most homework. I didn't realise Sean was drawing on my shoe until the damage was done, not that I minded. Now it's one of my favourite things. Well, it was until this second.

"Don't worry. Your secret's safe with me," he says with a smirk as he bumps me with his shoulder.

I bump him back, a little harder than needed. "I don't know what you mean."

"Exactly." He adds an overdramatic wink and as much as I want to roll my eyes and keep a straight face, I can't help but crack a smile.

The next few days of school go by fast and drama free where we're concerned. Hardly anyone cares about the rumours of Jackson and me anymore or if they do they don't talk about it which is nice, I can finally get back to normal. Everyone seems to have moved on to the next round of rumours about a girl in the year below being pregnant. Of course, no one's talking about the guy though.

"Thank god we're almost done with exams," Cassie's muffled voice echoes from behind the cubicle door.

We're in the clothes shop that Cassie drags me into every time we come to town. I once saw a cute top in here but when I checked the price, I had to check all of them to make sure they hadn't accidentally added an extra zero on the one I'd picked up. Ever since, I haven't even contemplated buying anything when we come in.

"I can't wait to never do physics again," I say as if I'm daydreaming about brownies not escaping the hell that is GCSE science. I am kinda sad though, this is the last week of school with all my friends and then we're off to different places. I'll still have Sean and Abby but they'll be doing different subjects and we'll hardly see each other. It won't be the same.

"Only a couple of days left and then we're free. How does this look?" Cassie asks as she steps out of the cubicle. She's wearing a red, sparkly mini dress that drops off one shoulder and a pair of black heels with a little bow on. It hugs her in all the right places and shines like a disco ball under the changing room lights. She looks amazing. I try not to think about how much the outfit costs but I know the shoes alone probably cost more than half of my wardrobe combined.

"Have you tried this on before?" Abby asks from beside me. We're sitting on some fancy-looking seat that the saleswoman called a pouffe. To say it's one of the poshest seats I've ever sat on, it's definitely the least comfy.

Now that she mentions it, the dress does look awfully familiar. I just thought Cassie might've pointed it out last time we were here.

"I made a copy a few months ago. I wanted to see if the shoes looked alright with it," she says to her reflection in the full-length mirror.

Ah yes, she wore it to the Valentine's Day party we went to and spent half an hour before we left constantly swapping her shoes, asking after each pair if they looked alright. I thought they all looked fine but apparently, I was wrong.

"They're nice," I offer but she doesn't look convinced.

"I like them," Abby agrees.

She scrunches her face in the mirror. "No. The ones I wore last time looked better, I'll leave it," she says on her way back to the cubicle to change.

"Have you finished your drawing yet?" Abby asks. She attempts to lean back but the seat starts to move so she quickly sits back up.

"You haven't sent it yet?" Cassie screams from the other side of the door causing the saleswoman to rush in and shush us. She quickly apologises, popping her head out of the cubicle. "The deadline's in a few days, isn't it?"

I feel my face drop as my heart momentarily stops. "Dammit! I knew I'd forgotten something." I finished it last night and planned to send it when I got in so it would get there on time but with us deciding to go shopping, I completely forgot about it.

I search for my phone in my bag and as I stand to leave, I do a little prayer that Dad hasn't gone out. He's been spending more time with Uncle Joe which is great but right now I really need him to be in.

"I'll be back in a min," I say, stepping out into the corridor.

"Hey! Speak of the devil," Dad's voice beams down the phone.

"Huh?"

"I was just ranting to your uncle about you leaving your windows open. I kept telling you about those damn leaves and now guess who's had to clean them up."

Make that two things I forgot to do. "Sorry," I say with as much sympathy as I can gather whilst also wanting to move on to the drawing asap.

"It's fine, there weren't that many. Just, remember to close it next time."

"Will do." I take a breath, hoping Dad won't freak out like Abby and Cassie did. I know I'm really late but it won't take that long to get there, right? "So… I forgot to send off my drawing. It's in my room on my desk and the packaging stuff is in the top drawer. Can you post it for me, please?" I try to make it sound like no big deal but even I can register the desperation in my voice.

He sighs. "You're leaving it a bit late."

"I know!" I groan.

"I'll run down to the post office now and get the next-day delivery. It should get there tomorrow or Friday morning at the latest, you'll be fine." He's already heading to my room, the sound of my sticky desk drawer coming through the phone.

"Thank you," I say, letting out a breath. Finally, I can relax.

We leave the boutique empty-handed and grab some milkshakes on the way to a more affordable shop.

"I can't remember the last time I went on a shopping spree," Abby says, eying up a new pair of trainers.

"Me neither." If it wasn't for these gift cards, I might've made it to my three-year anniversary of not buying a new article of clothing. It would've been closer to four but I was in desperate need of a new bra.

I've been messaging Jackson on and off for the past couple of days, it turns out we have more in common than I thought, and if it was anyone else, I'd say we're becoming friends. I sneak a photo of me and the gift card when they're not looking to send to him.

Did you know they were giving out gift cards at your concert?

My wardrobe thanks you.

"Finally, something good has come out of this whole Jackson thing," Cassie says. She's holding a plain black halter-neck dress and smiling at me like I'm her prey. "You have to get it, it'd look so good on you. Plus, it's on sale."

The dress *is* pretty but it's not exactly what I had in mind when Cassie said we should go on a shopping spree. "I don't know. I was thinking of getting more practical items."

"Didn't Jackson ruin your only going-out clothes?" Abby asks.

Cassie's smile thickens as she points at Abby with her milkshake, nodding like one of those dogs on a car's dashboard when it goes over a speed bump. "Exactly! And it's black so if it ever happened again it wouldn't matter."

How many times in the next couple of years will I need to wear a nice dress? The probability is so close to zero that it barely even counts as a number.

"Come on. It's a good investment, just in case you need to dress up. If you don't buy it then I'll have no choice but to get it for you as a present for when you get accepted to art camp." She raises an eyebrow, her smile not faltering.

"Fine," I sigh as I snatch the dress. It's actually a good price and I suppose it is cute. Plus, I should have enough money left over to get what I wanted, so I don't mind.

My phone vibrates in my pocket.

You got them!

Tell your wardrobe no worries, I owed it some clothes anyway.

He knew about them? I thought it might've been something the arena or his management team did, something he wasn't involved in. It sounds as though he's a little shocked we got them though, like maybe he doubted we would. Could it have been his idea? Like he said, he did owe me. Why does the thought make me so happy? If anything, replacing my ruined clothes is a bare minimum given how much he gets given for nothing.

"Are you coming?" Cassie asks, a few clothes racks away. She tilts her head, her mouth one step away from a frown.

"Yep." I quickly add a wide smile as I rush to join them.

She continues to eye me until we turn the corner and Abby spots a tiny pink, shimmery princess dress. She grabs one, inspecting it, and then holds it up for us to see. "Do you think they'll have one in Sean's size?" she asks as seriously as one might be when discussing coffins.

"I don't think my legs work anymore," Abby complains, dropping down into the chair opposite me and letting her bags fall to the floor. "Why is shopping so tiring?"

I take a big gulp of my berry smoothie, wiping my mouth with the back of my hand. "I don't know how Cassie manages to do it every week. And find it fun."

"We had fun!" Cassie says defensively, looking from me to Abby for confirmation.

Abby slowly nods her head. "Yeah, but I couldn't do it again."

"Me neither." I take a bite of my toastie. "I would if it meant I got to see you trying to walk in those shoes again though," I joke and try not to choke on my mouthful.

"They were stupidly high! They should come with a warning, someone could get seriously hurt."

"They were barely three inches."

They continue to argue over how high the heels were but I'm distracted by my phone vibrating in my pocket. My stomach flips and the corners of my mouth pull up before I've even checked it's him. It is.

Hey, there's a party on Friday and I can get you and your friends in if you're interested? They're usually pretty boring so I get it if you don't want to but it would be a lot more fun if you were there.

"Right, Lorri?"

"Huh?" I'd bet my life that my face resembles that of a little kid that's just been caught with their hand in the cookie jar.

"I said 'They were taller than the ones Cassie wears, weren't they?'" Abby asks, starting to look a bit concerned that I'd blocked out most of the conversation.

Cassie starts to laugh causing Abby to stare at her in confusion. I'm not. I saw her eying up my phone, smirking.

"You're messaging him, aren't you?" She makes a move to grab my phone but I pull it back, just out of her reach. "Come on, you were blushing! You definitely have a secret boyf."

I have a few choices. I could try and deny it again knowing damn well that she won't believe me, I could tell them everything- yeah, no chance-, or I could try and change the topic, cross everything and hope for the best.

"We should go out on Friday. As a celebration for surviving high school. We could get all dressed up and I can wear my new dress," I say, looking pointedly at Cassie. I grin widely, hoping I can bribe her to move on with the mention of some of her favourite things: getting dressed up, partying and using me as her own life-size, less stereotypical, barbie doll.

"Sure. Sean'll be in too. You could come round to ours to get ready," Abby suggests.

I nod and risk a peek at Cassie to see if she's buying it. She hasn't lost her smirk, she probably thinks she's figured it all out.

She sits up straight. "Oh, I'm in alright." She leans forward and folds her arms on the table. "Will he be there?"

Rolling my eyes, I pull my phone back out and quickly let him know we'll come. His response comes through less than a second later.

Great, I can't wait x

Twenty-Four

That's it. I'm done with high school forever. It's kinda weird that every weekday, every crazy sub teacher, every anxiety induced mock exam and every annoying parent's evening has led to this point. All the things we've ever been told or ever done to this day was for this moment. It's massively underwhelming.

We did have a little leavers assembly which quickly escalated into a shirt signing where not even the quietest of our peers were safe. It was nice. It was also the last time I'll see a lot of them though, the last time I'll step foot in that building. Well, it is if I somehow win the spot at the summer program, if not then I'll probably be back for my results.

Hanging my blazer and bag up, I shut the door behind me. Dad was going to leave work early to pick me up but I told him not too. I know it's my last day and all but it's not that big of a deal, plus he's already on thin ice with his boss because of the past few weeks. The other day was the first fully skipped day but he'd been late a lot more times than he should've been.

My blazer pocket vibrates against the mirror creating a short tap on the glass. I wonder what special surprise is waiting for me this time.

As soon as I open our chat my screen fills with a picture of a nauseated Jackson with lettuce cascading out of his mouth.

Help. They've replaced everything in my mini fridge with lettuce and taken away room service. I give it 24hrs before I turn ravenous and make my first kill.

He's gotten good at this, sending random photos at random points of the day. I don't know when but I started counting the minutes between them, their arrival as certain as the sun's. *Seventy-two.*

Now that he mentions it, I'm pretty hungry too. I've had nothing since breakfast and was going to settle for a meal just as disappointing as Jackson's, but where's the fun in that.

I've broken out of school early and can be at Piece of Cake in ten?

I didn't have time to change, his reply came straight away. *'Last one there's buying.'* I'm not sure if it's my excitement to see him or my genuine fear of not having enough to pay for both our orders, but I'm approaching the cafe at a mad pace. I slow as I round the corner and, glancing through the crystal storefront, notice the huddle of customers, all of which are around my age.

Ah, I almost forgot about the leaver's deals. There's not as many as there are on results day but they seem to be working at bringing in the new customers, I guess people really do love a bargain.

"Beat you," he teases as he whizzes past. *Great, at least the deal means I won't have to pay anymore than usual.* "Technically, I cheated so I already got our stuff. Zac said you like his special paninis but I can get something else if you want?"

The only 'special' part is that he adds a heap of paprika, otherwise it's just a normal cheese and ham panini. I don't know why he doesn't put it on the menu, it tastes amazing. "That's fine," I shout as I follow him through the loud crowd to the back of the cafe, away from my usual table.

The large group of cackling girls barge through the exit and Jackson turns at the quietness. His shoulders relax and he heads back to my table, making sure not to meet my gaze as he passes me.

It hadn't even crossed my mind that they'd recognise him, I guess that explains his unusual outfit choice though. He's wearing the same brown pants he wore the last time we were here but this time he's paired it with an oversized white hoodie, the hood pulled up so all his soft curls are stuffed away and half of his face is masked. It wouldn't be so odd if it wasn't boiling out and even worse in here. Who am I to judge, I look like I'm wearing an infant's colouring book.

He puts my mocha and panini down as I pull back my chair and then places his own on his side of the table. "Thank you. So, how did you cheat? I don't recall us making any rules."

He tilts his head back slightly to sip his coffee and as he does, he reveals the small smile under his hood. "True. But it hardly seems fair that my hotel is a few doors down."

"Oh." I should've guessed, that's the biggest hotel in town and definitely the poshest within our area. "Yeah, that does sound like something that should've been mentioned before," I say, matching his cheeky grin.

"Well, I thought it was an easy way of getting a free panini but I felt too guilty, I couldn't go through with the crime."

"Why? Because it would damage your image?"

"No." His smile vanishes but his tone stays light. "Because I like you."

I'm not sure what to say to that. It doesn't feel like we're just joking anymore, his voice might be saying 'calm and casual' but the statement feels anything but. If I admit I like him too I wouldn't just be agreeing that I enjoy his company or think he makes good conversations, it would be agreeing to something beyond that, something different entirely.

"I liked the outfit you wore in your new Insta pic. Very avant-garde." It was for the cover of a big fashion magazine and he was wearing a pink suit of sorts with many cutouts.

He chokes on a laugh, his face filling with relief. "You can talk. It looks like a box of crayons exploded on your shirt."

"Maybe, but at least my outfit doesn't include a neon green feather boa."

"Fair."

There's a screech as Zac knocks into one of the few empty tables next to us. His face is tinged the same shade as the cherry cheesecake and a drop of sweat flies from a strand of hair as he doubles over near our table. "How long have you been here?" he tries to scream but his lungs won't allow it. "I know we were hoping for more customers but I think this deal might kill us off."

The bell above the door chimes and Zac deflates even more, his eyes filling with dread, but before we even have time to glance in the new customers' direction Seth's voice travels over, already eagerly greeting them.

Zac rolls his eyes. "Well, it might kill *me* off. Can I get you anything else?" He wipes his forehead on his apron before recovering to his full height, his voice a lot steadier. "Another drink? Sauce? Brownies? Or…" His eyes go wide as they flit between me and Jackson. "Maybe you have something for me?"

I know he's after the 'tea' on us but there isn't much to tell, and even if there was this definitely isn't the time or the place. I don't think Jackson's quiet caught on to what he means as he regards him as if he's some kind of dealer or criminal. The only thing he's dealing is gossip. And killer paninis.

"We're good thanks."

"Well, if you need anything I'll be trying not to pass out in between making iced coffees," he says with a tight smile.

The bell goes again and Seth shouts for three more iced coffees. Before leaving, Zac gives us a silent cry for help and as he makes the journey back behind the counter he drags his feet, his tea towel trailing close behind. He always gets like this when it's really busy, the lack of gossiping time eats away at him until he's a hot mess. I turn to explain as such to Jackson but he's slumped in his chair, his face angled slightly towards the wall.

He catches me watching and sits up. "What is the story with the top? Art project gone wrong? Protest?"

"You've never seen a leavers shirt before?" He just gives me a slight shake of his head. "Oh. Basically, when you leave high school you get people to fill your shirt with messages that you can keep and look back on. Like your yearbooks."

He smiles but it doesn't quiet reach his eyes. "I wouldn't know, I've been homeschooled for as long as I can remember."

"Even before?" He's only really been in the spotlight for the past six or so years, I would've thought he'd had a pretty normal life up until then.

"Yep," he replies, his smile weakening. "My parents thought it would be best so I could spend more time on other projects. Before this I was doing dance comps, before that I was doing tv ads, and before I'd even learnt to walk they put me through modelling."

I couldn't even imagine what it must be like to have lived a life where something is constantly expected of you, even before your old enough to expect anything of yourself. No wonder he tries to hide from everyone or snaps at fans that are just returning his phone, he's always powered on and his off switch never got fitted.

He eyes my creased brow and mirrors it as he shifts in his chair. As much as I want to ask questions, push him to realize that the standards he's had set for him aren't normal, I know that's the last thing he wants. "I'm sorry, dance comps?"

His whole body lets out a sigh as he gives a nervous laugh. "Trust me, the feather boa has nothing on some of the outfits I had to wear back then."

"You wouldn't happen to have any pics to back you up would you?"

"God no, I took care of all the copies a few years back." The corners of his mouth pull up. "They really would have damaged my image."

"Shame. I would've loved to see them," I say, keeping my face as neutral as I can manage. "To test your theory of course."

He grins with a glint in his eyes. "Of course."

He asks about rugby and finishes his panini as I rant about our current season. I think he's regretting his decision and trail off but he only asks more questions, the glint only getting brighter as he meets my wide eyes.

Halfway through our third coffee the cafe starts to fill up with the rush of students finishing at the normal time and the tables quickly become overcrowded. Jackson's seemed okay up until now but every time I look at him, he seems to have shrunk further into himself, anymore and he'll be under the table.

"How about we grab a drink to take out?" I ask, leaning over the table to find his face.

Despite the awkward sitting he jumps up at a rapid pace, hooking an arm through his bag on the way. "Sounds great."

We decide on bottled drinks after a quick glance at Zac running around the machines and wait to pay for them in silence, Jackson keeping his eyes glued to the floor. As we step out onto the street, he lets out a breath. "Sorry about acting weird it's just... people," he says as if I'd understand. And in a way I do.

"When are you leaving?" I ask and his mouth gapes as he glances down the street towards his hotel. "Back to America, I mean."

"Right." He casts his eyes down to his bottle, the corners of his mouth following. "Soon. We only have this party and a photoshoot or two and then we're heading back."

Another couple of girls wearing the same uniform as me appear beside us as they try to get into the cafe. We step apart and they head towards the door.

I knew he'd be leaving at some point, and it's not like we've hung out all that much whilst he's been here, but, surprisingly, it stings to know there won't a chance of seeing him around anymore.

The chatter of the cafe disappears along with the girls and he rejoins me with that award-winning smile of his. "I would walk back with you but my managers found out about my cheat meal and is flapping. If I'm not back in my hotel room in five she's going to extend my lettuce sentence, and I really hate lettuce."

I wonder how she found out. Maybe he was spotted, although with all the precautions I doubt anyone could tell it was him, or maybe she somehow has access to his bank account? I'd say that's a little far but after everything I've learnt I wouldn't put it past them. "Do you want me to come with you? I can tell her I kidnapped you and forced you to buy me food. I have the rep for it."

His smile stretches wide. "I think I'll be alright. If I ring you later though you might need to answer and repeat all of that. Just for science."

"Oh okay," I laugh. "I'll be waiting then."

He goes quiet as he nervously shifts from side to side. He looks as though he's debating something, either that or he's suddenly desperate for the toilet. Making up his mind, he slowly leans towards me, his arms enveloping me. It only lasts a second or two, before he quickly springs away, but it's long enough for me to catch the hint of spice and the sweet undertones of his cologne, and notice his unsteady heartbeat as his breath hitches. "See you," he beams as he turns to leave.

"What was that for?" I shout after him, a similar smile playing on my own lips. It's not that I didn't enjoy it, it was just unexpected.

His shrug is only just visible under his giant hoodie as he shouts over his shoulder, "In case I don't make it out alive."

I met up with Sean and Abby after I left Jackson and we headed to Cassie's. We put on a movie in the cinema room and ransacked the snack cupboard but we didn't concentrate on it much, we were too busy reminiscing on the last five years. At least, that's what I was trying to do but it was a little hard with my phone and Jackson's potential call breathing down my neck.

I didn't mention him or any of our meeting to them, after all he's leaving soon so what's the point. Plus, Cassie would flip, she'd freak out and want to meet him again or maybe she'd be mad at me for not telling her sooner. And then there's the teasing I'd get off Sean, it's not worth it. Not when he'll be gone just as quick as he came.

Still, I'm waiting for his call. I got back over an hour ago after feinging a bad head and I've been waiting ever since. I know I shouldn't, and I'm not even sure why I am, it's not like he meant it. He was probably just joking yet the possibility of it makes me feel like fireworks are being lit inside of me with nowhere to go. It's incredibly annoying.

"Ah!" I cover my mouth even though I'm the only one in the flat, Dad left for Uncle Joe's earlier and promised to bring me back some supplies for my 'bad head'.

My phone light's up in my hand, Jackson's Finsta pic of Hugh Jackman in The Greatest Showman filling the screen. I splay out on the couch and then roll off. I look more like I'm giving birth than getting forty winks, I'll just sit. People sit.

"Hey." My voice is so high that the only species that could possibly hear it are dogs.

He doesn't reply, only raises an eyebrow.

Did he actually not hear me? Maybe the sound cut out? "Hey," I try again, my voice a little closer to normal. He widens his eyes in that 'go on…' sort of way and his mouth pulls into a smirk. What is he waiting for? Maybe he's on voice rest, that's a thing singers do, right? Although, if he was on voice rest his manager probably would've taken his phone off him, taped his mouth up and locked him in. Ah, his manager! "I didn't kidnap you and you ate all the food," I say with the same assurance a child might have when telling their babysitter their parents said they can eat ice cream for breakfast. "That's what we agreed on right?"

"I can't believe it," he shouts, his mouth falling agape even though his smirk still lingers in his sparkling eyes. "You would've sold me out. Just like that."

"Well, I'm trying to get on her good side so I can grab some more free tickets. I have a friends birthday coming up."

"You were just using me. I thought we were friends." He says it different this time, his tone less jokey with a hint of something more serious, like he's asking a question he's scared to hear the answer of.

Smiling, and realising I mean it, I reply, "We are."

Twenty-Five

"You have to!" Cassie demands as five different pairs of heels dangle impressively from her wafting hand.

We're getting ready for the party at Abby and Sean's, and trying not to make a mess in the process. We're kinda on a high off the fact that we've just left high school forever and might have already had a small drink to celebrate. Both of which are making Cassie slightly bossier than she usually is.

"What's wrong with my trainers?" I ask, pushing her other hand and bag of high heels away from me. Yes, bag. She decided to bring half her wardrobe so she could decide what looked best. We would've been better getting ready at her house instead of her bringing it with her but she insisted we come here. Apparently, her room's a mess which coming from Cassie must mean that it's *really* bad.

She stares at my feet in disgust and then up at the black dress from the other day. "You can't wear them with that. It would be a crime to the dress. And all fashion gods." She holds the bridge of her nose as if the shoes are causing her physical pain to look at. "Can someone back me up here?" she asks the others. "Sean! You're a guy, won't her secret boyfriend prefer heels?" She's trying to secretly nod at him encouragingly through the mirror, her eyebrows doing a kind of mad waltz.

"Heels would look a lot better." He ruffles his hair and then smooths it back before turning to us. "But you shouldn't choose to wear them just for a guy. Wear what makes you comfortable." He adds a shrug at Cassie and the death stare she's undoubtedly sporting.

"Now's not the time to be a feminist Sean," she says, frustrated. She turns to Abby who's making nachos in the kitchen. "Abby?"

The microwave pings and she takes the bowl out, placing it on the table. "I hate to say it because heels suck, but she's right. You can't wear those with your dress, not where we're going anyway, they have a dress code."

"Ugh." I roll my head back, careful not to mess up the hair Cassie just spent the last half an hour doing. She's somehow pulled it back into a half-up-half-down plait-ponytail concoction and I'm still not a hundred per cent sure it's going to stay put. I grab the shortest heels I can find and slip them on, thanking the universe when they fit. Not that it'll make me hate them any less by the end of the night.

"How is it we're getting in this place again?" Sean asks, moving towards the kitchen table as if drawn by the nachos.

"Lorri's boyfriend invited us. Apparently, he can get us in," Cassie answers. A smirk grows across her face as she mentions my 'secret boyfriend'. Would it still be there if she knew who it was who invited us?

"Oh. When are we leaving?" He tries to eat a handful of the cheesy nachos, leaning forward to stop any dripping onto his new shirt.

I see they've all accepted that I have a secret boyfriend now. I search for my phone and check the time when I find it hidden under Albert. "The taxi shouldn't be long."

They turn their attention back to the nachos and move on to more pressing matters like discussing what dance moves they're planning on showing off on the dance floor.

I check for any new messages from Jackson, my shoulders dropping when there aren't any. I messaged him a few times earlier today to ask some questions about the party and when I got no answer, I sent a few more just to check that everything's okay.

I haven't spoken to him since our video call last night. We ended up watching one of his favourite films when I admitted to having never heard of it, he put it on Netflix so I could watch it with him through the screen. It was more than a little shaky, especially when it got to his favourite scenes, but I didn't mind. We laughed together and almost cried together, and it wasn't until he gazed into my sleepy eyes to wish me goodnight that I realised I didn't want it to end.

"Oh Lorri, you look beautiful!"

I almost drop my phone on Albert's head, catching it just in time. He continues to snore away, kicking his leg occasionally while he dreams.

"Sorry love, I'm not that scary, am I?" Emma, Sean and Abby's mum, jokes. She's in her wheelchair, wrapped up in a blanket despite the warm weather.

I shake my head, more for myself than for her. "Sorry, I wasn't paying attention." It's not her that's scary, it's the illness. I'm not scared *of* her, I'm scared *for* her. And for what it'll mean for Sean and Abby.

"You're not the only one." She points her head towards the others in the kitchen who still haven't noticed her enter the room and gives me a look to say 'teenagers'.

I plaster on a smile, reminding myself to focus on the now instead of worrying about the future as I take in her own freshly done hair and make-up. "You look nice. Are you going out?" I ask, casually. I already know that she is, Sean told me earlier today, but I know she'll appreciate me asking like I normally would before.

Her face lights up as she thinks about her plans for the night. "As a matter of fact, I am," she says, smiling brightly. "We're going for a meal with some friends that I haven't seen in a long time."

My smile evolves into a real one as her excitement is pumped from her to me. "That sounds nice."

"Yeah, it's nice to get out more." She watches as Sean lets out a proper belly laugh, crumpling over to clutch his side. She smiles but it doesn't fully reach her eyes as they start to glaze over. "I'm glad you're all going out tonight. I know I should be telling you to behave and not to drink, and to be back early or whatever. But it's nice to see them being teenagers for once, you know?"

I don't nod or disagree, I just meet her sad eyes with my own. I know what she means, but I don't want to agree with her because I know she blames herself for that, which she shouldn't do. I know they don't.

"They're lucky to have you two, you've always been there for each other. Promise me you'll always stick together. No matter what." Her voice threatens to crack and she tries to cover it with a cough. It spirals into a fit, finally catching the attention of Abby, Cassie and Sean. The room falls silent, the laughter gone, the only noise her cough before everyone jumps into action.

Her nurse rushes out of her room and down the corridor, holding meds and other gadgets I've seen lying around the house a few times but have never learned the name of, and Sean runs to the sink to grab some water, his face failing to hide the panic. After a few minutes, she gets her breath back and risks lifting a shaky hand on top of Abby's.

"Are you sure you're okay to go? We can all stay here and watch a movie?" Sean asks. He looks around the room and we all nod.

She stretches her arm out to pat his chest. The action looks as though it causes her pain as she winces but she does it anyway. "I'll be alright. Go and have fun."

He tries to object but she reminds him that Ellen, her nurse, will be with her the whole time and that they won't be out long. A car beeps from outside and I check to confirm that it's our taxi before alerting the others. Even though he no longer wants to, Sean grabs his stuff, along with Abby, Cassie and I, and hugs his mum goodbye before heading for the door.

"Lorri," Emma croaks in a low voice as I'm about to leave. "Promise?"

I can't picture life without her. I know she's ill but we never really talk about what that means, what will happen after. Whether she'll get better or not has never really been a question, we've all come to an unspoken agreement that it'll happen because it's just impossible to even suggest anything else. *A stupid thought.*

I mirror her sad smile from earlier. "I promise."

"Thank you," we shout, one by one, as we file out of the taxi, our voices only just audible over the noise of the nightclub and the crowd that has gathered outside.

He looks us over and side-eyes the club before shaking his head as he speeds off. I guess warning us about underage drinking and trying to sneak into nightclubs isn't in his pay grade.

"Are you sure this is the place?" Sean asks. He spots the small huddle of paps behind a rope barrier next to the door and turns back to me, eyes wide.

"Unfortunately," I mumble and try to steady my clammy hands. The gang of paps looks identical to the one that met me that morning, which feels like an age ago. They all dress the same like they're in some kind of weird cult where it's not illegal to be stalkers. I wonder if I could suggest going back home, they'll probably recognise the back of me and chase me down the street like last time.

"Are we going in?" Abby asks, watching us with quizzical brows.

I nod, raise my chin and make a move towards the door. I'm going for 'confident' and not 'fighting-against-everything-in-my-body-not-to-barf-everywhere'. After all, *I* barely recognised myself in the mirror so maybe they won't.

The music gets even louder when we get closer and the paps turn their heads, readying their cameras as we climb the steps. I instantly angle my face the other way, trying to make it look as natural as possible like I've seen so many real celebs do before. *Oh, what's that? A flying pig?* Climbing the last few steps to the security guard, the others stay behind me, nudging me forward to give our names.

"Hi," I say, my voice shakier than I'd like. "Lorri?"

He wears a constant frown as he scans over us. "Second name?" he asks in a voice that says he thinks this is a waste of time.

"Uh, Johnson? Lorri Johnson?"

He flips through the pages attached to his clipboard and I nervously peek at the others. The paps have moved on to some influencer that I recognise but don't know the name of that's just turned up and is basking in all the attention.

"Sorry, you're not on the list." If there's a hint of surprise in his voice, only the best detectives could find it. He moves to the influencer who's now waiting in line, expecting us to leave.

I shift from one sore foot to the other. "Are you sure?" He crosses his arms as he towers over me, not impressed that we're still here. "It's just that..." Should I mention Jackson? I could but he wouldn't believe me anyway, I've heard Cassie mention multiple times about crazed fans trying to get into events that he's at. Plus, if the paps got a waft of it it wouldn't be long until it was in every magazine in the country. Scrap that, every magazine across the globe. "My friend's in there and he said he'd put our names on the list."

He doesn't make a move to check the list again. "Well, he didn't. Look, there are people waiting that are actually on the list. Why don't you move aside so I can let them in."

I don't have time to even think about arguing with him before he starts talking over us to the people behind.

Someone grabs my wrist, pulling me away. "Come on, screw him and his list," Sean says as he drags me down the steps. We walk back to the pavement in silence. The paparazzi's cameras go off and we scurry around the corner to hide from their flash.

Abby surveys the dark and dirty alleyway with a frown. "Now what?"

"I'll get us an Uber," Cassie replies mournfully, pulling out her phone.

Sean places his hand on her arm holding the phone. "Don't." He's staring down the side of the building, at a side door near the back. There's no handle on the outside otherwise I would think he's suggesting we sneak in. "Is he in there?" he asks, turning to me.

I assume he's referring to Jackson. "Uh, he should be?" I still don't understand where this is going.

He breaks into a smile. "Then it's fine. Who said we need to go in the front door?"

Abby clocks on, probably from twin telepathy, and mimics his smile, looking eerily like Sean. "Ring him. He can come and sneak us in."

Phone Jackson and get him to let us in. Right. To be honest, I'm not sure what my plan was for when we got in there and they saw him, maybe pretend I didn't know him? Or maybe I thought it would be too busy and we wouldn't run into each other? Why did I think this was a good idea, again?

Now they're all looking at me expectantly, I can't let them down. I can't let their mum down. Internally sighing, I hit the call button next to his username and the three of them watch with wide smiles. They look like they belong in a horror movie. We wait for it to ring out three times, their smiles fading even more after each unanswered call.

"He probably can't hear over the music," I say with a shrug. I try a small smile as I push down the disappointment.

A taxi pulls up, more influencers spew out, and we head towards it, Sean yelling for them to wait. Cassie opens the door at the same time the side door to the building swings open and Jackson slips out, glancing down.

"Hey!" I shout over the music.

He hears me, grinning when he spots us, and starts to walk towards our end, unaware that the door's one-way.

"The door!" I point at it and try to catch it before it closes, going as fast as I can in these death traps.

He grabs it just in time, holding it open while I continue the rest of the distance. I reach him first, glancing back at the others still near the pavement. They walk slowly, wearing a mixture of confusion and shock. And maybe a tad starstruck. Well, apart from Sean who looks like he's watching a good episode of the big bang or something. *Does he want some popcorn?*

"You look… You look beautiful," Jackson says, drinking in my appearance. He catches himself and his cheeks glow red, his eyes darting to the bins across from us.

My face burns from the compliment and a smile tugs at my lips. I smooth out my dress and tuck a stray strand of hair behind my ear, hyper-aware of his eyes as they find their way back to me. "You too."

I shake my head as he laughs. What's wrong with me? My brain didn't turn to mush when Sean and Abby's mum said the same thing. "I mean you look good too," I correct myself, my face now fully on fire.

He's gone for a grey top instead of white and thrown on a thick silver chain to differentiate from his usual Jackson Peters day-to-day look. His hair's a little more tame than the last time I saw him, probably due to a trim and a handful of products, and his face is slightly flushed, a sheen across his forehead. I take it the party inside is just as warm as outside, if not worse.

"I was about to call you back," he rushes, waving his phone as proof. "The music's too loud in there to hear anything." He peeps over my shoulder at the others as he pockets his phone and scratches the back of his neck with his free hand. "I should have messaged you earlier, I couldn't get you onto the list, but I can sneak you in here. There are so many random people in there that no one will notice you're not on the list," he says, his voice small and far away.

If you only knew him from the interviews and headlines, you'd think he was a party animal. Heck, *I did* think he was a party animal before this very second. "Why come if you don't enjoy them?" I ask, twiddling a charm on my bracelet.

He offers me a shy smile. "I don't have a choice, it's my party."

"Your party!" Cassie gasps, signalling her arrival. She quickly covers her mouth, the rest of them now standing next to me, and whacks my arm. "You never said anything."

"Ow." I rub where a red mark is already forming. Maybe Abby should see if there's room for Cassie in the martial arts class, she'd excel. "I didn't know," I say defensively.

"It was Cassie, right?" he asks. She nods, her mouth hanging open, and I can't help but find her nervousness entertaining, I have to look down at my feet just to hide my grin.

"It's nice to properly meet you. I'm sorry about how I acted when we last met, as the Brits say, I was a twat." He meets my eye and shares a quick smirk.

Cassie laughs it off like it's long forgotten. "That's okay. Everyone's a twat sometimes." She plays with a strand of hair, twirling it around her finger. She notices my raised brows and her eyes widen as she sees what I'm looking at, unaware she was doing it herself, and tosses it over her shoulder.

She takes a breath, straightening her spine. "This is Sean and Abby, they're twins."

Abby, smiling sweetly, greets him whilst Sean only offers a blunt 'hey'.

"Nice to meet you." He smiles shyly, adding a nod, before opening the door all the way. "Follow me."

Twenty-Six

He leads us down a dark corridor lined with blank black doors on either side, informing us that they're dressing rooms and pointing out which one's his. With us being underage, none of us have been before but I've heard of artists making surprise appearances and performances. Apparently, Taylor Swift was here a couple of months ago but I never found any evidence.

When we reach the end, he checks that the coast is clear before pushing the door open and letting us slip through. Standing guard, next to the door, is the same bodyguard from our date dressed in black and tangled with wires. As we pass, he barely pays us any attention. In fact, he doesn't even bat an eyelash at us, no one does.

It's packed. No wonder the security guy wouldn't let us squeeze in, any more influencers and they wouldn't have any room to take their selfies. The room's a sea of colourful garments that must be custom-made specifically for tonight. Or maybe they wear neon ballgowns all the time, who knows?

"Do you want something to drink?" Jackson shouts over the music. We all nod and follow him around the edge of the room to the bar near the entrance, trying really hard not to accidentally stand on anyone's dress or feet.

It's a lot bigger inside than it looks from the outside. At the opposite end of the room there's a giant elevated stage that's currently occupied by a DJ I recognise the name of. He points in a direction above my head where there are even more people upstairs. The bar's long and has more seats than I can count, yet all of them are taken and every gap is filled, meaning Jackson has to squeeze past multiple layers of people to get to the bartender.

"Here," he says, passing us our drinks whilst also politely taking photos with the group that has gathered by his side. They turn their attention away from him as they check over the photos, his presence now forgotten. He doesn't seem to mind. Either that or he's used to it. "Order whatever you want, it's an open bar."

"Sweet," Sean says, taking in his surroundings as he sips his drink. "So, this is your life, huh?"

Jackson lets out a hollow laugh. "I guess it is."

"Must be nice," Cassie drools as she admires the diamante-covered dress of the woman next to us.

He stares into his drink. "Uh, yeah, it's great." He might as well be talking about the weather, not a life of wealth and luxury. Maybe it's not just Jackson Peters' music he's unhappy with. He catches my worried stare and creases his brow before averting his gaze.

"Actually, I should probably go and greet some more people." He gulps half of his drink and glances at me before continuing, "Thank you for coming."

The others thank him for letting us in and for the drinks, and he stops in front of me as he leaves. "I'll see you around." It comes out more like a question so I nod in agreement, a tight smile on both our faces.

Someone shouts his name, beckoning him over, and he rushes off to meet them. When he reaches them, he transforms into Jackson Peters; his smile looser and his posture relaxed to give him more of an 'I don't care' attitude. They eat it up as they snap photos with him and laugh at the same stories he tells the next group, and then the next. He moves through the crowd, giving each person the same facial expressions and hand gestures as the last.

This isn't a life, this is his job.

"Can you at least pretend you're having fun?" Sean says, laughing at my face.

"She's probably looking for her secret friend," Abby teases.

Cassie perks up, quickly turning away from the woman in the dress. "Is he here? Can you see him?" she squeals, her head whipping from side to side as she surveys the crowd even though she doesn't know who she's looking for.

Sean narrows his eyes, his lips twitching into a smirk. "I think we just met him." He searches my face for a reaction and I feel the heat travel across it, covering my cheeks. Luckily, the room's dark, the only light source is the coloured strobe lights, so I think I'm safe.

I know he knew it was me in the photo but surely he doesn't go around analysing and remembering everyone's shoes. Or maybe he only figured it out now, after all, he did let us in, no questions asked.

"What? Jackson?" Abby asks, her head snaps from me to the direction he left in.

"No," Cassie laughs. "It's not Jackson Peters, don't be ridiculous."

"Why would that be ridiculous?" I half choke, the question more loaded then it was intended to be.

She stops laughing as she takes in my scrunched brows. "I didn't mean anything by it. It's just…" She searches for the right thing to say, something that won't push me over the line of being offended. "Well, you don't even like him, do you? And I could never picture you with someone like that, you said it yourself he's a 'stuck up twat'. You're just so different," she shrugs.

That was before I got to know him. Before I got to know the Jackson who watched the rugby just so we could continue talking about it, who is so obsessed with musicals it's actually kinda cute, who's an incredibly good photographer, who writes the most beautiful songs (even though he's not allowed to sing them), who makes me laugh without even trying and whose smile can make a bad day a little less bad. Yes, I said that, but I was wrong.

"You can't help who you like," Abby offers with a shrug and a reassuring smile.

"Yeah, but it's not Jackson," Cassie says, her voice rising.

"Anyone want another drink? I need another drink." Sean doesn't wait for us to answer before turning towards the bar. I'm grateful for his effort in trying to change the subject but that doesn't hide the fact that he started this.

Cassie lets out a frustrated sigh as she twirls a piece of hair. "Because if it was him then you would have said something, right?" she asks so quietly I have to strain to hear her. Her eyes are big, pleading. "Because if you were dating Jackson Peters that would be a really big freaking thing to keep from me." I can feel the hurt threatening to spill from her eyes and all I want to do is stop it.

"Of course, I'm not dating Jackson Peters," I reply with a weak smile. Well, it's not a lie. "You would know if I was."

Letting out a short laugh, Sean returns with something stronger looking. The song changes to a remix of 'Girls just want to have fun' and Cassie gasps, grabbing mine and Abby's arms. "Let's dance! And just forget about boys, who needs them?" she scowls at Sean.

We follow her out onto the dance floor, laughing as we leave Sean standing alone. We twirl each other around until the song finishes and when the next starts, we make no move to evacuate the dance floor. A few songs later we're a sweaty mess from jumping, spinning and laughing at each other's attempts at dancing.

The music cuts out creating a collective groan from the crowd, everyone's heads searching for the disruption. A very flustered woman walks onto the stage holding a mic and the whole club turns in her direction. When she enters the spotlight, I recognise that it's the woman who gave us the tickets to Jackson's concert, his manager.

"Good evening everyone, I hope y'all are having a good time!" she shouts across the speakers and the crowd goes wild, probably thanks to the open bar. She quickly glances to the side of the stage as if waiting for someone to arrive, but who, Jackson? I search for him in the crowd but he's nowhere to be found. He was somewhere on my right the last time I saw him but that was at least three songs ago, I stopped checking on him when Cassie attempted the robot.

Where is he?

"Well, I guess this is what y'all have been waiting for." More whoops from the crowd. "So," she continues, getting her confidence back. "Y'all aren't just here for a simple album release." She shakes her head, her nose scrunching up as if the idea is ridiculous. "Oh no. We brought y'all here tonight so you could be the first to know that *not only* will you get two now albums from Jackson before the end of the year, but y'all also be getting a brand-new WORLDWIDE TOUR!" As soon as the words leave her mouth the DJ starts back up but gets lost in the cheers. She goes into details of the tour, barely audible over all the noise as everyone either goes back to dancing or whips their phones out to race to be the first to post about the news.

"Lorri, you're psychic," Abby shouts in my direction, a laugh in her eyes.

Cassie doesn't look as amused by the 'coincident'. "How did you know?"

I wrack my brain for an excuse and laugh it off to buy myself some time. "I told you I thought I read it somewhere. Someone must have leaked it." I add a smile and a shrug, praying she won't ask any more questions.

I can tell she's contemplating whether or not to believe me, chewing the corner of her lip as she debates how likely it is that the news could have been leaked. Very, hopefully. She stops chewing, her slit eyes meeting mine and she sits on one hip as she crosses her arms.

Oh no.

My hand searches for my bracelet out of nerves but stops short when it only collides with more skin. I look down at my wrist expecting to see my silver charm bracelet but find nothing of the sort. "No. NO." *Great, one more thing for Cassie to be mad at.*

"What?" Abby asks.

Cassie's face falls and she unfolds her arms, her shoulders slumping. "Your bracelet." It comes out more like a gasp than a sentence. "Did you have it when we left the house?"

Had I put it on before we left? I know I brought it because Albert tried to chew the pouch that it's in, he always has ever since Sean spilt pickle juice all over it. Maybe I forgot when I was talking to Sean and Abby's mum.

"You did!" Abby exclaims, pointing at me. "I saw it when we got out of the taxi."

"Okay. So, maybe it fell off outside?" Cassie suggests.

Outside. When I was talking to Jackson. My cheeks burn and I avoid Cassie's eyes. "I had it when we ran into Jackson. I was messing with it, maybe I accidentally undid the clasp?"

They both consider it and then nod in agreement. "We should look for it before it gets damaged or taken," Abby says already scoping the ground.

"Ok. Abby, you check here. I'll go and look on that side." I point towards the side of the room where we came in from. "And make my way back to the alleyway. Cassie, can you go and ask if anyone's handed it in and check the bar?"

She nods in the direction where we left Sean what feels like ages ago, her eyebrows creasing. "Yeah, I should probably go and check on Sean anyway. I'll get him to help too."

I thank them and we part ways, deciding to message if any of us find it. Pushing past people, I scour the dance floor for the bracelet in case it's been kicked around and after a while of awkwardly pretending to dance, and trying not to get winded by stray elbows, I decide to walk back the way we came and see if I find it there.

It's my own fault. I used to wear it every day, only taking it off to wash, but then the clasp started to loosen and we couldn't afford to get it fixed. Now I only wear it on special occasions when it would feel too weird not to, but I know it's always a risk.

It's not on the edge of the dance floor. Or under any of the tables around the edge. Or near the door we came through.

"Excuse me," I start gingerly to the tall security guard. "I've lost my bracelet and I think I might have dropped it down there." I point towards the door that he's guarding.

He doesn't speak, just lifts his chin to squint at me, crossing his arms. He's going to tell me to get lost. What did I expect, I'm a nobody trying to get into the backstage area, he probably thinks I've made this up just to sneak into Jackson's dressing room and steal his hairbrush so I can clone him or something.

A smile breaks across his face. "Don't worry, I know who you are." *He does?* "Nothing gets passed me, if it did, I'd be pretty bad at my job."

"Oh." Does he mean he knows me from earlier or from the photos and the date? To be honest I don't care as long as he lets me through. "So, can I check for my bracelet?"

"It's fine, you don't need to make excuses. I think you're really good for him."

"Uh, thanks?" I didn't think anyone knew about us hanging out. Well, not the way we have been.

He glances around before leaning in, his voice as close to whispering as you can get in a nightclub. "It's been hard for him. They're hard on him. A life with so many secrets and such high expectations is a lonely one, but I'm glad you're helping change that."

I'm not sure what to say so I just nod. I knew things weren't great for him but they aren't that bad, are they? And even so, how am I changing anything?

"Sorry, I shouldn't have said anything," he says, noticing me glance at the door. "Your secret's safe with me," he winks and opens the door just wide enough for me to slip through.

Twenty-Seven

The door clicks shut behind me and the music suddenly dulls, sounding as though my ears need to pop. I let out a breath, finding comfort in the quietness, and turn to start my search down the corridor.

I remember the day I found it like it was yesterday. Mum had lost it a week before and I helped her look for it. We searched the whole house. Three times. She loved that bracelet, it was passed down from my grandma as a wedding gift before she died. It didn't have many charms, Mum never added to it. She said less is more and if it was full there'd be no space for me to add to when she passed it on.

The day she lost it was the last time I saw her.

After that, Dad was a mess and, after a few days, so was the house. I wasn't great either, my mum was missing and no one would tell me why, but Cassie had said she'd come over and I didn't want her to see the house a mess. So, I picked up the take-out boxes and the cans, I learnt how to do the dishes and the washing, and I cleaned the house the best I could through sobs.

Cassie was early and I'd just had some toast, so in a desperate attempt to clear the crumbs I pushed them down the side of the couch, catching my hand on something sharp. I pulled it out and gasped at the lost bracelet, it was one of the charms I'd stabbed myself with. Mum's charm. Me and Dad had picked it for her for Mother's Day. It was a spoon in a mixing bowl and on the front it said 'made with love'. When we gave it to her she turned to me and said, 'That's what you are'. Now I'm not too sure.

I put it on straight away, smiling at the memory, and opened the door to let Cassie in. She must've noticed the bracelet because when I finally got told the truth she got me a new charm. It was an infinity symbol that said 'You're stuck with me for'. Apparently, it was supposed to say 'forever' but she ran out of letters, I think it turned out perfect. Since then, she's given me many more. Ones that she, Sean and Abby have all picked out for me. She's probably spent more on it than anyone else, not the price that matters, if someone went and bought an exact replica it wouldn't be the same.

Sometimes I wonder what it meant. Was it just a coincidence that she lost it the day she left or was it all planned? Walking down the corridor, I survey the bright floor, checking everything shiny that catches my eye. *It would be a lot easier if the floor didn't contain these stupid silver flecks.*

I'd like to think it was a coincidence. That it was a spur-of-the-moment choice to leave me and not something she knew she was going to do. Because if so, why didn't she say goodbye? Or offer to stay in touch? Beg me to go with her? Explain? *Something.*

I pass the middle of the corridor as my sight starts to blur, the floor, ceiling and everything in between fusing together. I swipe at my eyes, batting the memories away.

I knew I shouldn't have put it on, not to go to a club, but I wanted to feel like Mum was here with me. It's at this point in your life that you need a mum the most. She's supposed to be here to talk to about boys and college, about what you want to do with your life and to tell you the dangers of underage drinking whilst helping you get ready for prom in the dress she helped you pick out. She's not supposed to be hundreds of miles away starting a new family and forgetting all about you.

I just about make out the door we came through in front of me and fall against it. I try to steady my breath and stop the tears from falling but they, along with my thoughts, have a mind of their own. "Stop it," I get out between breaths. "She's not worth it."

As my vision starts to comes back, and my chest rises and falls at a normal rate, I push off and open the door, only walking out far enough to check if the bracelet is there. I better keep hold of the door so I don't accidentally lock myself out, that's the last thing I need.

Scanning the floor from the door all the way down to the street, my eyes aren't met with anything shiny other than a few empty cans and a torn-up crisp packet. I close my eyes and take a few deep breaths of fresh air before re-entering the building.

Maybe one of the others found it and they're just waiting for me to get back. Yeah, that'll be it. I just need to hurry up and get back to them, and then everything will be okay. I start marching towards the door at the opposite end of the corridor but as I pass halfway a glass smashes and I stop short. I twist my head, trying to determine where it came from and notice that one of the doors to my right is open ajar.

Holding my breath, I wait for another sound to come from behind the door and inch closer. As I peer through the gap, the glass rattles against the floor as if someone's trying to pick it up. "Fuck!" they growl, dropping the bits they'd picked up and shattering them further.

Maybe I should check that they're okay, I could do with topping up my good karma. As the door creaks open, my heart stops. In the centre of the room, in front of a dressing table, a deflated Jackson is kneeling on the floor, cradling his left hand as warm red liquid drips into a puddle. He's imprisoned by broken glass and it glistens under the lights, warning those stupid enough to go near to back off. I ignore them as I rush towards him, tiptoeing through the maze, and grab his hand. My heartbeat relaxes as I realise the cut's not as deep as I originally thought.

"What happened? Are you okay?" I squat down in front of him but he doesn't tear his eyes away from his hand. "Jackson?" I whisper, softly, placing my hand on his upper arm.

"They're giving up," he slurs, his eyes starting to fill. "And they want me to pretend that everything's fine. But it's not." He lifts his head, slowly, and his eyes bore into mine. "It's not," he repeats, his voice cracking as the tears roll down his warm cheeks.

I squeeze his arm. "No, I know. I know." I'm not *really* sure what he's on about, but I do know that when people are drunk *they* barely know what they're on about, so it's better if I just go along with it. "Come on, let's clean up your hand."

I pull him up by his arms, making sure that he steps around the glass, and drop him onto the black leather couch at the back of the room before successfully guessing that the door next to the sofa is a bathroom. I locate a crappy first aid kit and take it back to where he's slumped, his eyes already closing. "I think this might have been here as long as the actual building," I joke, taking the seat next to him and accepting his damaged hand.

He sniffs and tries to sit up straighter. "Did they send you to look for me? Is that why you're helping me because I'm needed again?"

"What?" I stop wiping the wound, the almost dry antiseptic wipe hovering above his skin. "No, of course not." *If they were going to send anyone it definitely wouldn't be me.*

"I heard you, you were looking for someone in the corridor." He stares at the door I came through, his thoughts distant.

"Oh." The lonely syllable hangs in the air as I remember my bracelet. "I was looking for something I lost but it doesn't matter right now." There's a half-empty glass of water on the dressing table and I smooth the sides of the plaster onto his palm before getting up to grab it. "And I'm helping you because, believe it or not, I care about you."

He strokes the plaster with his right thumb.

"Now, drink," I say, thrusting the cup at him.

His head snaps up and a smirk crawls across his face. "You wouldn't be saying that if you knew what was in it," he mumbles, pointing quite shakily at the glass with his good hand.

Highering the glass to eye level, I inspect the liquid. *Yep, definitely clear.* I slowly bring the glass to my mouth, his eyes following it, and I wait for him to object or jump up and knock it out of my hand as if it's full of poison. He doesn't so I take a mouthful, and as soon as the glass leaves my lips everything starts to burn. In a desperate attempt to make it stop I swallow the liquid, the burn following it as it travels down my throat.

Jackson falls back into the couch with laughter as I choke on nothing, slapping his good hand on his knee. "Your face!" he says, clutching his side with his other hand. "It was all scrunched up!" He gasps for air during the breaks of laughter. "It looked like a butthole. On your face!"

Honestly, I don't know how he hasn't accidentally fallen off the couch with all the rolling around he's doing. "Well, I'm glad you found it so funny," I say, a hint of annoyance in my voice.

I empty the cup in the bathroom sink and swill it out with tap water before filling it up. He continues to laugh whilst I do so and when I return, he's wiping under his eyes, a little giggle stuck in his chest. It's like he's *begging* me to empty the glass over his head. "Here, you need to sober up."

He immediately stops laughing as he takes the cup. Do they have magic water here or something? Has it been blessed by a priest? You just have to hold it and you turn sober. He takes a sip and stares into the liquid. "Why? So I can go back out there?"

"No. Not if you don't want to." I lower myself onto the couch next to him, a piece of stray glass crunching under my shoe. I kick it towards the other bits. "Was it a bottle of vodka you smashed?" I ask quietly.

He takes a long, slow sip from his glass. "Yes. I took it from the bar, they were too busy to notice. They always are."

I watch the glistening shards and notice the lack of liquid, no puddle in sight. "You drank it all?" I exclaim, not bothering to hide my disappointment.

His cheeks flame and he lowers his head. "There wasn't *that* much left."

I take a deep breath. This isn't Jackson. The last time this happened, on our 'date', he said there was a reason, maybe it's the same now. "Jackson," I start softly. "What's happened?"

He meets me with crossed brows and tight lips. Maybe I shouldn't have pushed. He's made it clear multiple times that he doesn't want to talk about it with me, why would now be any different?

He exhales before downing the last of his water and slumps against the back of the couch. "My parents. I just found out they're getting a divorce." He lets out a laugh that's more of a cry. "I didn't even find out from them first, I saw it online almost twenty-four hours before they bothered to message me."

I don't know what I was expecting but it wasn't that. I remember the day I was told my mum had left and how utterly lost I felt as I watched my whole world implode around me with no way of fixing it. "I'm so sorry." I lay a hand over his and give it a squeeze. His glazed eyes land on where they're resting on his knee and he squeezes back.

"That's not even the worst part." His voice trembles and the first set of tears start to spill over. "I could have stopped it. It's *my* fault. This is all my fault."

I sit up straighter, fuelled with anger for both Jackson and myself, and the fact that I've allowed myself to think that way before. "No. None of it is your fault," I say, sternly.

He gives his head a quick, dismissive shake. "The day of our date I found out that my dad had been having an affair with my manager. I should have fired her and taken her out of the equation, but I don't know what I'm doing. I don't know who I am without her." He takes a deep breath, steadying himself, and wipes his chin just before a tear has the chance to drop off. "I get up and she sends me a timetable of everything I'm doing that day, minute by minute. I act like the character *she* created, the character people love. I mean, if you take the author away from the character then they're just words on a page, no one knows how to bring them to life like they do. They don't know what to do or what to say, where they're supposed to be or how they're supposed to act. She made Jackson Peters and I don't know how to be him without her."

"Just be you, like you've been with me." He doesn't give himself enough credit. In the time I've spent getting to know the actual Jackson I've gone from yelling in his face to defending him, I'd see that as a win but what do I know? "Anyway, they're grown adults, they would've carried on no matter what you did. Trust me," I say, picking at a thread on the couch.

"What is it?" he asks, offering me the closest thing to a reassuring smile that he can muster whilst being completely hammered.

I clear my throat. I can probably count on one hand how many times I've said these words out loud. "When I was younger, my mum met someone else too."

"I'm sorry." He cringes at his return of the words and gives my hand an apologetic squeeze.

"It's alright, it was a while ago. She was seeing him behind my dad's back for a while, no one knew, but he needed to move for his job so she had to choose between him or us."

"She chose him?" he asks, with something between anger and disbelief.

I feel a tear fall despite my best efforts to stop them. "It didn't matter what you did. You could have sent her to a different planet but you couldn't have stopped him from going after her."

He watches our intertwined hands, stroking mine with his thumb. "Does it get better?" He asks under his breath.

I should lie, tell him everything will be okay and he'll get over it eventually, but that's not fair. That's what everyone else will say, but it's not the whole truth. "Sometimes it feels like it does. You think you're over it, that you're used to the new normal, but then something happens. You see a family or you remember a memory or you do something new and you're reminded all over again just how different your life is now and that it'll never go back to normal ever again."

He continues to watch our hands, his thumb frozen. *Oh god, I'm scaring him.* "It'll get easier. The time you spend upset over the reminders will get shorter until they're barely noticeable. You'll always mourn your old life, but you'll get used to your new one." He meets my eyes and I offer him a sad smile. "Eventually."

He lifts a hand to my face, never taking his eyes off of mine, and carefully wipes a tear. His hand is warm and comforting, and I welcome it, falling against it as he cups my cheek.

I've never spoken to anyone about this, like this, before. Sure, Sean and Abby's dad was never around but it's not the same, he was a one-night stand so they never knew him. They never had everything tipped upside down and told to keep walking in a straight line like nothing had happened. They didn't stay up at night wondering why they weren't enough, why one of their parents needed to go in search of a new family to give all their love and attention to instead of the one already tucked in bed at home. They never felt it, not like me and Jackson.

A curl falls across his face as he moves closer and I use a finger to guide it back across his forehead, my hand finding a place at the side of his head that feels at home for it to rests against, not wanting to leave. His eyes flit between my eyes and my lips, setting the butterflies loose and enticing me to move forward. We're so close that his breath tickles the invisible hairs across my face.

The noise from outside floods in and a shadow forms at the door, breaking the connection and causing us to spring apart. "Are you joking me?" Cassie croaks. "I can't believe you," she laughs as the door slams behind her.

Jackson's leaning back against the arm of the sofa but his legs haven't moved. We were so close you would've been lucky to squeeze a flat hand between us. What's wrong with me, it wasn't long ago I hated the guy and now I'm thinking about making out with him. *Lorri, pull it together!* He looks just as surprised, and only manages an understanding nod before I stumble off after Cassie.

Twenty-Eight

"Cassie!" I yell, skidding around the door and almost breaking an ankle. "These damn heels," I mutter as I exit the security door, noticing the lack of security. He's probably on the hunt for a made-up fight caused by a weirdly fast teenage girl in a very tight sparkly dress. I yank the heels off, hopping from one foot to the other as I do so and breathe a sigh of relief when they're both off, then instantly regret it as my feet stick to the floor like Velcro. Cassie's blond head bobs up near the bar and she grabs Seans arm, pulling him towards the door with Abby on their tails. I sprint after them before they end up leaving me behind.

"Guys?" I shout after them but it's no use over the loud music.

I follow them through the exit to the foyer and the level of the music lowers significantly. I take my chance and shout after them again just as Cassie's about to open the main door. Abby and Sean hear me and turn back, Cassie still pulling Seans arm.

"Come on, we're leaving," she says, not looking at me.

"Cassie, please. It's really not what it looks like," I beg, halving the space between us. Maybe it is, but Jackson's bladdered and clearly going through some stuff so it doesn't really count. *Does it?*

"Really?" she yells, quickly turning on her heels. "So, you weren't just about to kiss Jackson Peters?"

I quickly glance around, hoping for both of our sakes that no one can hear us. Luckily, we're the only ones here, everyone else is inside with their night only just beginning.

"What?" Sean and Abby choke, sharing a look. "I knew it," Sean adds with a smirk that's full of… pride? Well, at least he's not mad at me as well.

"We were just talking," I lie. "He was upset because of something that's happened and we were talking about it, that's all." I throw my arms out in a half shrug, the heels flying about.

"Don't, I know what I saw. I asked you." She jabs at me with a pointed finger. "I asked you if it was him and you *lied* to me. All these years and we've never kept anything from each other, *never.* Even the stuff we don't tell each other we still know because we're family, *or so I thought.*" She dabs under her eyes to stop her tears from ruining her makeup. "Why didn't you just tell me? What, did you think I'd be jealous or something? Stop you from being with him because I have 'dibs'."

"No," I cry. I would never think of her like that. To be honest, I wasn't thinking about her at all. I don't think that would be much use for my defence though. "I'm not 'with him' anyway, it's not like that. And as for not telling each other everything," I laugh, remembering that day I saw her in Mr Lawrence's. "You're one to talk." I cross my arms, copying her.

She side-eyes Sean, confirming my suspicion. "What do you mean?"

"So, you have been hanging out behind my back." I raise a brow. "Don't think I haven't noticed all the looks you give each other, acting all weird. And you have the audacity to be mad at me for doing the same."

"This is different and you know it."

She scowls at me with tight lips whilst Sean struggles to defend them, his smirk completely vanished. "I-It's not what you think." He eyes Cassie, either looking for backup or checking he's got their story straight.

"Don't," she growls. I'm not sure if it's aimed at me or Sean, but she has her eyes locked onto mine. "We're leaving, come on." That's definitely not aimed at me. She turns, nods at Abby to follow them, and opens the door. I watch as she leaves, Sean running after her, not even offering me an apologetic look.

"Actually, I'm going to head back with Lorri," Abby shouts to them. She explains before Cassie can say anything back, "Safety in numbers, right?" We've had many chats over how bad it can be for girls to be out on their own, especially at night, so I know Cassie won't argue with her. No matter how pissed she is at me.

I hear her sigh from around the door and imagine her nodding in agreement as Sean tells Abby he'll see her at home. "I'll ring us a taxi," Abby says, her phone already to her ear.

I match her smile, grateful. "Thank you."

"Will you be alright walking back on your own?" I ask her as the taxi speeds away. It's not that dark thanks to the streetlights and the longer days, but it's still pretty late.

Her phone screen's lit up and I notice she's already pulled up Sean's number. "Yeah, I'll be fine," she replies, showing me the phone screen.

I nod and search for my keys, causing the heels I'd forgotten about to whack against my side. "Can you give these to Cassie if you see her?" I ask, holding them out to her.

"Or... You could give them to her," she tries, taking them anyway. "She just needs some space. She'd had a few drinks, she'll come to her senses when she can think properly."

I feel a pointy stone under my foot and kick at it. "Thanks for the socks. Wish I'd thought to bring some." She gives me a stern frown. "I know," I whine. "But she lied to me too. It's not like I actually did anything wrong, nothing happened between us. And, even if it did -which it didn't- she doesn't actually have dibs on him. She doesn't even know him!" I let out a big puff of air and fold my arms.

"She's not upset because she's jealous, you know that," she starts, her voice that of a warning mother. "At least not of you. She's just upset you didn't tell us it was him, you had plenty of opportunities." She looks down at the heels in her hands, fiddling with the straps. Is she hurt that I didn't tell them too? When all of this started, I didn't plan any of it, I never meant to start anything with Jackson and I definitely didn't mean to hurt anyone by entertaining it.

"Are you embarrassed by us?" she whispers to the shoes.

"What? Of course not." My voice raises slightly higher than it should at this time of night. The memory of pouring my drink over that girl outside Mr Lawrence's comes to the front of my mind, causing me to feel sick. Or maybe it's just the alcohol. I shake my head, violently. "Definitely, not. I wasn't really thinking, I didn't think any of you would care and I didn't think it would matter since he's leaving soon."

"If it was someone else, would you have still done the same? If it wasn't Jackson?" It's less of a question, her tone making it more of a trick.

"No, I don't know. It all just happened," I shrug, the action being the only way I can express how I feel about the whole situation. "I didn't plan on actually liking him."

Her face lights up for the first time since we left the club. "So, something did happen?"

I hold my hands up, quickly backtracking. "No, no."

Her face deflates and I feel bad for ruining the mood yet again. *Sod it.* I exhale, rubbing my head as the start of a headache pounds my skull. "Well, we might have almost kissed." She gasps. "I think. I don't know, we were just talking about our parents, and he was drunk," I add to express that this isn't something we do all the time. "And it just happened. But it didn't. Cassie came in, just in time." She *was* in time, if she had come later there'd be no going back for me and Jackson. Plus, then I'd be keeping a lot more from Cassie which would've made it way worse. She was in time, so why do I wish she wasn't.

She nods, studying my face as her brow arches, and then breaks into a grin. "Well, if something *had* happened- I know it didn't, I believe you- but if it *had* then that wouldn't be a bad thing, would it?"

The wind picks up, blowing my hair, and a stray strand whacks me in the face. I tuck it behind my ear, just like I did with Jackson, and it calls all of the butterflies back. I smile, annoyingly. "I guess not?" My voice goes so high at the end that it sounds like a strangled cat.

She practically vibrates with excitement. "Ah! You like him," she shouts in a sing-songy way.

"Shut up," I say, whacking her, even though I have a huge smile on my face and a warm feeling in my chest. "He was drunk, he doesn't like me like that. We're just friends."

"Mhm," she says, raising her brow further. Her phone goes before I can respond, a photo of baby Sean pulling a face whilst dressed up as the little mermaid filling the screen. She answers with, "One sec", and turns back to me. "I'll try and speak to Cassie if I see her. Don't worry though, she'll come around, she always does."

We hug and I thank her before she sets off back towards their home, her phone at her ear. I climb the steps to our flat, my keys in hand, and unlock the door. I try not to make any noise as I lock it behind me, seeing that dad's already in bed, and tiptoe to my room, slowly closing the door so it doesn't bang shut. I place my bag on my desk and meet my reflection in the mirror for the first time since I left the Crawford's.

I look awful, my foundation's already separated despite it only being light coverage and my mascara's created panda rings around my eyes. And to no one's surprise, my hair's doubled in size even though most of it is tied up. Jackson only almost kissed me because he was drunk and upset, it was just a case of the right place at the right time.

And now we've probably ruined our friendship, as well as mine and Cassie's.

I can't wait to go to bed and pretend that today never happened. I should at least take my make-up off before getting under the covers, a big red zit would be the universe's joke of a cherry on top of the damn cake.

I check my draws for my wipes when I don't find them in their usual spot on my desk. I bought a new double pack when I went to town with Cassie and Abby as I'd just ran out. I definitely put them on the desk when I got back but they're not there now.

And they're not in the drawers. I get down on my hands and knees, and move my chair out of the way. It wouldn't be the first time they'd fallen down the back. The main drawer's been broken since we got it, getting jammed every time I open it so I have to yank it open, pulling it away from the wall. *Bingo.* The pink packet's lying in a pool of crinkled paper that's also fallen down the back of the desk. I'll get around to fixing it one day.

I pull out the nest of paper as well as the wipes and place them on top of the desk. As I get up, one of the drawings catches my eye. I frantically pull it out of the pile, smoothing it out, and feel my heart sink as I take in the picture. It's my application. The one that's supposed to be miles away right now. The one I got an email for today, thanking me for submitting. But how is it there if it's still here?

I place it behind me on my bed and quickly scour through the other drawings on my desk. *Oh, please no.* Then the stack on top of my wardrobe. *Nope, not there.* Then in my portfolio. *Or there.* Maybe I put it in my bag, I wonder, tipping my backpack upside down so the contents spill out onto the floor. No luck.

My drawing of Jackson's missing.

And my application's not.

Maybe it fell down the back as well and I just didn't see it on the first look. Yoah, that'll be it. I duck down and move my boxes full of old pens and pencils around, hoping it's somehow hiding underneath one. Nothing except a leaf.

A laugh escapes me, sounding awfully like a sob. Dad always warned about the damn leaves. The drawing must've blown off the desk when I left the window open, leaving Dad to think the one underneath was my application. Yet another thing I've managed to mess up.

I kick the boxes back under the desk and slump down onto the floor, my back against the bed and my knees tight to my chest. I open the new pack of wipes and pull one out, wiping aimlessly at my face. It doesn't dry out.

Once my face feels rubbed raw, and the wipe gets too full to handle, I throw it in the direction of my bin and crawl up into bed, not caring about what happens to the application drawing anymore, or the fact that I'm still fully clothed. Pulling my duvet over my head, I quietly cry into my pillow until eventually, I drift off to sleep.

Twenty-Nine

I spent the whole of yesterday either in bed feeling sorry for myself or on the couch, also feeling sorry for myself, whilst trying to contact the competition organisers to explain that I'd sent the wrong piece. They didn't want to hear it so I finished off the pot of ice cream from the back of the freezer instead.

I tried to get out of coming to the picnic today, I had planned to fake bad period cramps but Abby said she and Chen would still be swinging by and she'd try to get Sean and Cassie to come too.

"Lorri, can you pass me a lemonade dear?" Grandma croaks from her deck chair.

I move from my spot in the only little bit of shade I could find and squint as I'm blinded by the sun. If anyone was to see me, they'd mistake me for playing a game of Twister as I try not to stand on any of the food.

Auntie Tanya decided to make enough food to feed the whole park, which thanks to the warm weather currently contains the majority of the city. It's so packed we had to stand around for half an hour searching for a spot and the only reason we found one is because I noticed the previous family were packing up. Grandma had to fight off another old couple who were eyeing the spot. I think she was fed up with walking around because letting them have it definitely *wasn't* an option for her.

"Thank you, honey," she says sweetly, accepting the plastic glass of cool lemonade from the cooler she brought. "Are these your friends?"

My heart sinks. I don't know why but a part of me hoped Cassie would wake up today and randomly decide to forgive me. I know she's not here, if she was my grandma would be halfway across the park by now. Still, the sight of Abby and Chen cheers me up. "Yeah."

Their hair's a mess, lopsided ponytails with defying strands sticking out all over, but they look badass in their white outfits. They spot us and start to walk over, waving their hands over their heads. A smile cuts across my face as I wave back.

"Hey, sorry we're sweaty," Abby says, hugging me.

Chen jokingly sniffs her armpit and pulls a face. "Who knew martial arts would be so much work."

Abby rolls her eyes, the biggest grin on her face. "You loved it."

"I know." She returns the grin before turning on me. "You should come to the next one. And Cassie and Sean. Heck, tell everyone to come."

Abby's eyes roll again. "She's decided to be the spokesperson for martial arts. We went to the shop to pick up some bits." She holds up a white bag full of snacks. "And she tried to recruit everyone in there. I'm pretty sure they started scanning our stuff quicker just so they could get rid of us."

"Well, I'm glad you guys enjoyed it," I laugh.

They say hi to everyone and my grandma quickly warms to them, but only lasts two minutes before asking about Cassie, and my cousins demand a demonstration when they hear where they've been. Then we grab some food and drinks and head back to my spot under a big willow tree.

"We can't stay too long, Mum's gone out with Ellen but we need to be back before she leaves her."

I try not to look too bothered, picking at a few blades of grass. "Where's Sean?"

"Er... I think this might be him now." She points in the direction behind me, down the other side of the hill.

As soon as my eyes land on him and his tray of half-melted milkshakes my stomach relaxes. He hadn't been ignoring me but he might as well have been with his one worded replies in the group chat. The drinks might look like normal milkshakes to everyone else but to me they're the biggest and best peace offering I've ever seen.

"Hey," he says, his mouth pulled into his usual grin. "Sorry I'm late."

He could've turned up ten hours late and chucked the drinks over me and I'd still be happy to see him. "We're good?"

He stops mid sit, looking like he's attempting some kind of levitating meditation. "Of course, we're good." *Could've fooled me.* He takes his seat next to me and starts distributing the goods. "Cassie needed someone on her side, even if I didn't fully agree with her. I thought it'd be easier to sort out that way. I spent yesterday with her, trying to talk her round, and I think I'm getting somewhere. She was alright with me coming so that's something."

I take a sip of the cool yellow liquid. "I thought you were angry with me too. For not telling you."

He lets out a short howl of a laugh, the couple on the other side of the tree turning to stare. "I thought you knew that I knew."

He did? He knew that I was hanging out with someone but he couldn't have known who, right? He takes my silence as an answer and continues, "Come on, I know you. You really think I wouldn't have picked up on the way you've changed since you met him?"

I sit up straight, caught off guard. "I have?"

"Yes," all three of them say as if I'm crazy for thinking anything different.

"He got so under your skin, but then you didn't mind that much after a while," he explains. "And you knew about his tour and new albums, the old Lorri wouldn't even absorb that information if she was told about it multiple times and her life depended on it, *and* you knew it before Cassie. The party just confirmed my theory. But I had a feeling way before," he quickly adds as if looking for praise.

"Oh." I stare out over the park, the trees blowing in the light summer breeze. "Why not say anything?"

He thinks for a minute, eyes staring out at the same place as mine, and shrugs. "I was happy for you but I could see you were still figuring it out, and I knew you'd tell us when you were ready. Everyone's got at least one secret that's just something they haven't figured out how to put into words yet."

I wonder what his is, and if he'll ever figure it out enough to tell us. "Thank you, for not pushing me. It was weirdly kind of you."

He snorts, his eyes crinkling. "I'm kind."

"Sure," I smile back, glad everything's back to normal. Well, almost everything. "How is she? She's fine with you, right?" I turn to Abby.

She tries to nod but loses it. "I don't know, I guess. She's just upset."

"But you did nothing wrong." She can be mad at me but all Abby did was make sure I got home okay, it wasn't a declaration of war with her.

"Neither of you did anything wrong," Chen argues, placing a friendly arm across Abby's shoulders. "She's just grieving that she'll never get to make out with Jackson Peters. Sisters before misters or whatever." Her eyes go big as they frantically flit between me and Abby. "Sorry. Abby told me but don't worry, your secret's safe with me. Also, congrats," she adds, wiggling her eyebrows.

I try to shake my smile as Abby pushes Chen away, laughing, and Sean pulls a face. "So, what's he said?" Chen asks, brushing her hair off her face as she gets back up.

I look confusedly between them both. "What do you mean?"

"About the kiss!" she exclaims.

"Oh." I pick a daisy and pluck the petals off one at a time like Cassie showed me when we were kids. He loves me. *He loves me not.* "Well, he hasn't messaged me. I sent him a message yesterday morning, just to check he was okay, but he never opened it."

She shares a worried glance with Abby, offering me a wry smile as she notices I caught it. "He's probably busy, there must be a hundred things they have to do to prepare for the tour. It must be tiring."

"Right," Abby agrees when Chen elbows her. "Wasn't he going back to America soon? Maybe he's on the plane," she offers with a shrug.

"America's far but it doesn't take two days to fly there," Sean mutters, his brows drawn. I pretend I don't hear him.

"He did say he was leaving a few days after the party, so maybe." I add a shrug hoping they can't tell I've been checking my phone every hour and spent half an hour last night overthinking it before bed. "Scotch egg?" I ask, holding out the large packet we bought, putting an end to the subject.

After food we play a few games of football with my cousins, Chen letting them win every time, and then when the football pitch starts to get invaded by the more adventurous picnic goers, Sean says they should get going.

"Thanks for coming," I start, turning to Sean. "It means a lot."

"Don't mention it." He knocks my shoulder with his own. "And don't worry about Cassie, she'll get bored soon and apologise."

"And if she doesn't then I'll go and show her some of my new moves," Chen says doing some kind of kick as she punches the air. She somehow makes it look cool but I imagine if I was to do it, I'd end up flat on my face rather than intimidating my opponent. "Jokes. I know we're not supposed to use our knowledge for violence, please don't tell Sensei Dominik I was threatening people," she pleads with Abby.

"Thanks," I laugh, picturing Chen begging her Sensei to let her stay in the class. "And thanks for coming as well, I know you'd much rather be practising." I try to copy what she did and confirm my suspicion, thankfully we're outside so hopefully people will think I'm just sniffing the grass. Or sunbathing, that's probably more likely. Although, I doubt people have their face buried in the ground when trying to catch a tan.

They try to stifle a laugh. "No worries, I had a lot of fun. Thanks for inviting us," Chen says, with a grin. "Oh! Abby told me about the summer camp comp, when will you find out?"

Great, I almost made it a couple of hours without thinking about it. I guess I have to tell people at some point. "Um. It's in a couple of days, but I've not got a chance. I accidentally sent the wrong drawing in."

All three of them stare at me with creased foreheads, waiting for an explanation. "Don't ask, I've already spent the last thirty-plus hours kicking myself."

Chen throws their carrier bag of rubbish over her shoulder. "Their loss, your stuff's amazing and if they can't see it then they clearly don't know talent."

Abby nods, pointing at Chen. "What she said."

"You're going to win, I know it," Sean smiles, throwing an arm over my shoulders to pull me into a half hug.

I thank them one last time before they say goodbye to everyone else, having to fight off my cousins so they can leave. Then it's just me and my thoughts again. And my message-less phone.

With no school, and Cassie not speaking to me, I have nothing to do other than sulk around the flat until it gets unbearably warm, and then find somewhere outside to sulk.

"Lorri! We haven't seen you in a few days, how are you?" Seth asks from behind the counter.

The cafe seemed like an obvious choice; unlimited caffeinated drinks, free desserts and a whole heap of fantastic customer service. What more could you want when you're feeling low? Well, fewer customers would be great, there are hardly any available seats.

Zac, who was cleaning a table near the window, turns at the mention of my name and gasps, "You're not cheating on us are you?" He grabs his chest with his hand that's holding his cloth as if I've wounded him. *Always with the dramatics.* I wouldn't dare tell him for fear of growing his huge ego, but this is exactly what I need right now. "I noticed there's another new coffee shop in town. You know they don't even bake their food in-store. Why would anyone want warmed-up, store-bought pastries when you can come and get freshly baked ones? What do they have that we don't?"

I smile at Seth and he rolls his eyes before grabbing my usual cup. "Nothing," I reassure him. "I've had exams. And some other stuff." I sigh, joining them both at the counter.

Zac nods as if he's cracked the question of the century whilst placing his cleaning products on the side. "Ah. So that's why he looked so sad," he explains to Seth before turning back to me. "You broke his heart then? Deserves him right for the way he treated you."

"Huh?" Broke who's heart? The only person that comes to mind shouldn't be in the country. And even if he was, why would *I* have broken *his* heart?

Zac's barely listening as he carries on. "I wanted to spit in his drink last time he came in." He sends half-hearted daggers over to where Seth's pouring steaming milk into my mocha. "But someone wouldn't let me," he whines, sounding awfully like a toddler.

"Don't cut your nose off to spite your face," Seth sings as he perfects the art in my drink. "You can't go around spitting in people's drink just because you don't like them, they're paying customers." He turns, briefly, to hand me the cup with a smile. "Don't forget that," he says to Zac with a pointed look.

I thank him and pay for my drink. "Sorry, who are you on about?" I ask Zac, still confused.

He looks at me as if I'm stupid and then glances around the cafe before whispering, "That Jackson Peters, he's been here almost every day since Saturday. He always looks sad, though. Well," he starts but Seth shoots him a warning glance.

I try to figure out what they're saying in their silent conversation but come up short. "What? What happened?"

Seth throws his hands up, groaning, and stalks off into the kitchen, shouting back, "Don't say I didn't warn you." *Well now he needs to tell me.*

"I thought you knew by now that you don't have to do that with me," he says, making a circle around my face with his palm. "*I'll* happily tell you gossip, it's him that's like drawing blood from brick."

"Stone!" Seth growls from around the door. "And you know it is."

He smiles and I can't help but mirror him. "I just like to wind him up from time to time," he mock whispers.

Seth's head pops around the corner sporting his best fake grumpy face but the second their eyes meet, he breaks into a loving smile.

"Well, remind me never to tell you any secrets," I interrupt, taking a sip of my drink.

"I'd never tell any of yours," he exclaims, grasping his chest again.

Seth walks over and slips a brownie across the counter. "I wouldn't let him."

Their kindness warms me and I silently thank them, taking a big bite of the chocolate gooeyness. "Anyway, back to that boy," Zac starts, getting excited. "He *was* sad. Until Cassie met up with him."

I choke on the brownie, causing me to sputter with my hand around my neck as my eyes fill up. Seth lets out an aggravated, but worried, exhale as he lunges for a glass and fills it up. He throws it at me and I immediately drink it, feeling my throat open more with every sip.

I finish it and Seth takes it back, both of them watching me with anxious eyes. Standing back up straight, I rub at my burning chest. "I'm okay," I croak out, wiping my eyes.

They both let out their breath, Seth's slightly louder than Zac's. "That's your fault," he says, throwing his tea towel at Zac.

He catches it and wipes the counter. "Technically it would be Jackson's fault, no?" he asks, whispering his name. "Or even Cassie's. Don't shoot the messenger, I thought you knew that one," he adds, throwing the towel back.

"Sorry," I start, trying out my voice. "Cassie was with Jackson?" My eyebrows shoot up, my head tilting as I try to process the new information.

Seth shakes his head and goes to greet a new customer, clearly over the conversation, as Zac's head moves in the opposite direction. "I can't remember when it was now, but he came in like he usually does, just watching the cafe. It's a bit weird but I thought 'Hey, maybe he's writing a song about people in a cafe' who knows," he says with a shrug. "Artists are weird like that." He flashes a grin.

"Cassie went past and I was about to go and say hi," he continues, leaning on the counter, "because we weren't that busy at the time, but I wasn't the only one that noticed her." He raises an eyebrow, his grin not entirely gone. "He must've been looking out the window as she walked past because he ran out, shouting after her. And I mean *ran out*, he left most of his drink."

"He ran after her? Why?" I ask, more to myself than anyone else.

I notice Zac shrug out of the corner of my eye. "No idea. I thought she would have told you by now, you guys don't breathe without the other knowing."

Taking a sip of my drink, I skim the tables noting the regulars and the newbies. "She's not talking to me." I side-eye him. "Because I almost kissed Jackson."

All traces of a smile leave his face, his eyes dimming as he rest a hand on my shoulder. "I'm sorry. She won't keep it up for long, you two are basically sisters. And sisters fight sometimes, but at the end of the day you'll always come back to each other." He takes his hand away. "I should know, I have an army of them."

"Thanks," I mumble. It's always a little weird to see Zac without his signature cheeky grin, it's like a cake without any frosting.

A timer goes off in the kitchen and Seth asks Zac to tend to the new customers whilst he checks on the pastries. "Don't think I missed the part where you said you almost *kissed* him!" he barely whispers as he leans in, back to his usual self.

Rolling my eyes, we share a smile as he goes behind the counter, making his way towards the till, and I finish off my brownie as I catch my thoughts. Cassie and Jackson. Jackson, who's supposed to be in America, and who hasn't replied to me in days after more texts than I'd like to admit too. And Cassie, who's mad at everyone just because I spent some time with '*the* Jackson Peters' without telling her. I suppose Jackson never could do anything wrong in her eyes.

Why is he still here though? He definitely mentioned he was leaving over the weekend, he should be long gone by now. Maybe he woke up, remembering everything from the night before, and realised that he'd made the wrong choice. So now he's ignoring me and going after Cassie instead.

Still, if Cassie has what she wants, why is she still ignoring me?

Thirty

My phone dances across the counter and Seth, coming to join me, catches it just in time. "Where were you?" he comments on my dazed expression and hands over my phone. "Here."

It's Abby. "Hello?"

Even with the new customers spilling in and the music cranked up, I have to pull my phone away from my ear. "Congrats!" two voices shout.

"What?" I ask them, shrugging at Seth's quizzical scrunched brows.

One of them, Abby, gasps, "You haven't heard yet?"

I hold in a sigh. "Heard what?" I ask, reproachfully.

I can hear the broad smile in her voice. "You won! You did it, I knew you would! Have you not received an email or anything? We sent you a million messages but we figured you didn't reply because you were on the phone with them."

No, she can't be on about... What day is it? "Won what?" I ask, quietly, still locking eyes with Seth.

Zac, with no more customers to serve, joins us, catching the end of the conversation. His face matches Seth's confused expression before they both follow the same path I went down, their eyes lighting up as their lips pull into excited grins.

No, I'm not getting my hopes up. Not when it's something that could be *that* life changing. Most of the people that go there end up with an art show within the next year, the rest within five. "Won what?" I repeat, a little more urgently this time.

"The summer program, duh!" Chen shouts. "Your drawing's everywhere. And Lorri, I don't know what you were so worried about, it's beautiful. Really, it almost brought a tear to my eye, and I don't say that often."

My heart picks up and I have to grab the countertop to steady myself. Seth instinctively moves towards me but freezes when I look at him. "I won," I tell them, testing the sentence on my lips, not quite believing it. "I won!" I repeat, matching Abby and Chen's excitement.

Zac and Seth start to freak out too, both of their arms waving about as they try not to jump with joy. Seth mutters something about making a celebratory cake whilst he speed walks to the kitchen, waiting to wipe his eyes until he thinks I can't see.

"Ooo, does this mean we get to see it now?" Zac asks. He doesn't wait for me to answer as he whips out his phone, already tapping away.

My hands shake as I put Abby on speakerphone and check my notifications. I received an email from Vivian herself about fifteen minutes ago that I hadn't noticed. I open it and start to read aloud, my voice just as unstable as my hands, "'Dear Lorri, I'd like to personally thank you for entering my competition and I'm delighted to let you know that I've selected you to join us here over the summer. I feel you will be a great addition and that your talent will be able to grow and thrive with the help of my program. I chose your piece because it didn't just feel like I was there, but like I was truly seeing it from your eyes and feeling it within your heart. No matter how hard I tried, I couldn't let it go and I kept coming back to it every time. That's what even some of the greatest artists spend most of their lives trying to accomplish, and that's what I want at my summer program. I look forward to hearing back from you. Vivian Blanche.'"

Abby and Chen celebrate on the other end of the phone as I stare at Vivian's signature at the bottom of the email, the reality of all of this starting to sink in. Another voice travels down the line, bringing me back to the room, and I finally pick my jaw up off the floor as I take my phone off speaker to bring it back to my ear.

I can just about hear the other voice across the room. *Sean.* "She won?" There's shuffling, like the phone's being moved around, and it sounds like someone's running. "Lorri?"

"Hey," I say, trying not to cry from the scrabble bag of emotions.

"Congrats, I'm really happy for you," he says earnestly. He also sounds like he's holding something back, not sure if he should say anything more, but he doesn't.

I glance at my shoes, kicking at nothing. "Thanks."

He lets out a small breath, continuing, "I know Cassie will be too. She's a lot better now, less angry."

Of course she is, she's got Jackson all to herself. Grabbing my drink, I head over to my usual table, leaving Zac glued to his phone. He holds it up, my drawing on the screen, and gives me a thumbs-up paired with a giant grin.

"Really, she even asked about you this morning."

"She did?" I can't help but sound more shocked than someone that's just been struck by lightning. I would've thought she'd be spending all her time with Jackson now, not still hanging out with Sean and definitely not talking to him about me.

"Yep. It wasn't much but she's coming around. She can't stay away from you for too long, it's hurting her more than she'd like to admit."

It can't be that bad. She could stop at any point, it's not like I'm the one refusing to see her, yet she's still sulking.

There's murmuring and he clears his throat. "I've gotta go, Cassie's here, but I'll talk to you later, promise. Oh, are you going to prom?"

I spin the little saucer that my drink's resting on. I got the ticket ages ago when Cassie got hers but with everything going on I'd completely forgotten to do everything else that goes into getting ready from prom. Maybe I'd be more bummed about it if I actually wanted to go, but I'm not too bothered. Especially now Cassie doesn't want me there either. "No, sorry."

He doesn't say anything and then there's a knock on the door. "Oh. No, that's okay. We'll come and see you at some point though, okay?" His sentence speeds up as I hear him weave his way around the living room to the front door. "I promise. Okay I really gotta go. I'll work on Cassie. Congrats again! Bye!"

The line goes dead, leaving me alone with just my mocha and thoughts to keep me company.

It's prom day and I've still not heard anything from Cassie. Abby says she's been over a few times and everything's back to normal between them, which is good, but she's still saying she needs time. If I give her anymore, she'll be able to open up a clock shop.

I went out for a meal with Dad, Uncle Joe and Auntie Tanya the other day to celebrate winning the competition and they invited Abby and Sean too. It was really nice until all the news articles started popping up about me winning and going on and on about how the guy looks awfully familiar. Honestly, if it had been drawn by anyone else then no one would have even noticed. Now it feels like I'm being thrown right back in when I've only just made it out. And this time I don't even have Cassie to go through it with, or Jackson.

"Lorri, are you listening?"

"Huh?" I break my stare with the blank TV to turn to Dad.

He gives me his best 'I know what you're thinking and I'm about to ask something that I know the answer of but you're going to try and deny it anyway' face. "Are you sure you don't want to go to prom?"

Translation: Are you sure you don't want to go and speak to Cassie? *Nope, I'd rather not go and be ignored all night.* "Yeah, I'm not really feeling it."

He does a single nod. "Right. Well, that means we can listen to the rugby together instead. Do you still have your old shirt? I think I'm going to get mine on and then I'll make our tea before it starts." He rubs his hands together, jump-starting the massive grin that spreads across his face.

A wave of deja vu rushes over me, creating a warm smile. "I'll go and see if it still fits."

I head to my room, feeling as though I've made the right decision. After all, I'd much rather cheer on our team than go to a dance in annoying heels. Maybe I'd think differently if Cassie wanted me there.

I close the door behind me and perch on my bed, opening Instagram. My feed immediately fills with photos of Cassie, Sean and Abby in Cassie's bedroom. They haven't posted any outfit posts, probably because Cassie wants it to be a surprise, but from what I can see they look great. Both Cassie's and Abby's hair is up, Cassie's a more extravagant version of Abby's, and Cassie's given Abby a simplistic but elegant make-up look which, although it's a big contrast, looks just as beautiful as Cassie's colourful glam.

Sean's not in as many photos, and the ones he is in, he's in the background sitting in front of the TV. He's the only one that's showing off his outfit, although he doesn't seem very bothered. He hasn't done much, just shoved some products in his hair and put on a classic black suit with a bright blue tie, but he looks better than he ever has before.

I wish I was there with them. Not necessarily because it's prom but because it's the last milestone we'll be able to do together for a while, and as much as Cassie's cold shoulder hurts, it's nothing compared to what the next year without her by my side is going to be.

After spending at least ten minutes scrolling through all of Cassie's pre-prom posts, I go in search of the account that I've lost track of how many times I've looked at over the past couple of days, finding it like clockwork. Still no posts. Not even any reposts from photo shoots. It seems I'm not the only one that's wondering where he is, the comment section of his last post is overrun with worries from fans.

I find my way to our chat, almost by muscle memory at this point, and send another message that's along the same line as all the others.

Hey, where did you go? How's it going?

Chewing my thumbnail, I stare at the screen, willing him to message back. Although a part of me tells me not to, I let my heart take over and fire off another message with little hope of him seeing it.

I'm worried about you. I know how shitty it can be right now and all I want to do is be there for you. Damn it, I miss you.

I hit send before I even realise I'm crying. I'm not sure if the tears are for Jackson or Cassie, or both, but they come all the same. Grabbing a tissue off my bedside table, I wipe my eyes with a sniffle. It's infuriating how much I miss someone that was only a part of my life for a short time, especially when I never really liked them in the first place. If only I had known the real Jackson then. I suppose I'll still see him every now and again if he's with Cassie, that's if Cassie ever forgives me.

"Spag Bol or curry?" Dad's muffled voice shouts from the living room.

One more sniff before I attempt a reply, shouting back in as cheery a voice as I can muster, "Uh, Spag Bol." I push my phone away and dive into my wardrobe in search of my shirt, deciding I need a distraction from anything Jackson or Cassie related.

Maybe he just wanted to fix things with Cassie and check that everything's alright. Although, if that was the case, why hasn't he responded to any of my messages? Maybe he was waiting at the cafe to try and catch me in person to tell me that whatever we were doing was over, and when he saw Cassie he thought it would be better coming from a friend so he chased after her and told her to let me know. Cassie would've been around here straight away, though. *Unless she wanted me to suffer.*

This isn't working.

"Ugh," I groan, frustratedly, as I try to pull my top over my head. It takes a minute, and I'm almost certain I hear a rip, but I finally get it on. It's a little tight and looks more like a crop top, but it'll do.

I go to grab the door handle but there's a soft knock. "Can I come in?"

Cassie.

Thirty-One

My heart feels like it's going to break out of my ribcage as I check my reflection in the mirror. My eyes are a tad swollen but I don't think she'll be able to tell I was crying.

The door opens timidly and she creeps in, her dress coming into view before she does. It's a giant ball gown made from the royal blue fabric she showed me before all of this started, and she's surrounded by layers upon layers of delicate tulle, on top of which are beautifully hand-stitched embroidered flowers of almost the same blue. The fabric is the perfect shade to compliment her icy eyes, making them appear bluer than they've ever been and as she steps into the light, they set alight along with the dress that sparkles all over as the thousands of tiny diamantes refract the light.

"Wow," I breathe out, meaning to say it in my head rather than aloud. She looks like a princess.

She looks down at her dress, as if only just remembering what she's wearing, and blushes. "Thanks, I'm glad the weeks of blood, sweat and tears paid off," she laughs nervously.

I absentmindedly pick at one of my nails and mirror her awkward smile. "You look amazing. Really," I add, scared that I might have fully lost her trust.

My compliment is met with another nervous smile and the room fills with an awkward silence. How did we get like this? More importantly, how did we let ourselves get like this over a boy? I don't think there's been one awkward silence between us the whole time we've known each other, which is basically our whole lives. Well, until now.

"I hate this," she blurts out, reading my mind because that's what sisters do.

I take a tiny, hopeful, step towards her, the tears from earlier starting to resurface. "Me too."

She throws her hands up, her posture finally relaxing, and her face breaking. "No, don't! I spent way too long on this makeup to ruin it."

"Sorry," I half cry, half laugh.

We take a minute to pull ourselves together, both of us stood in silence as we dab under our eyes, the only sound our sniffles. Actually, now that I think about it, that's the only sound in the whole flat.

Cassie notices me watching the door. "Your dad let me in on his way out, he said he's gone to get some hotdog buns for tea."

"Of course he has," I mumble, the corners of my mouth pulling up. I bet the fresh buns in the bread bin feel awful.

She almost asks me to repeat but her face changes and a wave of understanding comes over her. It's not the first time he's created a task so he can leave us to our 'girl talk' as he calls it.

I take a seat on my bed. "I'm really, really, sorry. I should've told you I just didn't know what to say, I didn't know what was happening between us. *If* anything even *did* happen between us."

"No, no. *I'm* sorry," she says, rush-shuffling to take a seat next to me. "I barely know him. And even if I did, our friendship is worth more than any boy, no matter how hot and famous he may be."

I laugh at her honesty and she pulls me into a tight hug. I try my best not to disrupt any of her outfit but still end up with some of her hair in my mouth, seasoned with tangy hairspray, not that I mind. I'm just glad to have her back.

"I was never mad because you didn't tell us you were dating someone, you know," she says into my shoulder. "I was really happy for you. Plus, you know I live for the drama and a bit of mystery. It's just crazy that it's him, I needed time to get my head around it. I think it's the first time I didn't know something major about him and it was about you too."

"Wait, so you're not seeing him?" I ask, letting go of her. "Because it's totally okay if you are," I add hastily, scared she might try to hide it as I did, I wouldn't blame her.

"Who?" she quickly asks, her eyes so wide I can see my whole reflection.

I pull my eyebrows together. "Jackson," I say, the same way one might say 'duh'.

"Oh." She reddens and messes with a loose strand before tucking it behind her ear. "God no, not after finding out that you like him like that. Why'd you think that?"

My turn to go up a notch on the lobster scale. I guess it was obvious to everyone but me that I liked him 'like that'. "Well, it's just that Zac said he saw Jackson run out of the cafe, calling after you."

She doesn't try to deny it, she just nods slowly, glancing down at her dress as she smooths it out. "Oh. He must've gotten it wrong, it must've been a look-a-like, because I don't remember seeing him." She's still nervously playing with a bit of the tulle. She catches me looking at it and stops, quickly dropping her hands. "Have you not spoken to him?"

I know when she's not telling me the whole truth and I have to will my brain to focus on the question instead of what she could be hiding. "Urm, no. I've messaged him multiple times but I've had nothing back." The last message, as well as the others, cloud my head. That, along with the fact that he's been here the whole time, causes my eyes to fog over and my cheeks to burn with embarrassment.

Cassie looks into my eyes and instinctively grabs my hand. "Hey," she treads softly. "Maybe he's busy, or still figuring it out for himself, or lost his phone." She shrugs.

I guess they are all reasonable excuses. Plus, if he lost his phone that would explain why he hasn't posted anything on his socials. Or maybe not considering how little control he has on what goes on there.

"Or he could just be a stuck-up twat," Cassie blurts, breaking the silence with a huge grin spread across her face. It catches me off guard, Cassie too by the looks of it, and we both fall into hysteria.

"Shouldn't you get going soon?" I ask once we've calmed down, glancing at my plain, round clock on the wall.

Turning to look at it, she gasps, excitedly. "Omg, I almost forgot." She turns back with the same wide smile she had when we were six and she wanted to show me her new kitten. "I brought you a gift," she says, pulling herself up and running as fast as she can out of my room in her dress. It's less of a run and more of a stumble, that thing must weigh a tonne.

"A gift?" I ask, alarmed. "What've you gotten me a gift for?"

She's back at the door, already out of breath, carrying a huge white bag over her shoulder. "For being a crappy friend. Also, to say congratulations! I can't believe I almost forgot about the competition. Honestly, so good," she says, throwing her spare hand around, still panting to catch her breath. "I should have called or messaged to say congrats but I didn't want to apologise before I'd finished this." She struggles for a second to fit her own dress and the dress bag through the door, almost tripping but catching herself. When she's safely in the room she brandishes the bag, the excitement filling her eyes.

"What's that?" I ask, cautiously, with a slight feeling I know exactly what it is.

She starts to unzip it, opening it wider and wider and I feel my jaw do the same as she reveals the emerald gown inside. The silky fabric cascades out of the opening, revealing a modest slit down one side. She pulls it entirely out of the bag, showing off the open back. It's far more simple than Cassie's but it's definitely not plain.

"I- Wow. Cassie it's... beautiful," I gasp.

Her face sets alight. "Well, go on then," she starts, pushing it towards me. "Try it on."

I should say no, stay in my old rugby shirt and hope it doesn't cut off my circulation whilst listening to the game with dad, but how can I say no to that, I think it might be the prettiest thing I'll ever get a chance to wear.

Cassie claps as I stand, laying the dress on my bed and then shuffling out of my room so I can get changed. The fabric is a welcoming cool sensation on my skin, slipping on and fitting me perfectly, and as I head to my mirror, I notice that it's almost the right length for me, it would be exact with some short heels.

"Everything okay?" Cassie's slightly muffled voice calls through the door. "I know it's a little different from your usual style but I couldn't help myself. We might have enough time to do up the slit if you want?"

"Come look," I shout at the elegant girl in the mirror.

Cassie rushes through the door, her eyes welling up as soon as they land on my reflection. "Do you like it?" she asks over my shoulder after a minute of silence.

"I love it," I reply, finally pulling my eyes from the mirror. "Really, it's perfect. Thank you." I pull her in for another hug, our fabrics meshing together like water and earth.

"We don't have time to do your hair or makeup properly but you look perfect anyway." The front door goes and Dad calls that he's back. "Here." She hands me a pair of short silver heels. "You do whatever you need to do and I'll go and fill your dad in."

"On it."

"You got a limo?" I ask in disbelief as we reach the vehicle outside the flats. I don't know why am that surprised, of course Cassie got a limo.

She watches it with raised brows, her hands on her hips, almost as surprised to see it as me. "Uh," she says, her chest falling. "Yeah! Well, I borrowed it. Family friend." She turns to me to give me an odd smile, ushering me into the open door.

Once I've climbed in and made sure not to stand on my dress, I take a seat and gawp at how beautiful the inside is. If it was full of water, I could swim laps in here. "Since when did you have a millionaire as a family friend?" I whisper, feeling as if I should be quiet to respect how amazing it is, like you do at an art gallery.

She holds her hand out for me to help pull her and her dress in. "I think you might've actually met them once or twice," she says with another odd smile and a twinkle in her eye.

I've met a few of their family friends at barbecues and when her parents have held dinner meetings, but I don't recall her ever mentioning any owning a limo. And it's definitely not something that would slip her mind.

"Karaoke! Did I tell you we have Karaoke? We should do Karaoke!" She finds the remote on one of the shelves under the glasses rack, and turns the giant flat screen on just as I feel the limo pull away from the pavement. "What song?"

Thirty-Two

"You came!" Abby shouts when she finds us, running across the hotel car park and wrapping her arms around me. She pulls away to get a better look at my dress. "Wow. It looks great Cassie."

"Doesn't it?" I give them a small spin so they can get a full view.

Cassie glows pink, the tinge of colour only just shining through her makeup. "Oh, stop."

"So," Sean says, his grin wide on his face. "The band's back together?"

They glance between me and Cassie before landing on me, eagerly awaiting confirmation. I try to drag it out, cupping my chin as if I have to think it over first. "Hmm, that depends," I say, remembering Cassie's face when I asked about Jackson. "Are you going to tell me who you thought I was on about before?" I playfully raise an eyebrow and Abby and Sean make matching confused, yet slightly amused, faces.

"Uh," Cassie starts, her chest rising and falling at a much faster rate than one's should. "Well," she sputters as she slowly wipes her hands over her dress, pretending to smooth it out. Her eyes dart frantically from me to Sean, his face changing as she does so as if finally understanding what's happening.

"Sean?" I half yell. "You're dating Sean?"

I wait for either of them to object but both of them regard me with half-open mouths, not sure what to say.

"Finally," says Chen as she joins us. "It took you long enough. What?" she asks their bulging eyes. "Come on. I saw all the little touches and the lovestruck glances." She impersonates them, dramatizing every move.

Now that she mentions it, so did I. I just thought it was them being them, nothing out of the ordinary. Sure, it was more often and a little less jokey than usual but that's just what they're like. "Is that why you've been hanging out more?" I ask, following my train of thought. "Why you've been to Mr Lawrence's more?"

Slowly, she nods. "I wanted to tell you, I just…" she trails off, searching for words.

"Didn't know how to put it into words yet?" I quietly finish for her, sharing a warm smile with Sean.

Her face relaxes and I almost feel the relief flooding out of her at my understanding, all her features smoothing and the corner of her lips tugging up, thankfully. "Exactly."

"Oh, I think they've opened the doors," Abby says as the crowd moves towards the huge entrance of the Bridgerton-esque hotel.

"Well, we better get inside then." Chen grabs Abby's hand and twirls her around. "Let's go and get our party on!"

We all laugh, Abby the hardest as she tries not to lose her balance, and follow the others like a group of ducklings towards the entrance. Abby and Chen start rating everyone's outfits, but I only catch bits and pieces due to the surrounding people all doing the same.

"So… We're dating?" I catch Sean's voice above the rest. I don't need to look to see the childlike grin shining across his face.

Inside we head for a giant golden ballroom, not an old-fashioned one you'd find in a castle but a more modern, sophisticated one, full of glowing white drapes hiding magical fairy lights. The room's been sectioned into two halves to make space for round tables layered with crisp sheets and centred with vases filled with dainty flowers and more fairy lights hidden within shimmering diamantes.

We pick the table closest to the dance floor, as per Cassie's request, and I take the seat facing the stage to follow her seating plan. *Of course, she has a seating plan*. I think she's put more time into planning this than the school has.

"This is crazy," I state as I run my hands, softly, over the silk-like tablecloth.

The others nod in agreement just as the first set of waiters appear from behind one of the drapes carrying multiple plates of piping hot food. It wouldn't end well if they dropped one as they came out, the permanent stain would look like a different kind of accident.

Chen notices me watching them emerge from the swaying fabric. "Waiting for them to drop one?" she asks me with a challenging raised brow.

"No," I lie, turning away from that side of the room and matching her devilish grin. "I'm just really hungry."

"Hmm, sure."

Our plates arrive- basically a posh version of a Sunday dinner- and we wolf them down, rating each item as we go. We get a small bowl full of, what we assume is, a dessert and ultimately decide that it's vile, Sean spitting his first mouth full back into the bowl and refusing to take another bite. As waiters pass, carrying bowls from surrounding tables, I notice we're not the only ones that thought so.

Once all of the tables are cleared, the lights dim and the disco ball comes out as the DJ starts up his set. It doesn't take long before the first group makes their way to the dance floor, led by Natasha, and then one by one everyone else migrates their way over.

"Come on, you guys didn't just come to watch, did you?" Chen asks flatly, already pushing her chair back.

Smiling, Abby takes her hand, standing with her and I push away from the table to follow but stop mid-stance when I spot Sean nervously watching Cassie. Something's caught her attention on her phone and she's determinedly typing back and forth with someone, causing her not to notice all of our prying eyes.

"Cassie," Chen says quickly, startling her. She glances my way, Cassie's eyes following hers. "Dancing?"

"Yep," she chimes, a little too cheerily. "What are you all waiting for? Come on!" She stands, grabbing Sean's hand, and pulls him towards the already packed dance floor. She takes her phone with her.

"Okay then." Abby turns to me and Chen. "Are we joining them?"

We jump around to the usual disco songs, creating the biggest snake for the conga I've ever seen, until there's sweat on my forehead and the start of fresh blisters on my heels. I'm not built for this, the most exercise I do is trying to rub out a stubborn pencil line.

Cassie always carries powder, I think she buys a new one every time she buys a new bag. I search for her in the crowd, finding her huddled near one of the drapes at the side of the room with Sean, her arms flapping about as his eyes flit around the room.

Maybe I should go over and check that everything's okay. They've only been officially dating for two minutes, they can't break up already. I turn back to tell Abby and Chen where I'm going but they've invaded another group, screaming the lyrics to the song that's just come on.

As I get closer, I can just about make out what they're saying. "You were supposed to be here earlier!" Cassie whisper-shouts towards the drape, side-eyeing Sean.

I approach them slowly. "Are you guys okay?"

Both of their heads snap my way in unison. "Yeah. We're great, you?" Sean replies, moving his body so that he's standing in front of the drape. They both watch me with wide eyes, waiting for a response.

I put all my focus on Cassie and the weird smile she's giving me, ignoring Sean. "What's going on?" I ask, slightly annoyed.

Her shoulders sag and she lets out an agitated sigh. "Nothing."

She comes and hugs my arm, ready to pull me back over to our table. "We're going to do what we came here to do," she says, louder than she needs to considering I'm standing right next to her. She continues in a lower voice as we leave Sean. "Have fun and look good while we do so."

"Here," she says when we reach our seats. She pulls out her powder and applies some.

I take her spare puff and, using her extra mirror, wipe it over the majority of my face, watching my reflection instantly matt down. "Thanks. You guys *are* okay right?" I don't know what we would do if it went wrong between them. I guess Abby would have to side with Sean and I'd have to side with Cassie, what with us growing up with them, but at this point, we're all like one big family.

She snaps shut the powder and shoves it into her bag, avoiding eye contact. "Honestly, we're goo-" She stops at the same time as the music cuts out.

She lets out an excited gasp and her face, along with everyone else's, swivels towards the empty stage. The little bit of light we have also goes out, the room going into almost complete darkness, and a few people let out squeals. *Great, a power cut*. I didn't even know hotels could have power cuts.

There's static and then someone's voice plays through the speakers. I'm not sure what they're singing, I've never heard the song before, it doesn't help that there's no backing music either. It sounds beautiful whatever it is, their voice is incredible, it's sounds so familiar but I can't quite put my finger on it.

My foot starts to slowly tap in time. Wait, don't I know this? I force my leg to stay still, lean forward and open my ears as much as possible, straining them to catch the one bit of the song that I know I know. The only bit that someone else, other than the writer, has heard. *There's no way. It can't be.*

My heart drums louder and louder in my ears, adding the missing beat. The line comes and my ears almost miss it, they would have done if they weren't happily waiting for it, and the hairs on my arms stand on end as if reaching out for him.

Everything comes back on in a flash, right after our line, and he comes into view. He's watching me from the stage, his eyes locked on me and nobody else. I'm sure many people on the dance floor are gawping at him right now, heck I'd probably hear them screaming if I weren't giving him my full attention, but he doesn't seem to notice. Or he doesn't care. Instead, he offers me a contagious smile, impossible to fight off, not that I try.

He's dressed in an outfit similar to what he wore to the cafe and his hair's messy in his 'I-didn't-do-anything-but-it-still-looks-good' way, and everything about him is glowing under the warm lights.

The song comes to an end and he lowers the mic, finally giving some attention to the rest of his audience. They hardly notice Jackson thanking them though as all eyes on both sides of the room are turned on me, the voices behind them a buzz of gossip.

Feeling my cheeks redden I try to hide from their glares, but there's nowhere to turn. My breathing quickens as I try to subtly wipe my wet palms on the tablecloth next to me.

I thought I'd just gotten over everyone whispering about me, yet here we are.

Cassie gives my hand a squeeze, not fazed by its dampness. "Are you okay?" She mouths, partnered with drawn eyebrows. *'Did I do something wrong?'*

I find the rest of my friends huddled in a group nearby, all asking the same question. I nod, adding a smile so she knows I'm answering the spoken question and not the one her face is asking me and she relaxes, giving my hand another friendly squeeze. *'I've got you.'*

I squeeze back. *'Thank you.'*

There's movement behind Cassie and I glance over her shoulder, finding Jackson heading our way, the sea of people parting for him like the red sea did, except this sea's all shades of the rainbow. Once again, his eyes never leave mine as he closes distance between us. Cassie moves out of his way, just like everyone else, and joins the others but not before throwing us both one of her biggest grins.

I look at Jackson, really look at him. How did I not realise how beautiful he is before? I mean I knew he was good-looking, he models all the time, I wouldn't even be surprised if parts of him are insured, I've heard some celebs do that. I guess it's just different when you get to truly see someone and who they are on the inside, it helps you to see them in a new, beautiful light. Like unlocking the best version of that person, for your eyes only.

He watches me watch him and tries to stifle a nervous chuckle. Timidly, he lifts a hand, stopping when he catches himself, but as I make no signs of refusal he continues, lifting his hand to slowly swipe a stray strand of hair behind my ear. His hand grazes my cheek, sending sparks down my spine and lighting a fire in my stomach, adding to the glow of my cheeks.

He pulls his hand back, quickly, twisting his head to meet the prying eyes behind him and when he turns back, he's slightly redder than before. Raising his eyebrows, his eyes go wide. "What're they waiting for?" he whispers.

I lean in close, causing him to copy me so we're inches away from each other. "I think they're waiting for me to start screaming, get down on one knee and confess my undying love for you. You know, the usual." Despite everything, I can't seem to stop the devilish grin or the playful tone from taking over.

His eyes sparkle as the corners crease and his mouth turns up. "I've missed you."

His statement and its sincerity hit me by surprise, and I take a tiny step back. He missed me. I feel a rush of warmth and... relief? Have I been hoping that he felt that way? I know we haven't known each other long, but in that time we've grown close enough to open up to each other about things no one else knows, and when I thought I'd never speak to him again it hurt surprisingly more than I'd ever admit. "I missed you too."

I can almost see the relief being poured over his face, cooling and smoothing all of his muscles. There's a stray 'Awe' from somewhere behind him that causes him to visibly cringe and I try not to laugh as he searches around the room. "Can we talk?" he asks in a low voice, nodding towards the closest exit.

I give him a single nod. *After all, if you missed me, why not reach out?*

Thirty-Three

As the door closes behind us the music starts up again, the party carrying on. We've ended up in an empty side corridor with a comfy-looking dusty grey loveseat opposite the door which we take a seat on.

"Why didn't you reply?" I start after he doesn't, getting straight to the point. "I thought you didn't want to speak to me again after the party. That you regretted it. Regretted letting me close," I quickly add. After all, I could've misread the situation, maybe he wasn't going to kiss me. "Not that I would blame you, yo- *we* had been drinking. But you could have replied and let me know you were okay." I lay my eyes on my lap and nervously pick at my nails.

He immediately shifts his whole body to face me, knocking the pillow behind him to the floor. "I wanted to. You're the *only* person I wanted to talk to." I glance up, our eyes finding each other like they always seem to. "But I didn't have your number, and my manager found out about my account when she saw us together at the party. She asked me why you were there and I was too drunk and upset to even attempt an excuse, I think I just wanted to annoy her." He shrugs as he glances away, his cheeks flaring. "She took my phone, changed the login details and logged me out. By the time she gave it back and said I couldn't see you again I was beyond pissed so I yelled at her, called her some names, and fired her. Along with everyone else on my team."

"Everyone?" I quietly echo. All this because I was seen with him.

"Yeah…" he draws out with a hollow chuckle before shaking his head, unfazed. "I was just lashing out. I know that, they know that. Still, the quietness and normality of this week has been nice. It was almost perfect, there was just something missing." His eyes bore deeper into mine, allowing him to reach in and add a couple of logs to that fire in my stomach, the heat spreading all over my body.

The door we came through flies open and Cassie's the first to come barrelling out, followed by Sean, Abby and Chen. "Sorry! Did I do it again?" she shrieks, her face full of genuine sorrow.

I quickly stand, feeling a bit embarrassed to have been caught once again having a moment with Jackson. "Nope, we're good. You're good!" I hastily correct myself, going crimson.

She smirks. "Okay... good."

"Have you told her yet?" Sean asks, checking his watch.

Jackson shakes his head. "I was getting there, but I got a bit distracted," he replies, shyly rubbing the back of his neck.

I glance between each of them, Abby and Chen also checking the time on one of their phones. Told me what? Is he going to turn into a toad when the clock strikes seven?

Cassie impatiently shifts from one leg to the other. "Well, you need to get 'there' quicker because it's going to start soon." She adds a warning look that says if he doesn't tell me soon then she'll blurt it out.

He holds his hands up, surrendering, and quickly turns to me. "Okay, okay. I'm really hoping I did the right thing," he starts, anxiously wringing his hands.

"You did," Cassie adds, vibrating from the excitement.

He gives a taut smile. "If not and you'd rather stay here then that's fine, we can go a different time. But you mentioned that this game was a big one and that you hadn't been able to go in ages," he rambles.

Wait, 'game'. 'Game' as in "Rugby?" I ask, thinking out loud.

"Yes?" he replies, unsure. "I got us tickets. If you want to go?"

"*If I want to go,*" I repeat, my eyes wide. Does he even need to ask? "I'd love to!" Cassie and Chen cheer, both of them clapping like seals. "You guys don't mind?"

"No! Girl go get it," Chen says at the same time Cassie shouts, "We helped make this happen."

"You were all in on this?" I knew Cassie was being sus and I guess Sean was being weird too, but all of them?

They all nod with the biggest of grins, proud of their work. "Cassie did most of it," Abby confesses.

"Everyone helped," she shrugs it off. "So, turns out I lied about not seeing Jackson outside the cafe," she explains with a smug smirk. "He came and explained everything, I'd already gotten over it all so I said I could help. I was just going to walk with him to your flat but then I remembered the dress and my plan, so I filled him in. He wanted to be a part of it so we put our heads together and came up with a new plan. We only had a couple of days so we had to come up with something quick but it worked in the end. Jackson gets full credit for the rugby tickets though, that was all him."

"Really?" I really do have amazing people that I'm so grateful to be able to call my friends. *No, family.*

Jackson watches me through his lashes as he glows red. "Yeah."

"Seriously though, you guys need to get a move on if you want to get there before it starts." Sean turns to Cassie, speaking in a softer tone. "Do you have the clothes?"

Cassie chews her lip. "Clothes?"

He rubs a hand over his face, Abby copying in a less disruptive manner. "Cassie," they both chorus.

"Sorry," she defends herself, "I forgot to grab some. You don't have enough time anyway. You look great, now come on." No one has time to argue with her, or even attempt to suggest a change to the plan as she immediately turns on her heels and heads down the corridor towards the exit. She reaches the end, shouting back without looking, "Are you coming or not?"

"So, it's yours then?" I ask after we're both shoved into the limo that Cassie and I came in. "Of course it's yours." How did I not realise before? None of Cassie's family friends have seemed like the type of people to have a limo and personal driver. To be honest, though, neither is Jackson. Not anymore.

"Guilty," he admits. "I don't use it all the time, but I owed you a ride." He picks up a bottle of champagne, offering me some, and puts it back when I decline.

"We've come a long way since then." I laugh at the memory and how different everything is now.

"You can say that again." He rakes a hand through his hair, the playfulness leaving his voice. "I think I'm ready to be me. To show the world the *real* me," he says, searching my face. "I had Sean record me at the dance. I'm sure a few others probably got some snippets too, but I thought I could upload it, officially, and start releasing music I'm actually proud of."

I scooch towards him. This is a big decision for him, especially now with so much going on. "Wow, that's great. Really, they're going to love it." I can't hide the joyous grin on my face.

"It's all thanks to you." I begin to shake my head but he hurries on. "Seriously, if I hadn't met you, I probably would've carried on with the act for a hell of a lot longer. You've made me realise that I am good enough, that being just Jackson is enough. You stuck around after getting to know me, same with your friends. And you were the first to make me feel like it might actually be possible to make my own music. That's why I wanted you to hear it first." He lowers his voice. "Why I want you to hear all of my songs first."

I'm not sure how to respond so we both sit in silence, searching each other's eyes. His somewhat resemble those of a gazelle standing in front of a pack of lions at feeding time. "What. Like an official role as 'song listener number 1' or something?" I tease. I make my eyes as wide as they can physically go before it hurts. "Do I get my own limo?"

He cracks a smile, letting out a carefree chuckle and relaxes. *Mission accomplished.*

"I'd love to," I say after a beat, explaining at his drawn brows, "hear your music."

For a second, I think I see his eyes shimmer, almost glazing over, and he opens his mouth to say something, fighting with himself about whether or not he should, but the driver beats him to it.

"We're here Mr Peters," he shouts through the little opening.

We both rush to peer out of the window, gazing up at the giant stadium. I've been past this place countless times during my life, always pining to go in and only making it a handful of times since Mum left. I always forget just how magical it is on a game night, all the lights and people dressed in matching colours making it easy to tell if they're friends or rivals. And that's what they are, at least for the night. For the next eighty minutes or so.

I survey the crowds outside. A large number are gawping at the limo, probably wondering which of the celebs that occasionally come to the games are inside, but the majority are laughing and cheering, singing the chants that will carry our team to victory.

I catch our reflections in the window, my heart swelling from a mixture of what's happening just outside and also inside. Jackson's wearing an expression vaguely similar to mine, one full of awe, wonder and something more. Except he's not looking out the window anymore, maybe he never was, he's looking straight at me.

The temperature starts to rise and I feel my throat dry up. "Can I ask you something?" I croak, waiting a second before turning to him. He doesn't try to hide what he was doing, just nods so I go on, "That day when you saw Cassie, were you looking for me?"

There's not even a fraction of hesitation. "Yes. I went as often as I could and sat at our table. But I never saw you."

Our table. For some reason, it sets off fireworks. Before him it was always *my* table, Zac and Seth would even put out a reserved sign if they knew I'd be popping in, now I don't mind sharing it with him. "If only I knew you were there." It would've saved me a lot of worry. *And embarrassing, emotion-fuelled messages.*

"Speaking of knowing where people are," he says with a nervous short laugh. "Do you want to hear a secret?"

I lean closer, intrigued. From the outside, we must look like two kids sharing the latest playground gossip. "Go on."

He scratches his neck, avoiding my eyes, and takes a deep breath. "So, you know after the concert? When you were in my dressing room?"

Oh great. "Yeah…"

"Well. I kinda, sorta, knew you were there," he says quickly, tripping over his words.

"What?! How? Why didn't you say anything? Wait, weren't you shirtless?" My mind races back to our unfortunate meeting, filling with a thousand questions.

"Ah." He drops his head into his hands, shaking his head. "I was," he cries, half-laughing. "I saw you when I came around the corner, you were just going in, and I was so excited. I wanted to impress you because I felt bad about everything and feared you hated me or thought I hated you, but I only knew how to do that the Jackson Peters way." He smiles and clutches his chest. "My ego did take a bit of a hit when it didn't work."

All the photos of him shirtless that Cassie's shown or messaged me over the years come to mind. "Can I let *you* into a secret? It wasn't my first time seeing you shirtless."

Surprisingly, he's very surprised. "You're shirtless at every photo shoot," I half joke.

His back straightens. "Not *every* photo shoot," he laughs. "Hang on. So, you've been checking out my photo shoots? Or just the shirtless ones?"

I lightly punch his chest, pushing him back into his seat. "Shut up." But he doesn't, he just continues to laugh. Rolling my eyes, I find myself copying him, falling into a fit of laughter.

When we stop, we just stare at each other, smiling. He leans in and after being here before, I follow his cue. This time we don't get interrupted as his lips meet mine, him pulling me closer. I feel warm under his touch, warmer than I thought was even possible.

We finally pull apart, our breathing heavy, and out of the corner of my eye I notice the crowds have almost completely disappeared. I gasp, "They've gone in!"

He swings his head to follow my gaze and sits up, already rushing to get the door. Stopping, he remembers something and grabs two pairs of designer sunglasses out of a white plastic bag. He pops a lopsided pair on me and the other on himself before grabbing the last thing out of the bag and shoving it on his head; a curly two-toned wig with our team's colours on.

He gives me a wide smile and a shake of his head causing the giant wig to wobble from side to side before jumping out and offering me his hand as he bows like a true gentleman, fuelled up with the excitement of a first kiss. "Will you be my date?"

I can't hide my giggles as I accept his hand. "Why of course."

Epilogue

Opening my eyes, I jump, knocking one of my earphones down the side of my temporary bed as Jackson's smiley face stares through the screen. "Why didn't you wake me?" I protest as loud as I can get away with without waking my new roomie.

       I arrived at the camp a couple of weeks ago and I've had the best time. Don't mistake me though, it's been tough, we have breakfast at seven and then non-stop lessons till the sun's gone down, I think my calluses have calluses at this point. Some are more for fun though, like pottery or the odd water sport activity, and the other campers are really nice too. My roomie's no exception, not unless she's woken at two in the morning.

She doesn't stir, her still quilt kept peacefully tucked under her chin. *Well, at least we know the earbuds we got work.*

"I didn't want to disturb you, you have to be up early." The closing credit music stops as flicks his laptop off. "Plus, you're cute when you're sleeping."

I feel my cheeks burn and tuck a stray strand of frizzy, bedhead hair out of my face. We're just getting to the stage in our relationship when it's normal to say things like this to each other.

"In a donkey-snoring kinda way," he snorts.

As I said, we're *just* getting to that stage. "I do *not* snore!"

Oh, you thought the earbuds were because of our nightly midnight calls? Nope. Amanda seems to think I snore loud enough that one day I'll blow the cabin down but I think she might just be getting me confused with the wind howling through the gap in the window.

"Whatever you say, Donkey," he says in a terrible Shrek impression. He's been trying to perfect it since he went to watch the musical last week.

"How's your ankle?" I ask, sitting up to rest against the wooden headboard.

Just as I was about to eat my breakfast this morning, I received a lovely photo of Jackson's mangled foot and a message that read 'Do you think it's broken?'. Turns out it wasn't but you could've fooled me, it put me right off my food.

He'd been doing some late-night rehearsals for one of the festivals and tripped, falling off the stage and knocking out one of the guys that were carrying heavy equipment, which in turn crushed his foot.

He sulks. "Still hurts. And I just got confirmation that I have to cancel my performance tomorrow. After that, I'm good to go, but I'll have to stay sitting for my next few gigs." He shakes his head, his soft curls framing his tired eyes. "I would've felt awful if we had to cancel all the festivals."

It's only teatime in LA but he's been working like crazy for his new albums and shows. When he went back to America, he hired everyone back with the exception that he gets to make more decisions when it comes to his career, starting with his new song. Which, by that time, was trending on YouTube. Now they're switching out some of the existing songs on the albums for some from Jackson's songbook, which is amazing but it means spending double the time in the recording studio.

"We can stop these if you want, just until the albums are finished?"

"You're kidding right?" he asks, fighting a yawn. "Our Facetime is the best part of my day."

I fight off a yawn myself with a grin. I'm a hundred percent sure I look like a serial killer in this low lighting but he doesn't seem to mind. "Did you get my package?"

I eye the small box on the other side of the cabin, resting anxiously on top of my temporary fancy art desk. "I might've done," I mumble, my eyes trying to close again.

"Dad dropped something off this morning, he said not to open it until I was told to."

He looks at me expectantly. "Go on then, open it," he laughs when I make no move to grab it.

As excited as I am, I groan as I throw my covers off and my bare feet touch the cold wooden floor. Grabbing the goods, I check Amanda before tiptoe-running back to my bed. I place Jackson down so he can witness my reaction and rip open the packaging.

Letting out a breath, my voice catches. "You found it." I pull the bracelet out of the new jewellery box and instantly put it on, my eyes filling with emotions. "You fixed it too?" *Now, all the 101 questions make sense.*

He nods as he lowers his head. "Yeah. I called the venue to see if they'd found any bracelets and they said just one with charms, so I had it sent over. Once I checked it was the right one, I got it fixed."

I can't believe it. It's been months now, I thought it was gone for good. He clears his throat, rubbing the back of his neck. "I also added a charm, I hope that's okay."

What?! I quickly scan them, trying to find the odd one out, and land on a shiny, tiny camera. "You know," he starts at my confused expression. "In a weird way, we have the paps to thank for our relationship. If they hadn't taken that photo, we wouldn't be here right now."

It's more than okay, it's perfect. "I still hate them," I smile.

He chuckles. "Oh, me too."

I stare at the tiny pendant. "I love it, really. Thank you."

We lock eyes as we fall into a comfortable silence and he whispers, "No biggie."

"God! Get a room," Amanda groans, turning over to reveal a grin.

"Sorry!" I half-whisper. "I'll wrap it up, promise."

"It's fine," she says rubbing her head against the pillow, her eyes still closed. "Tell Jackson I said hi."

I do as she says and tell her he said hi back but I think she's already gone back to sleep. "Oh, are you still coming to Abby's fight?" *It still sounds weird to say.*

"I haven't missed any of her other wins," he grins, resting his head on the studio's couch pillow. "Is your dad going?"

"No." *Thank God.* He went to the last one and was cheering so loud we almost got chucked out. "He's got a therapy session and then he's going with Uncle Joe to pick out some clothes before he starts at Joe's place."

Dad's continued his AA meetings and therapy sessions and there haven't been any incidents since. I know we won't ever be totally in the clear, but right now things are good.

He opens his mouth to speak but there's a voice in the background as someone shouts his name. "One sec," he replies to them holding up his index finger. "How's Cassie and Sean? He messaged that she was driving him mad but then never responded when I messaged back. To be fair, it was an hour or two later."

"Ah." I got a similar one from Cassie. "They were arguing over what movie to watch for date night."

He laughs, the screen shaking. "That makes more sense. I was worried for a sec."

"Nah, they're good. Actually, they're probably great if he never responded."

He goes to agree but the same voice cuts him off. "I have to go," he yawns, stretching. "I'll see you on Saturday." The voice calls him again and he rolls his eyes.

"Can't wait," I wave and he waves back just before the screen goes blank.

I remove my earphones, placing them along with the package on my bedside table, the bracelet jingling as it taps the side. I still can't believe it's here. I find the new charm and hold it to my chest.

My phone buzzes.

New message from @HughJackmanSon

Night x

Acknowledgments

I wasn't going to write one of these because I thought they were just for 'Real Authors' (whatever that means) but this book probably wouldn't be here without the amazing beta readers that helped me along the way and I just wanted to say a massive thank you to them. Natalia, Carolyn, Victoria and the others that dipped in and out along the way, thank you so much for taking a chance on my first novel and believing in it enough to help turn it into the book that it is today. I really couldn't have done it without you guys helping out when the words turned to mush and lost their meaning so thank you.

Printed in Great Britain
by Amazon

29909561R00192